'How do you know I'm not already fully a woman?'

'Don't be more of a fool than nature made you,' he retorted, knowing it from the bold bravery with which she met his eyes.

Even his certainty reminded him he'd once been a rake and knew far too much about women for a simple countryman. She was far too good for him in every way he could think of, even if he'd had his old self back and could offer her so much more than a cottage in the woods and a life of toil and obscurity.

'I'm a realist, not a fool,' she said softly.

Her breath stuttered, as if *not* being his would hurt her in some drastic fashion, and he kissed her with a curse that shuddered through him and into her as something broke.

She was tangled around every sense and scruple Rich had. He raised his head to look at her at last, a desperate question in his eyes, seeking an answer he shouldn't ask for and she shouldn't give.

AUTHOR NOTE

Welcome to the third and last in my series of *Seaborne* books. If any of you are new to this rich and powerful family this story reads perfectly well as a single book in its own right, but if you enjoy this book you might like to find out more about the Seabornes in THE DUCHESS HUNT (Jessica and Jack's story) and THE SCARRED EARL (Alex and Persephone's story), which are available as eBooks.

Ever since the idea for the Seabornes came to me I have had a soft spot for Rich Seaborne, the family rogue and unwitting cause of so much trouble for the rest of the Seabornes. Even while I was weaving the stories of bold Jack and troubled Alex and their eventful journeys to happiness I was itching to get on with Rich's story as well.

While those of you who have read THE DUCHESS HUNT might remember Lady Freya Buckle as being the least popular of Jack's guests, I had no idea she would turn out to be Rich's match back then. It wasn't until she dashed into the first scene in a most un-Freya-like state of disarray and took over that I realised she was the perfect lady for a man convinced he could never love again.

So I hope you enjoy this tale of love against the odds, set in the midst of a series of secrets and misunderstandings, and agree that Freya and Rich truly do deserve each other by the time they finally manage to bring the Seaborne family the happy ending they have all been longing to see.

THE BLACK SHEEP'S RETURN

Elizabeth Beacon

First published in Great Britain 2013
by Mills & Boon, an imprint of Harlequin (UK) Limited.
Harlequin (UK) Limited, Eton House, 18-24 Paradise Road,
Richmond, Surrey TW9 1SR

© Elizabeth Beacon 2013

ISBN: 978 0 263 89845 3

Elizabeth Beacon lives in the beautiful English West Country, and is finally putting her insatiable curiosity about the past to good use. Over the years Elizabeth has worked in her family's horticultural business, become a mature student, qualified as an English teacher, worked as a secretary and, briefly, tried to be a civil servant. She is now happily ensconced behind her computer, when not trying to exhaust her bouncy rescue dog with as many walks as the Inexhaustible Lurcher can finagle. Elizabeth can't bring herself to call researching the wonderfully diverse, scandalous Regency period and creating charismatic heroes and feisty heroines *work*, and she is waiting for someone to find out how much fun she is having and tell her to stop it.

Previous novels by the same author:

Chapter One

Rich Seaborne stretched his long legs towards the glowing fire and gave a contented sigh as he finally allowed himself to relax. It had been a long day crowded with tasks and responsibilities, but they all were nowadays. He wondered what his old friends and family would say if they could see him now and marvelled he'd ever been the man they would remember. Mr Richard Seaborne had also gone to bed late and never risen early for the simple reason he was seldom even home by the time most of humanity were ready to begin a hard day's work.

'Idle young idiot,' he chastised his old self, feeling as if his very bones gave a sigh of relief at the luxury of sitting still at long last.

The careless young wastrel he'd once been

seemed a puzzling stranger to him now. Despite the hard work and heavy responsibilities, Rich couldn't imagine going back to his old, useless life of a careless beau about town. Back then he never knew the satisfaction of earning his family's bread by his own labour. He'd never earned a penny in his life until he had to learn how, or starve and watch them go hungry as well.

He leaned back against the well-worn cushions his wife had made to soften the larger of the two Windsor chairs he'd crafted with wood from the forest. Content by his own fireside, watching a fire fuelled with wood he'd felled, seasoned and chopped himself, he let himself enjoy the pure pleasure of sitting still for ten precious minutes before he climbed the steep stairs he'd built when they restored the derelict cottage so deep in the woods he hoped everyone else had forgotten it was here and sought his bed after a hard day's work.

If the old Rich could see himself six years on, he'd marvel at this homespun fellow with marks of labour on his hands, a day's growth of beard on his chin and a streak or two of dirt across his face where he'd rubbed his nose when thinking. A bittersweet smile lifted his mouth as he recalled his Anna doing her best to break him of the habit with a combination of tenderness and nagging, but at the end of the day he would look in the small square of mirror over the mantel and see the proof that, whilst his ears heard her, his mind went its own way as soon as he was intent on something else.

Without her at his side to encourage, chide and push at him to be a better man it felt as if he was trying to move the world with a teaspoon. There wasn't any balance to it all, even with their children asleep and reasonably clean, decent and well fed upstairs. No wife on the other side of his fireside, no warm body and acute mind relaxing in the smaller chair he'd made for her to wrap herself snugly into at the end of a hard day. No lover in his bed at the ultimate end of that day to welcome him, love him and, after they made love softly so as not to wake the baby, snuggle against him and fall so absolutely asleep he used to marvel at the quick neatness of her slumbers.

He felt the familiar deadening pall of hopelessness drive out his earlier contentment and frowned at the fire, shifting impatiently in his chair as if he might physically fight off the darkness his life could become without her. For months after Anna died he'd sat and brooded alone over the fire at the end of the day and despaired. In those dark days he felt no satisfaction in his isolated life. He'd silently rail at God, the devil and the world in general for letting his wife die and leave him behind, a useless hulk who couldn't even quiet his crying children, let alone make up the loss of their mother in some way he still couldn't fathom.

During those endless nights it had sometimes seemed stupid to carry on, looking over his shoulder and battling to be father and mother to two tiny mites who shouldn't have to grow up in a hovel in the forest. Night after night he'd sat here and agonised over his decision to walk away from his loving family and privileged youth. If he went home, he told himself, his mother would raise his two motherless children so they hardly felt the loss he could barely live with.

Lady Henry Seaborne could fill the gaps left by a mother they lost so young with all the love they would ever need. His younger brother and sisters would enjoy their niece and nephew and help bring them up as a Seaborne should be raised—with full knowledge of a long and proud tradition at their backs, and a sense of responsibility their father had lacked until he met Anna. He wanted his son and daughter to possess the steadiness of character he would probably have mocked as tedious in another until the memorable day he met his fate in the Strand and his whole world changed between one breath and the next.

He sighed now for the hugeness of losing her, but three slow, hard years had gone by and somehow he'd learnt to go on from day to day for the sake of his children and not fume quite so hard or so often at her, the world and the devil about her untimely death. Now he could even recall meeting his love with a smile, not feel that terrible wall of grief tumbling on to him every time he triggered the slightest memory of falling in love with his wife. It had all begun as a gallant impulse to help a lovely but painfully young girl in dire straits; after five minutes in her company he had continued in heady exaltation at finding the love of his life and the memory woke an echoing thrill in his heart even now.

Even romantic love couldn't sustain itself on fairytales, but somehow they had truly grown up together and it had only made them stronger. Once he and Anna had realised they would have to make their own way in the world, neither had had much of a clue how, he recalled with a wry grin. Yet they were stubborn, passionate people and managed to make new lives by hard work. Somehow it had built even firmer foundations as their feelings grew beyond that first heady passion for each other into a true, enduring love he doubted could ever fade, even with Anna's death yawning between them like some unbridgeable void.

Their love had stood every test when she was alive, he reflected, and thanked God for it, although their time together was painfully short. He missed his wife so much it physically hurt at times and the only way to take the edge off his longing for her wisdom, loveliness and sheer, bright optimism in the face of hardship was to work so zealously he didn't have chance to linger on how little his life felt without her.

She'd been slender as a whip when she wasn't with child and so small a fool might take her for a child at a distance, but she'd proved as strong as steel when life tried them as they had never been tried before. Anna was a lioness in defence of her own and her own lay upstairs fast asleep—his own now, both of them. Her child, and her child and his child, two children he loved as dearly as he could ever imagine any father loving his brood, king or pauper, and Rich Seaborne lived as a poor man, despite the rich estate and comfortable fortune awaiting him if he ever dared reclaim them.

He reminded himself exactly why he was still living the life of a woodsman and bodger of everyday furniture and necessities in a remote cottage. He *could* go back, of course. Then he could be a gentleman again, return to his birthright as eldest son of the late Lord Henry Seaborne and his loving and gracious wife. Set in the Seaborne heartland, poised between the last of England and the first of Wales, he could take up his rich inheritance. The land there echoed with the challenges of the warrior princes and insurgent robber barons who had fought over it for centuries and he loved and sometimes longed for it as if it had a soul that cried out to his. He felt a familiar yearning to stand once more on that rich soil that was almost beyond reasoning away.

It wasn't simple homesickness—nothing as straightforward as that for a Seaborne in exile. No, it felt like a deeper sense of connection to the beautiful land of his birth, so nearly into a Celtic land and not quite fully within rich England either; which was pretty much how the Seaborne clan regarded themselves, now he thought about it. They were very nearly subject to their king, so long as he didn't interfere with them and theirs, loyal to their country, passionate about family and as determined to go their own way as any of the old Marcher lords, who had ruled their fiefdoms as if they were their own states and had often proved as stubbornly independent in thought and deed as the Welsh so-called rebels they were sent to awe in the first place.

He could go back and be welcomed like the Prodigal Son and, once he explained this isolation was not chosen but forced on him, his family would forgive all the years of not knowing he was alive or dead and he could take up his old life. No, he wouldn't go back to that hedonistic existence, but he could take responsibility for Seaborne House, accept the joys and burdens of a large landowner and lift some of the responsibility off the shoulders of the head of the family.

They were broad enough in all conscience, but Jack, Duke of Dettingham, currently carried out Rich's duties as well as his own. Jack was married and two of his own sisters and his little brother had wed since Rich had left home. The urge to see them and meet their husbands and wives was sometimes so strong he wanted to pack up his family in the cart he used for taking his goods to distant markets and drive back home, so he could watch Hal and Sally run wild with their young cousins.

Yes, he could do all of that. He could live in his comfortable home, amidst his prosperous acres, within the protective circle of his family—where he could sit like an animal in a trap and wait for the devil to find them and tear it all apart. So he was still here, work boots resting on a battered fender used to rest the fire-irons against and dry the kindling for the following day. He would still be here tomorrow and next year and however many years it took for his family to grow up and face the world alone. None of which stopped him being afraid some harm might come to him and leave his children alone, or that he wouldn't give them the sort of childhood Anna would want for them.

Sighing as he damped down the fire for the night, Rich set his battered old watch by the clock he'd painstakingly resurrected from a box of bits thrown out by the local doctor, who had discovered he was no better at healing broken clocks than patients. Rich hoped he'd hidden the wonderful Tompion timepiece his father had given him for his twenty-first birthday well enough for it to stay there until his son reached maturity and must be told the truth, but suddenly he longed for the luxury and comfort of it in his hand—a reminder of the good man who'd given it to him and he wished he even half-deserved to call father.

He recalled riding away from Seaborne after Lord Henry's death, thinking he could never fill his sire's shoes so there was no point staying, little realising he would never have a second chance to prove himself wrong. No point dwelling on old inadequacies—irresponsible young Rich Seaborne became a stranger when he met his future wife. Mature Rich regretted not a step that led him to Anna later that day, even though love had brought with it such untold depths of sadness and loss after she died.

Lady Freya Buckle had endured a day of wild exertion, misery and trouble and she was now very lost. It was about time she enjoyed her right to be warm, comfortable and well fed as befitted the daughter of an Earl, but there seemed little chance of any comfort at all in this endless forest. Her father's last and least acceptable daughter had been forced to accept that money and position couldn't buy happiness over the last few years, but losing even the small comforts of her everyday life was somewhere beyond ridiculous.

Now she was alone and penniless and it was dark and cold under these infernal, unending trees. Somehow she must find some shelter for the night to rest her weary limbs and take the weight off her aching, blistered feet until daylight returned and it was as safe as it ever got in this benighted forest. Freya wrapped the remnants of her once-fine cloak about her shivering person and only just managed to resist an urge to plump down on a carpet of dead leaves under the nearest tree and cry some of her misery out.

She was a Buckle of Bowland and that meant something, even if it currently meant she was exhausted, shivering and hungry in an ever-darkening world of trees that all looked the same. Nevertheless, Lady Freya could not sink into resigned indifference and sleep like a helpless babe lost in the wood as a lesser person might. A true Buckle did not crumble under misfortune, but it was difficult to stay regally resolute when her noble family didn't care what happened to her and she frowned into the gathering darkness of the June night.

If only she had been able to marry the Duke of Dettingham, she would have a vital, handsome husband to make getting children tolerable and all would have been well with her world, but he had contrived to avoid the honour. Aristocratic marriages were seldom based on love, but it seemed the noble Seaborne family thought otherwise. Freya sighed at the contrariness of gentlemen while she walked with less and less confidence into the unknown. The Duke pretended to be a rational man looking for a well-connected wife who was pretty enough to make filling his nurseries bearable, but he turned out to be a romantic fool who fell head over ears in love with an antidote and married her instead.

So the Duke married his unsuitable Duchess and a year later her own mother, the widowed Countess of Bowland, was dead and Freya had been learning hard lessons about the world ever since. Nobody could accuse the rigidly proper Countess of being unfaithful to her lord, but the family made it clear Freya was an outsider. Mingling their blue blood with that of an East India nabob's daughter might have been a deplorable necessity, since a Buckle could not take to trade and actually *earn* money, but it didn't make the result a true aristocrat.

When she had a chance of another suitor pleasing enough to endure marriage with she went along with her half-brother's plans, until she heard Lord George Perton tell his friends how he was about to suffer. She shuddered at the memory of hearing him describe her as a stubborn nag he would never ride given a free choice of mounts, but he'd take a gallop on her for her fat dowry. His friends laughed uproariously, then commended his courage.

'Dare say the bad-tempered filly will throw you into a duck pond, Per old man. I'd jib in your shoes, fortune or no.'

'Ah, but you ain't as poor as me and the old man swears he'll throw me out to starve if I don't wed a golden dolly. I'll marry her and tup her to get a brat or two, then my father can live with her while I take a ride with the fine fillies I can buy with her money. They might argue each other into an early grave, with any luck.'

So Freya had refused him and her half-brother's fury had been memorable, but it wasn't as if she had grown up with the illusion that her wider family looked on her advent with unalloyed delight. She accepted she was unlovable, but lately being accepted by society as Lady Freya Buckle, daughter of an Earl of ancient bloodlines and old renown, hadn't been enough to make her bend to her family's wishes any longer. Now Bowland was favouring a political crony with even less charm than

Lord George and Freya decided it was time to make a new life, before she was bullied into marrying a man she loathed. The thought of sharing a bed with Mr Forland made her shudder at the thought of his flabby body, greedy hands, mean little eyes and all the unthinkable intimacies she had no wish to learn with him.

A trip to her maternal great-aunt had seemed a good place to start an independent life. They corresponded dutifully and she'd been invited to Miss Bradstock's house, but Bowland would not hear of her accepting. As a first, wary step into the unknown her decision to go anyway had seemed safe enough, but now look where it had landed her. The shudder that shook her this time was so powerful it nearly left her in a shaking and hysterical heap on the forest floor. No, she was a Buckle, even if her old life was *over*, Freya reminded herself starkly, and Buckles didn't buckle.

She swished the skirts of her gown away from an encroaching bramble with some of her old panache, glared at it as if it was her worst enemy and finally let herself consider the idea she could have been going round in circles in the watchful silence of these woodlands for hours. If only she had done as Mama always insisted and travelled with armed outriders, who would have put off rag-tag scoundrels like the ones who had held up her hired carriage and threatened them with rape and murder. Freya clamped her hand over her mouth as she shook her head at the whimper on her lips and tried to hold back the terror threatening to turn her hysterical. She gulped in a huge gasp of cool, fresh air and reminded herself hysterics didn't get a woman anywhere, unless she was the current Countess of Bowland, of course.

An audible snort of exasperation made her wonder if her mouth had an independent life this time, but her brother Bowland really was an idiot—unfortunately one with a dream of power and not enough sense to see he was being manipulated by his wife, who was a clever rogue. If Freya had known how dangerous it was to steal away and travel lesser-known roads, she would probably have risked the fat politician after all. No, she felt sick at the very idea and would rather be torn apart by wild beasts than wed Mr Forland, then she remembered how close she'd come to just that today and her empty stomach dry-retched painfully. Again she heard the betraying sob in her breath as dawning terror, then desperate flight, replayed in her mind and she trembled so badly she had to bully herself not to simply give up.

Heaven send the coachman and guard had not been murdered by the brutes who'd attacked them, Freya prayed and shuddered again at their possible fate. She desperately hoped handing over the hefty purse she was carrying had allowed them to escape, but tales of unscrupulous men who banded together to prey on the unwary, such as Lady Freya Buckle, kept nudging at her as she wondered if she was a bigger fool than Bowland to believe paying the hired coachman extra to help her run away from home was as good an idea as it had seemed at the time.

She was alive and unmolested, thanks to her headlong flight, but the thorny underbrush was intent on destroying the very clothes she stood up in and robbing her of her last shreds of dignity. If only she'd sewn a few guineas into her petticoat, or stuffed one of Bowland's new-fangled paper bank notes into her short corset before she set out. She had been too intent on escaping to worry about what might happen along the way. One mistake she would never make again, if she ever managed to reclaim her true position in life.

She stopped to listen for any sound over

the racing beat of her own heart. Breathing as deeply as she could, she sensed she was alone out here and suddenly she really didn't want to be. If only she had been born in a different bed. A comfortable squirely one, perhaps, where she could have grown up as merely a passably pretty young miss. Then she might have made friends, gone on impromptu picnics and danced the night away at country balls with eager young gentlemen in search of a comfortable wife.

Dreaming wouldn't get her out of this endless forest and now it was getting dark. It took all her resolution to face the endless isolation and strange twilight noises without giving in to her fears. Lucky it was summer, she told herself, and this was England so no wolves or bears were running about the forest hungry for a well-fed young aristocrat. Of course there were still human wolves, as she had found out earlier today, but best not to think of them.

Freya struggled to see further than a foot in front of her nose and came to the unwelcome conclusion that she would have to find a suitably dry tree and curl up under it for the night, before she fell flat on her face into some sharp and clinging bush that would snare her fast in the darkness, or cut her to ribbons when she tried to escape. Failing anything better, it might be as well to stop before she did more damage.

Hesitating as she fought what felt like an ancient terror of being trapped in the forest by night, she snuffed the air like one of Bowland's hunting dogs and caught an elusive flare of scent made up of wood-smoke and manure and perhaps even a garden that told her she wasn't so far away from humanity after all. Unsure if that was good or bad, given the horrors of her day, she tried to creep closer as softly as she could. Shivering like a nervous racehorse as full darkness brought the threatening chill of night with it, she hesitated in mid-stride and tripped over a protruding root and fell awkwardly into a heap of felled logs waiting to be split by the forester she was trying not to disturb. She tried her best to get up as she flailed around to find a prop in the dark and grasped yet another bramble instead.

With hot pain from her new scratches bringing tears to her eyes she made herself splay her hands palms down to push herself up and discovered she couldn't endure any weight on her ankle as agony shot through it and she couldn't hold back a grunt of pain. At last tears were streaming down her face unchecked at the misery of it all and she couldn't seem to stop now she'd finally got started. Conscious of a huge and probably fearsome dog baying to be let out, so he could fight off the clumsy idiot come to attack him and his, she decided all she had left in her to do was to curl up as small as possible and hope she wasn't about to be savaged.

Sure enough, the vast-sounding hound was unleashed by his probably terrified owner and she could hear him howling with eagerness. Now she heard the soft pound of huge paws on the echoing floor in this dry part of the forest and she let herself breathe in the surprisingly sweet scent of old leaves, lichen and earth in case it was the last thing she ever sensed. Almost wishing the rest of her senses hadn't sprung into action now the darkness rendered her eyes useless, Freya heard the dog panting between growls and knew her fears were about to come true. Suppressing an irrational plea not to hurt her, she stiffened and waited as it bounded up to her and at least terror had stopped her crying. Almost resigned to feel its huge teeth close on her flesh, she heard a gentlemanly snuffle, then a puzzled whine as the huge beast lay down beside her and sniffed politely at her wildly disordered curls where she had buried her face in her arms in instinctive defence.

Chapter Two

Daring to raise her head half an inch from her sheltering arms, Freya ventured a hesitant look in the direction of a vast sigh, as the large hound decided it didn't understand humans at all and seemed about to go to sleep. She couldn't actually see much, but it was enough to know the animal was as large as its bark indicated. Wishing she knew more about dogs and her mama hadn't been so afraid of them that she wouldn't have the smallest lapdog in the house, Freya wondered how you made friends with an animal the size of a small horse.

She hesitantly held out a still-shaking hand and he sniffed it obligingly before putting his head on his paws and sighing once again as if all the cares of the world lay on his doggy shoulders. Biting back what she assumed would be a hysterical chuckle, she risked pushing herself up on to her knees before the shock of pain in her ankle made her collapse in an inelegant heap and wish she was brave enough to cuddle up to this apparently benign dog for comfort.

'What have we got here then, Atlas old boy?' a deep voice rumbled out of the darkness and nearly made Freya jump out of her skin.

'Who the devil are you?' she snapped, finally feeling anger burn away the tears and shock of these last horrible hours.

'I think it's the host's prerogative to ask that question,' he replied with lazy indifference to a lady's plight and she wondered if that burst of fury had been such a good idea when her safety and possible future might lie in this man's hands.

'You can ask, but I'm not promising I'll answer,' she muttered, supposedly to herself, but from the deep chuckle it won from him, he had amazing hearing.

'Let's start with what you're doing lying in the middle of my favourite coppice and work it out from there, shall we?'

'No, I didn't have the least idea it was yours

and you should keep it in better order if you don't expect strangers to trip over things in the dark and do themselves an injury.'

'Had I known you were coming, my lady, I would have made sure everything was ship-shape and neat. As it is, you'll have to excuse a working man for being just that.'

She almost leapt at that satirical 'my lady' and asked how he knew who she was, but stopped herself just in time when she realised her normal haughty manner had sparked his sarcasm and she should be more conciliatory, under the circumstances.

'I'm sorry, it's been a very long day,' she managed more graciously.

'Clearly, so let's get you inside and at least fed and watered, even if comfortable is beyond hope for a lady such as you with my slender means. It's far too dark to put you on the road to wherever you were going before you got lost now,' he said gently, as if he could hear the fear and horror in her voice despite her best efforts.

'I can't walk,' she explained blankly.

'I hesitate to ask how you got so far from civilisation then,' he teased as if it didn't really matter how she got here, here she was and he would deal with her as best he could.

'I fell over,' she explained earnestly and

wondered why it felt so tempting to give up fighting at last and let him take over.

'Better for you perhaps if you'd done so sooner,' she thought she heard him mutter, but it was lost in the sensation of his touch, as if he was learning her by feel since he'd failed to bring a lantern with him.

'Where does it hurt?' he asked and she marvelled that the authority in his voice had her pointing to her ankle, feeling more foolish than ever when she realised he couldn't see her in the dark.

'My ankle,' she said gruffly and yelped as he found out for himself which one.

Atlas whined his puzzlement that his master was hurting the surprise human he'd found him, then settled at a soothing word.

'I hope you're not heavy,' the man said as he rose to his haunches beside her and it felt as if he was towering over her as he insinuated strong hands under her legs and shoulders and lifted her in his mighty arms.

'Goodness!' Freya managed weakly as she found herself airborne. 'If you'd only let me lean on your shoulder, I'm sure I could manage to walk.'

'It would take all night,' he told her and

strode along the forest path with her in his arms as easily as if it was clear daylight.

'It's unladylike,' she muttered as she listened for the almost silent pad of Atlas's feet on the forest floor, surprised to find she already liked the huge animal and wanted his warmth and proximity as she didn't dare covet that of his master.

'Probably, but we don't worry too much about such delicate notions out here in the wilds,' he told her as if familiar with the dictates of polite society, which seemed unlikely.

Come to think of it, she'd taken him for one of her own kind when he first spoke and perhaps that accounted for this feeling she could finally relax and let a gentleman take care of her. It had been a very trying day, she assured herself, and she was probably wishing the world was how she wanted it to be. If she got through the night in one piece, no doubt it would lurch back to its proper order by morning. For now it felt oddly pleasant to be borne along in a strong man's arms. She could feel powerful muscles and sinews few gentlemen of her acquaintance could boast as she settled against his broad shoulder with a contented sigh.

'There,' he said at last, as he rounded what

seemed a deliberately serpentine last twist in the path and the faint glow of a small curtained window made her open her eyes wider. 'As well it was no further, perhaps, or you would have been fast asleep,' he whispered as he shifted her to open his door.

'What a cosy room,' she managed sincerely as she took in the still-glowing fire and companionable-looking chairs on either side of the fire.

Clearly his wife had gone to bed and that was why he was murmuring, for fear of waking her after a long day of hard work. She admired his consideration and let herself envy his lady for a moment, surprised how appealing the notion of being cared for by a very masculine husband at the end of a tiring day seemed to someone who'd never done a hard day's work in her life.

'It could do with being a little larger. With myself and Atlas to accommodate, one of us always ends up a little too far from the fire for comfort,' he said and gently set her down in the smaller chair before she could demand to get there on her own one foot and a stick.

'It seems truly comfortable to me,' she admitted as she shivered at the idea of all that lay outside this warm room and how deeply uncomfortable her day had been so far.

'We can argue about that when we try to decide how to find you a respectable place to sleep in such a confined space later,' he told her as he sank to his knees in front of her and insisted on removing her stained shoe.

He gave her an impatient look when she batted his hand away from her torn stocking and insisted on undoing her own garter after he turned his back.

'Done?' he asked irritably and stared into the fire as if it annoyed him nearly as much as his uninvited guest.

'Yes,' she admitted, once she wasn't biting her lip to conceal how much that small movement hurt her.

'Good, now let me have a proper look at it,' he said, as if mentally girding his loins for an unpleasant task. 'This will probably hurt, but I would be grateful if you could manage not to scream, since my children are asleep upstairs. They would normally sleep through cannon-fire, but I doubt a lady screeching at the top of her voice could fail to wake them and I don't need more complications.'

So he had children, did he? He'd made no mention of his wife so it seemed likely he was a widower and she went back to wondering if she was as safe after all. Yet there was no air of menace to this man such as she had felt so terrifyingly earlier today from the highwaymen and, once or twice, on the dance floors of Mayfair when a so-called gentleman insisted on brushing too close as they moved through the figures of the dance together. This man might not overtly threaten a young lady's honour, but he had surprising presence for the rough woodsman his clothes, cottage and everything but his voice proclaimed him to be. He sank to his knees in front of her again and she was determined to show him not all ladies screeched and fainted at the slightest provocation, or even, she revised with a muffled gasp, quite a lot of provocation.

He had dark-gold hair, she catalogued desperately, as the sickening pain of having her injury even this gently prodded surged through her with an oily chill. There was a touch of auburn to it in the firelight and it made for a distinctive contrast with the darkness of his brows and the golden tan of an outdoorsman under his end-of-day stubble of whiskers. He had strong rather than patrician features and a bony nose, but there was a hint of humour about his expressive mouth that saved his face seeming austere as a medieval monk's.

Since she had avoided his gaze when they came into the mellow light of what smelt like a luxurious wax candle rather than the stink of tallow she expected, she had no idea of the colour of his eyes. Such faint light probably wouldn't show it anyway, even if she somehow found the courage to meet his shrewdly assessing gaze, but he had the most amazingly long and thick dark lashes she had ever seen on a man. Meanwhile, the touch of his work-worn hand on her tender foot was surprisingly gentle and she let herself watch him prod and probe her poor battered feet to divert herself from the pain and noticed his fingers were long and sensitive, as well as clearly strong and very fit for whatever purpose he set them by day.

She took in the scent of him without the sort of indelicate snuffle she had allowed herself on smelling smoke from the blessed fire that was now thawing out her aching limbs when she was still in darkness and she decided he shared that oddly clean smell of wood-smoke and deep woodland she had appreciated with what she thought might be her last breath. Add to that a touch of soap and clean man and she concluded he washed of a night, perhaps at the same time as he bathed his children, so he could leap into action of a morning with only an early morning shave.

Only just restraining herself from adding touch to her exploration of him, she pulled her hand back in time not to explore his overlong thatch of curly hair and see if it felt as alive and wilful as she thought it must be under her probing fingers. Perhaps that was why he lived out here in the middle of nowhere, because the family who had made sure he was educated and taught the manners and speech of a gentleman then found they couldn't control him either. He looked like a man who went his own way, so why would that way bring him to a humble woodsman's cottage in the heart of the most remote forest he could find?

Everything about the man was a puzzle and when he met her eyes with cool resignation, she could see that he knew it. Whatever shade his eyes were there was no cruel, hot greed in them as there had been in the eyes of the men who attacked her coach today and those of her parliamentary suitor. She had been desperately frightened and on the verge of a very un-Freya-like attack of the vapours all day, but suddenly the world seemed to rock back on to its proper axis.

'You're probably wishing you'd never found me lying out there now,' she said as he knelt at her feet like a subject king.

'Shall we say you could prove a mixed blessing, Perdita, and leave it at that?' he said as he rose to his feet and moved into what she presumed was a scullery from the cool air that wafted in and reminded her how much night there was out there to be terrified of.

'Isn't she the heroine of *A Winter's Tale*?' she questioned and caught herself presuming cottage dwellers didn't read Shakespeare. 'I'm sorry to sound so astonished,' she added as he reappeared with a bowl and some rags. 'Out here in the midst of nowhere, I dare say you read to pass the long winter hours when you cannot work.'

'I dare say I do,' he said uninformatively and she began to realise there were areas of his odd way of life he refused to lay open for her to read and became even more intrigued.

'Pray, what is your name?' she asked with some of Lady Freya's haughty assurance.

He raised his eyebrows and went on soaking rags in the icy water as if only the slight wind getting up outside had disturbed the peace of the night, other than Atlas's lusty snores.

'It will seem odd if I address you as "sir" or

"you", will it not?' she said in this new Perdita's softer tone and found she liked it better as well.

'You can call me Orlando,' he said at last, kneeling at her feet again and startling a gasp out of her as he bound the ice-cold wet rags about her flinching foot.

'Oh, so we're galloping through *As You Like It* now, are we?' she ventured when the initial shock had passed and she felt every muscle and bone in her misused foot sigh in relief.

'We are wherever we choose to be,' he said quizzically, then got to his feet and looked down at her as if he could read her life history in her eyes.

'Thank you,' she said quietly, fervently hoping he couldn't.

'For giving you the liberty not to be yourself, or doing all I can to relieve the pain?'

'Perhaps for both?'

'You're very welcome, lady,' he told her with a courtly bow that seemed as sharply at odds with his humble circumstances as his educated accent.

'Thank you, kind sir,' she said with a regal gesture and a wry smile in return.

'Now there's only the problem of where you can bed down for the night to deal with,' Rich said, turning away from the temptation of this suddenly enchanting lost lady.

Left to his own wayward devices, he might linger half the night talking with her if he wasn't careful. She intrigued him with the odd contrast of dowager queen and lonely hoyden she seemed to switch between as her moods changed, or he got a little too close to the truth of who she might be for her comfort. He'd seen such mischief in her extraordinary amber eyes just now that he knew she was far more complex a person than either role allowed. He wished now that he hadn't plonked the candle so close to her that he could see the true glory of her unusual eyes when he rose from attending to her foot by its flaring light and felt as if he might fall headlong into them if he wasn't very careful indeed.

'If you can endure Atlas snoring all night long on the rug next to it, I think you'd best take the box-bed in the corner. My son and daughter will bounce out of their own beds on to mine before the sun is hardly risen tomorrow and I don't think your ankle would like two wild animals stamping about on it if I lend you mine for the night and sleep here instead.'

'After today it seems almost beyond wonderful to borrow such a cosy bed for the night.

I defy any thief or rogue who found this place by an unlucky accident to get to me before he got to them, so I'm very happy that your dog will bear me company,' his waif said cheerfully and clearly found his simple life an intriguing novelty.

After a few days his mundane existence would pall on a princess in hiding and he hoped he would be rid of her long before then, before they recklessly explored the daring female under all those rigidly correct manners of hers and complicated this inconvenient business even further.

'I'll make you a posset to take away the worst of the pain and while it's brewing I can make up the bed for you,' he said, in what he hoped was the detached tone of a dutiful host.

'Thank you, Orlando, you're treating me like royalty,' she said politely and he told himself it was a good thing the laughing rogue of a few moments ago was back in hiding.

He preferred her withdrawn and coolly polite, he assured himself. He preferred any youthful and even remotely attractive young woman to stay at a distance nowadays. Indeed, he had felt no more than a soon-dismissed masculine reaction to any other woman since he first laid eyes on his darling Anna. It felt like a betrayal of his own beloved that a feral part of him wanted to know far more about Perdita than the colour of her eyes. After the unmatchable joy of making love to his wife, the rest of her sex had faded into friends, or lusty females to be avoided. He told himself feeling even a hint of hunger for this intriguing female was an insult to Anna's memory.

'Are you a wise man?' she asked curiously as he went about the task of adding a pinch of this herb and a dot of that spice with a sweetening of honey to the pot over the fire until he had the right mix to bring her relief from pain, but not leave her drugged and lost in wild dreams.

'Do you think I would be living miles away from my fellow creatures if I had an iota of sense, Perdita?' he asked unwarily and saw reawakened curiosity light her fine eyes.

'You might, if you had reason enough,' she said shrewdly.

He distrusted the speculative glint in her eyes and set about finding what linens he had to spare for the box-bed that a previous owner of the cottage had built so well it was too much trouble to dismantle when they moved in. It had been all that *was* left, apart from most of the roof, the walls and part of the chimney, when he and Anna had found this place and claimed it for their own, since nobody else wanted it.

'Maybe I don't like company,' he let himself mutter loudly enough for her to hear and felt a pang of guilt at the long Seaborne tradition of hospitality he was betraying.

'Next time I run away from a pack of desperate and dangerous rogues, I'll be sure to bolt in the opposite direction,' she said with a cool social lightness that set him at a distance and he was contrary enough to dislike it.

'Were they really so desperate?'

'Of course they were—why else would I have run so far and so fast I got completely lost to avoid them?'

'I'm sorry,' he had the grace to admit, 'you have been through an appalling ordeal and all that matters is that you recover from your hurts and we somehow manage to reunite you with your friends and family as soon as we can. They must be desperately worried about you by now, so I could make sure a letter is delivered to inform them you're safe and reasonably unharmed, if you would care to write one.'

She was silent for a long moment and he began to wonder if she had fallen asleep by the fire. He reluctantly turned to look at her in time to see her shake her head regretfully and look a little mournful and sorry for herself for the first time.

'There is no one,' she said bleakly. 'It was a hired coach and the relatives I left behind will not miss me. I thank you, sir, but I will not put you to so much trouble on my behalf.'

'You were travelling alone?' he heard himself ask disapprovingly and wondered when he'd begun to care what rich and overindulged young ladies did to put themselves in danger nowadays.

'I'm of age, why should I not?' she asked as if a young lady hiring a carriage and travelling without either companion or protector was perfectly normal.

'For the very good reason it turned out to be such a disaster, I should think. You would have done better to travel post and enjoy the protection of an armed guard and the King's mails.'

'There's no post road to my destination.'

'Which is?'

'None of your business.'

'Do you expect me to set you on your way to the nearest village in the morning so you can blithely limp off into more ill-advised and plainly ridiculous escapades? How can I turn my back on a disaster in petticoats like you and leave you to wander about the country with no more idea how to go on than my three-year-old daughter?'

'I know how to conduct myself,' she informed him in her best mistress-of-all-she-surveyed voice.

'So well you just informed a complete stranger nobody will notice if you disappear for good, so I could make a quick getaway after foully doing away with you or having my wicked way with you, whatever you have to say about it? I begin to think my Sally has more sense in her currently very little finger than you have in your whole head, Princess Perdita.'

Chapter Three

For a moment the girl looked disconcerted
by the realisation he was right and she'd put
herself totally in his power. She rapidly re-
built her innate assurance she was right and
the rest of the world wrong and drew herself
up to give him a disdainful look worthy of his
grandmother, the Dowager Duchess of Dettingham, in her most formidable glory. Wondering if this aristocrat had ever met the one
lady who would be able to stare her down and
stand none of her nonsense, Rich tried not to
admire the stony dignity she was facing him
with. For some reason he liked his granddam
a lot more than the rest of the family did and
found his unwanted visitor's steely poise un-
expectedly endearing.

'I trust you,' she finally admitted very quietly. He felt another burden settle on his shoulders and suppressed a gusty sigh.

'You can,' he promised easily enough. 'I'm no killer and can imagine nothing more repulsive than forcing myself on a woman against her will.'

'Clearly my judgement isn't as bad as you think, then,' she argued gallantly, but he could see the blue shadows under her lioness's eyes and the stark pallor of her face and knew it was only her steadfast spirit that held her upright in her chair right now.

'Whether it is or not, mine currently tells me you're very near the end of your tether, Perdita,' he told her in much the same tone he used on his stubborn little daughter when she was about to fall asleep on her feet after a long day of mischief and mayhem.

For a moment she raised her chin and looked ready to swear she was fresh as a daisy and ready for her next set of misadventures, then she literally drooped, as if a great wave of exhaustion was about to claim her, much as it did his Sally, who had been known to fall asleep in her dinner only a second after insisting she wasn't a bit tired. Afraid she might tumble headlong into dreamland in a similar manner, he scooped her out of the chair and up into his arms once more.

'Quiet,' he ordered when her eyes seemed about to cross with absolute weariness.

She glared at him instead and he admitted she had a very effective glare by nodding ruefully at the ceiling to remind her they weren't the only people in the house who needed their sleep tonight. Feeling her relax against him for the short journey from his hearth to the box-bed, he felt that peculiar stir of interest in her as a very desirable young woman once more and sternly ordered his inner satyr back into retirement.

'I'd best unwrap you and bandage that ankle properly for the night, or you'll spend a very uncomfortable night in a damp bed,' he said as he set her down on the side of the bed and knelt at her narrow, but sore and scratched feet once more to do so. 'Keziah has an evil-smelling salve that will do wonders for these blisters. I'll get some from her in the morning so it won't be so painful for you to walk on them once your ankle has healed enough for you to hobble about on it.'

'Who's Keziah?' she asked and he thought her words were saved from slurring into each other only by her stubborn determination to fight the waves of shock and exhaustion finally catching up with her.

'Keep still,' he demanded grimly as he realised he was going to have to unlace her gown and strip her, since she was beyond doing anything but pretending she wasn't half-asleep. 'Lift up,' he ordered as if she really was Sally, and perhaps by believing that he could fool himself there wasn't a mature and very desirable woman under his questing fingers and control his inner beast long enough to get her safely into bed and asleep.

Freya huffed and told herself it was like being back in her nursery, but she managed to raise herself from the feather mattress long enough to feel pain in her ankle and blisters on her feet and flinched when he undid her sash and the side-lacing of her gown, then stripped her once-fine sprigged-muslin gown off in one neat and practised swish that reminded her he had a little girl upstairs he evidently tended himself.

'Have you other wounds you didn't tell me about?' he asked as she slumped back on the temptingly comfortable bed.

'No,' she said and had to stop herself tumbling back and falling asleep in front of him.

'Then stand up as best you can and I'll pull back the covers so you can finally lie down and rest,' he ordered abruptly.

'Yes, Papa,' she murmured defiantly, but did as he said, trying not to notice that a hot shiver threatened to streak through her as he reached round her scantily clad person to do so.

'Believe me, I don't feel in the least bit fatherly towards you at the moment, Perdita,' he warned gruffly.

Without visible effort he lifted her on to the clean cotton sheet covering the mattress before drawing the bedclothes over her and tucking her in as if it was far safer to have her covered up and neatly pinned into her bed for the night. Sighing with bliss at the feel of clean sheets and a comfortable bed, she opened her eyes long enough to mutter a thank you before tumbling headlong into unconsciousness between one word and the next.

'You're welcome, my lady,' Rich whispered as he watched the strain leave her face and sleep smooth her features into someone softer and younger than she tried to pretend she was when awake.

Shaking his head at the contrariness of fate in bringing her to his door in such a state he couldn't turn her away, he gestured to Atlas to come outside once more and relieve himself before they both settled down for the night. Reassured that his guest would hardly wake if a battalion of Boney's soldiers began manoeuvres in his vegetable garden, he waited for Atlas in the cool of the late spring evening and tried to forget he had just put a very adult woman to bed in the corner of his living room and he couldn't fairly be rid of her until she was strong enough to walk away.

If tonight was anything to go by, he would be raving mad by the end of the week that ankle probably needed for her to be able to put it to the ground for long without pain. He felt raw with unwanted longings, bewildered by the animal need he felt for a female he probably wouldn't even have liked if he'd met her as humble woodsman to her regal lady of high birth and position. The beast in any man could sometimes shock him, but his seemed to have taken on a life of its own tonight, even though he'd thought his Annabelle had tamed it and spoilt him for any other woman while she was about it.

Urges were there to be controlled, he assured himself, and his high-born waif had been through far too much to suffer from his, even if he wanted her to. He would offer her shelter, food and warmth until she was well, then he would set her back on her way with a huge sigh of relief. A week with a woman he wanted but couldn't have seemed like a lifetime at the moment, but Rich sighed morosely, whistled Atlas back inside and stole upstairs as quietly as a thief in the night. Closing the door of his narrow bedroom on the world and trying to sleep after a long day working hard, caring for his children and rescuing grumpy young ladies from their own folly, he tossed and turned until exhaustion finally overtook him and all the occupants of the isolated cottage deep in Longborough Forest finally slept.

'Is she going to sleep for a hundred years like the princess in the forest?' a shrill little whisper sounded so close to Freya's ear that she felt as if she was swimming from fathoms' depth of sleep to meet it coming the other way.

'Of course not, silly, that's a fairytale,' a slightly less shrill, but still very young voice replied scornfully. 'She's probably dead.'

She wondered if the second child might be right for a fleeting second as she tried to make sense of an unfamiliar bed and a world she'd forgotten to be terrified of while lost in slumber. The throbbing pain in her ankle, half-a-dozen lesser ones and the stiffness of her aching limbs made her feel half a century older than she was, but informed her she was alive and suffering for all the things she'd done yesterday to stay that way.

'Is not so, she just blinked.'

Freya felt the second child's breath on her cheek as he, for somehow she thought he sounded like a boy, stood on tiptoe to peer at her inquisitively, as if he rather hoped she might be his first real dead body and his sister was imagining that movement. Forcing open eyes heavy with sleep, she met the boy's brilliantly blue eyes at very close range and wondered if she might be in heaven after all. At first glance he could have sat for a cherub on an altarpiece; a second look showed the mischief and verve in his bright blue eyes and told her a very human boy was gazing at her as if he'd never seen anyone quite so odd.

'Move,' the tot at his side ordered and swatted him with the carved dog in her hand with such vigour Freya winced on his behalf. 'I can't see,' the little girl explained as if it justified anything she must do to change that sad state of affairs.

'I'll put Pod in the bonfire next time we have one and burn him to cinders,' the boy said as he rubbed his bruises and tried to grab her weapon.

'No, you won't, you won't, you won't,' the furious little girl ordered at the top of her voice and seemed about to bellow herself into a storm of tears at the very idea.

'I thought I told you two limbs of Satan to let the lady sleep,' Freya's rescuer of the night before interrupted what might well be an inexhaustible tantrum, given the way the tot had screwed up her face and seemed about to settle into a fine dramatic performance.

'We did, Dada, we did,' the little girl said with such a purposefully winsome smile Freya felt her heart melt at the sheer brass-faced audacity of her.

'I dare say you did, for a whole minute after I took my eyes off you so I could take that thorn out of Atlas's foot you said you were so upset about. Next time I shall have to leave it in, if that is what you get up to as soon as my back is turned.'

'Oh, no, Papa,' she begged and real emotion in her clear green eyes revealed what a fine little actress she was the rest of the time.

'No, for I wouldn't let a kind and decent animal like Atlas suffer for the misdeeds of a naughty little girl and her big brother, both of whom are old enough to know better.'

'We wanted to see if she was dead or not,' her brother said earnestly.

'As you woke her up to find out, you now know otherwise and may say your best hello, then beg the lady's pardon,' the now clean-shaven and disturbingly attractive Orlando said as coldly as he could with two pairs of wide and innocent eyes gazing at him as if their owners never had a wicked thought in their lives. 'I'm your father, don't forget. I know you two imps were sent from Hades to plague the rest of us, so there's no point pretending to be little angels with me. Make your curtsy, Sally, and you, young man, can give the lady your best bow for waking her when a big boy of more than five ought to do as he's told by now.'

'We're very sorry for disturbing your rest, lady,' the boy said with a quaint courtly bow that instantly enslaved Freya.

'Sally?' the tough little girl's father prompted and it looked for a moment as if he might have a revolution on his hands.

'We're thorry,' she said, as if expecting them to fall for the lisped sweetness of her false words so hard they would forget the rest.

'And?' her father prompted ruthlessly.

Sally sighed, a long-suffering gust that said *Do I really have to?* A quick nod from her father told her she wasn't going to get away without one, so she attempted a wobbly curtsy before plumping down on the floor with an annoyed huff.

'I can't do it,' she informed them crossly and sat there with her arms folded over her chest and a furious frown on her face as if it must be someone else's fault.

'You'll learn, if we both live long enough,' her unsympathetic father said and plucked her up, set her on her feet, then ignored her mutinous expression as he frowned at Freya.

'Go back to sleep,' he ordered brusquely before leaving the house with his children firmly in tow.

'Well, really,' Freya huffed at Atlas, who decided he preferred peace and quiet to being with his master this morning and settled on his rug with a relieved sigh.

Reluctantly amused by him, his master and the determined son and daughter of the house, Freya lay back and almost did as she was told. Deciding after five minutes she was now fully awake, she fought her many aches and pains to sit up in bed and wondered if the room would spin round or not if she tried to get up. When it stayed obligingly as it was, she risked pushing back the covers and, examining the grubby hem of her shift, she marvelled at herself for sleeping in all her dirt even after such a demanding day as she had had yesterday.

Wrinkling her nose at the idea of somehow getting herself clean, then having to put the mired and torn gown of yesterday back on, she carefully slid her good foot to the floor and stood on one leg. Her body felt stiff and sore and her ankle throbbed sickeningly, but she was whole and alive and the rumble in her stomach reminded her she was also desperately hungry. First she needed soap and water and a comb—oh, and a privy, her body reminded her as normal everyday needs collided with brisk reality. The expectation that all those necessities would be provided for Lady Freya Buckle without question made her feel alien and suddenly very alone and forsaken in this cramped cottage in the woods. She looked about for inspiration and saw only that the place was neat as a pin and surprisingly free of dust and dirt.

Hopping to the door 'Orlando' had opened last night to fetch cold water and binding for her foot, she opened it and found a spartan lean-to scullery with a cold and empty copper and two large buckets of water standing on a scrubbed deal table. There was an empty bowl and a metal cup on a long handle that she supposed must be used to scoop up water without the risk of spilling most of it by tipping the heavy bucket. Her nose wrinkled as she wondered how it would feel to wash in freezing cold water and she shrugged and looked about her for some soap and anything to use as a towel because even that was preferable to staying dirty for another minute. Cursing her absent host for being so remorselessly tidy, she ran a half-used washing ball that smelt of lavender and summer to earth in a box on the windowsill, then wondered if she could hop back to her bed and draw the curtains while she washed, or simply do so here when that would mean spilling most of the contents of the bowl on her way.

Improvising with the rough piece of un-bleached cloth he probably used for wiping the dishes for a towel, she made sure the door was firmly shut before unlacing her short corset and stripping off her ragged and dirty shift. The blessed relief of cool water and remarkably good soap on her skin made her sigh with pleasure and she washed the sweat and fear and grime from her face and upper torso before attending to her filthy and scratched legs and feet. It wasn't easy to get yourself thoroughly clean while standing on one leg, she found, and a sponge or flannel would have been a wonderful help.

Frowning at the very feel of her still half-pinned-up hair and the wild bird's nest the rest of it felt as bits tried to escape while the rest was still in a knot, she searched for her hairpins and piled them up on the table and sighed with relief when the whole heavy mass tumbled down. Oh, the sheer pleasure and relief of feeling the uncombed length of it flow down her back and the pull and tangle subside a little. Freya went back to her filthy feet and legs and found another bowl to fill with clean water when the soap scum and mire in the first seemed too disgusting to use any more.

At last she felt as clean as she could make herself without a hot bath and shut off the blissful thought of one of those with a regretful sigh at the very moment the door to the little kitchen-cum-scullery opened and Orlando strode in. Horrified and at the same time oddly frozen in her position, half-propped and half-sitting on the table so she could wash her good foot and take the weight off her bad one, she blushed so hotly it felt as if every inch of her must be covered in shame. Peeping at him from behind her tumbling mass of hair, she saw an arrested, almost shocked look on his face—as if he'd been hit on the head for no good reason. This time she noted numbly that his eyes were as clear and green as his little daughter's by daylight and full of contrary emotions as they fixed on her like a sailor sighting land after a long voyage.

'I beg your pardon,' he finally managed in a deeper and huskier voice than normal and turned sharply about and was out of the door before she could think of a word to say.

Since she still couldn't, it was probably as well he'd disappeared faster than a scalded cat, she decided, making herself finish her makeshift *toilette*. She was contemplating her grubby chemise and shift with disgust when the door opened the smallest distance it took for a vigorous male hand to squeeze through it, then drop clean replacements on the floor before shutting it firmly once more. For some odd reason it seemed funny and Freya gratefully pulled on the chemise as she tried not to giggle hysterically at the latest act in the farce she and Orlando seemed to be playing.

She looked ruefully at the shift before

scrambling into it and decided his wife must have been considerably shorter than herself. It seemed she would have to wear her own half-ruined gown to preserve any hint of decency, if only she knew what he'd done with it. The next time the door did its remarkable trick he produced a cotton bedcover she took silently and wrapped round her body like a bath towel, before stiffening her shockingly naked shoulders and hopping out to face him as best she could. It took every ounce of well-honed Buckle pride to meet his eyes as if he hadn't just seen her in the same state of nature in which she came into the world.

'I should like to borrow a comb,' she said loftily.

'These belonged to my wife,' he said with so little expression in his green gaze as he handed her a brush and comb she almost forgot to be deeply mortified for a moment.

'Thank you,' she returned and raised her eyebrows at him to indicate he should now make himself scarce if he was any sort of a gentleman at all.

'I have been promised an outfit that I doubt very much is up to your usual standards whilst your own gown is being washed and mended. I will see you have it as soon as possible now you are up and awake,' he said stiffly and took himself off.

Freya crossed to the bed with more painful effort than she liked to think about and sank down on it before pulling the curtain across behind her so she would have the belated illusion of privacy. She examined the brush as if it might give her some clue to the woman who once owned it, but not even one stray strand remained to tell her what colour hair the lady had rejoiced in. Freya sighed and began the long and frustrating business of combing out the wild tangles from her own heavy mane and heartily wished for the ladies' maid she had left at Bowland with not even a second thought how she would shift for herself without her. Of course she knew how to comb her own hair, everyone knew that, but she thought of the gentle patience little Mercy Dawkins had always shown her exacting mistress and felt oddly ashamed as she teased knot after knot from her rebellious locks.

She wasn't a fool, she decided as distance and the oddest of circumstances made her think hard about her day-to-day self, but Lady Freya Buckle had managed to go through life so far without thinking too hard about herself or those around her. The loss of her grandfather had hit her far harder than that of her own father and the sudden death of her mother two years earlier had shaken her world to its very foundations. Apart from those two heavy losses, the only event that had caused her even the mildest suffering until yesterday was the marriage of his Grace the Duke of Dettingham to Miss Jessica Pendle, and that certainly wasn't because her heart was broken.

No, she decided now with a preoccupied frown as she finally tracked down the piece of twig caught in the depths of her worst knot so far and set about removing it without pulling a hank of hair out with it, the fact that he preferred a lame spinster to the Earl of Buckland's pretty daughter had been the first indication the rest of the world didn't share her conviction she was entitled to all the best things in life that society had to offer her. For a while she had been so offended and furious she hadn't asked herself why Jack Seaborne, Duke of Dettingham, preferred damaged Miss Pendle to her pristine and noble self.

She and her mother had been a little too sure Lady Freya would be the next Duchess and the subsequent Little Season had been dogged by sniggers and snide whispers as she tried to pretend she didn't care that the new Duchess was still on a protracted wedding journey about the Lakes with her besotted husband. The most eligible bachelors had begun to slide out of dances with her and find themselves engaged when Lady Bowland organised an elegant supper party or visit to the theatre and Freya had somehow become a laughing stock to the very people she had so wanted to impress with her ancient lineage and proud good looks when she made her début.

It had taken Lady Bowland's death and two years of living at Bowland, instead of comfortably ensconced in the Dower House with Mama, to finally make her realise she was not some entitled being, blessed by every god of good fortune at her christening. Being stripped of the advantages of wealth and rank had forced her into her true self: Lady Freya, the glowing hope of her mother and grandfather's wildest dreams, was gone. Here sat a woman who must find out what she really wanted from life before it was too late to achieve it and suddenly she was determined to find out what that was as soon as possible.

She squirmed on the disarrayed bed and tried to tell herself it was the constant nag of pain from her ankle making her so restless, even as her fingers patiently continued the task she'd set them. It wasn't the fact she'd been seen mother-naked by Orlando, but she had to admit the sneaky idea it could be very pleasant indeed if he was entirely undressed too haunted her like a bad dream. She shifted impatiently again and had to suppress a yelp of agony as her injured foot reminded her how desperate her current situation was. Clearly it behoved her to behave like a lady for however long it took her to heal, then depart with as much of her tattered reputation and self-esteem intact as possible.

Despite her burning cheeks and the shock she should be suffering from, she wondered how she had looked to Orlando and didn't even notice her busy fingers had found the last knot in her nut-brown hair and she was now combing the heavy softness of it as if her life depended on it. Even allowing for the flattery her rank and fortune attracted while the *ton* laughed at her behind her back, she knew she was pretty enough and reasonably well formed. She was shaped like a nymph rather than a goddess and some might consider her slight and unformed, of course. Yet perhaps some men preferred subtlety to the obvious charms of more buxom women, she let herself wonder. After all, her legs were long and slender and her waist small above the long line of her hips. Feeling as guilty as if she was testing the ebb and flow of those very curves with her own hands to see if they could please a lover, she gasped at the thought of Orlando ever watching her with a lover's eyes and told herself it was with horror at the very idea.

Chapter Four

No use trying to pretend any longer she was essentially cold and passionless when she wasn't even deceiving herself. The leap of hot and vigorous fire at the heart of her, the quickening of what felt like every inch of the body, made this new Freya feel very different from the old one. Not sure she approved of the change, she laid down the wide-toothed comb and took up the brush with the vague idea soothing her abused hair into shining smoothness might somehow turn her back into the safe and certain Freya she had been before she found Dukes didn't obligingly fall into her lap like apples from a tree.

She had never felt this hot burn of curiosity towards the tall and strikingly handsome

Duke of Dettingham, of course, but had assured herself during that June when he'd set up a house party at Ashburton New Place to choose his Duchess that she was born and bred for marriage to the highest in the land. He was well enough and so was she and she assumed that would make their marriage bed a bearable place to beget a tribe of little lords and ladies.

Some determined remnant of the old Freya whispered she was right, but the idea of such a marriage with Jack Seaborne now seemed icy cold as she sat on the lowly bed of a lowly man and fought *not* to think about sharing it with him. Shorn of the stubble of the day before, his face had been sharply defined in the soft north light of the shadowy scullery. It wasn't as if he was starkly handsome like Jack Seaborne, she told herself crossly, or romantically dashing like the Earl of Calvercombe, who had married Jack's lovely cousin Persephone so soon after the ducal wedding that rumours of a dashing scandal had flown delightedly about the *ton* for weeks. Even young Telemachus Seaborne, known as Marcus, would outshine Orlando if he had cared to shine in anyone but his stormy-looking young wife's eyes, and everyone knew theirs was another love match.

Why on earth she was sitting here dwelling on the family who had begun her descent into the ranks of the unmarriageable she had no idea. Perhaps it was because Orlando struck her as a man of suppressed power, she suddenly realised, and her instincts were probably better than she'd realised back when so much was done for her she had never needed to test them. Or at least she hoped they were, because if he wasn't an honourable man she could still be in deep trouble. It was obvious he had deliberately marooned himself in the heart of this forest where nobody would find him except by the purest chance, but he didn't strike her as a man who would run from trouble. She could imagine him meeting it with guile and reckless courage, but not hiding where he could do no good except to his family and there, she decided with a triumphant sense of those instincts leading her well, was the key to the whole mystery.

For the wife she sensed had been more dearly loved by her Orlando than Lady Freya Buckle had ever dared dream of being loved by a man, he would have crossed oceans and fought every battle it took to keep her safe. The reason he was still here now had to mean there was some sort of threat to his children as well and she shook her head and frowned, dubious at the idea anyone would harm such bright and hopeful little mysteries in miniature. Had he eloped with Mrs Orlando in the teeth of powerful opposition? she wondered. He was clearly raised a gentleman, so maybe he had been tutor to a noble family and run off with some great lord's daughter? Or, worse still, could it have been the man's own lady he stole away from him? She would have been the man's legal chattel and he couldn't raise a bill to divorce her in the House of Lords, or drag her home by her hair to fulfil her duty and bear *him* a boy instead, if he couldn't actually find her in the first place.

Freya tried to be shocked by the very idea of such scandalous goings on, but found she couldn't blame the woodsman's wife if she had decided she preferred him to some fat old noble her family had forced her to marry. She had nearly been the victim of such a conspiracy herself, although she lacked the gallant rescuer who would make that marriage to the fat politician irrelevant. Finding herself guilty of the most shocking immorality as she wondered why the woman couldn't have taken a handsome and vigorous young lover to make up for the lack of both in her marriage bed, Freya reminded herself this was all speculation and even the prospect of a one-day lover could not have reconciled her to marriage with Bowland's latest repellent protégé.

Maybe Orlando was a follower of Rousseau, or a romantic philosopher-poet who preferred a simple life wrenched from the forest by his own hand? Yet the picture of him, austere and intent as he stood and watched her for one long moment with hot green eyes telling of unimagined delights in his bed, argued he had once been a more rash and hedonistic adventurer than any idealistic poet or shrinking recluse could ever be. For a quick and wickedly exciting minute she knew how it felt to be urgently wanted by a compelling rake. Then he doused the lust and longing and promise sparking between them before it could become a blaze and walked away as if she was dressed from head to toe in propriety.

Dropping the brush on the rumpled bedclothes as if it had become red hot, Freya fought off the most ridiculous jealousy of the woman who once owned it. Her now wildly flying imagination invited her to visualise Orlando brushing her hair for her with long, sensual strokes as he played with the heavy locks and arranged them over her naked body to his satisfaction, before satisfying her as royally as a woman had ever been satisfied by her man. Except she had no idea how it felt to be sensually seduced and satiated, she reminded herself sternly.

Nor did she want to know, if her lover had to be this penniless ex-pirate who hid in the woods from his own kind. A burn of curiosity tightened her suddenly very sensitive nipples under the bedcover toga and made her squirm against the surprisingly comfortable mattress under her, as she sought to douse the inquisitive fire at her feminine core. She told herself she didn't want a rustic lover with two bold and enterprising children dependent on him as both father and mother, who were likely to resent even the smallest sharing of his attention with her. As soon as she could put her foot to the floor with any degree of comfort she would walk out of here and not look back, ever.

So why did it feel as if she was on sabbatical from her duty once she'd plaited her hair a little clumsily and tried to put her foot to the floor once more? Pain shot through her as sharp and almost sickening as it had been last night when she first injured herself. Fool, she castigated herself as she tottered across the room in search of the next necessity of life and peered out of the door for a privy or con-

veniently secluded bush to relieve herself behind, since the problem was becoming urgent.
Spotting a rustic shelter some yards upwind of
the house, she blessed the fact she hadn't tumbled into his cesspit last night and told herself
Lady Freya Buckle could not afford to expect
comfort in this most basic form of country life.
She hopped towards the honeysuckle-covered
shelter with her flapping bedcover grasped to
her body with one hand, while she used the
other to prop herself upright with a stout stick
left leaning by the back door for her with a
consideration she refused to find disarming.

It didn't matter if he had been sensitive
enough to her needs to let her get on with
learning to do as much for herself as she
could. Yet Lady Freya seemed to be fading
into a stiff caricature of herself as she embraced being Perdita instead. She reflected
on William Shakespeare's story of a found-
ling princess left to be brought up by peasants.
How would she have been now if she had been
taken from Bowland Castle in some fanciful
start of her father's that her mother had been
unfaithful and his despised daughter was not
his child? A nagging suspicion she might be
relieved *not* to be Lady Freya Buckle seemed

unthinkable, considering her mother brought her up so proud of the ancient name she bore.

Luckily the privy turned out to be surprisingly clean and smelt of tarred wood and earth as much as it did of humanity. Observing the strange device her host had rigged up for his family, she shovelled what looked like dried earth into the hole after herself and hoped that would cover everything, then limped back towards the cottage feeling considerably better, if now left with one less distraction from being very hungry indeed.

'We're having Percy for breakfast,' the boy popped out of the trees at the other side of the clearing to inform her mysteriously and the little girl doggedly caught up with a squeal of triumph, as if she spent most of her life following her big brother about just in time to watch him disappear again.

'Who is Percy?' Freya asked distractedly as the delicious cooking smells emanating from the direction he had just come from began to tease her eager nostrils.

'One of last year's piglets,' he told her with a resigned shrug for the realities of cottage life that left Freya wondering if she really wanted to know the name of her food before she ate it.

'It smells delicious,' she managed as hunger fought her scruples for at least ten seconds as her mouth watered at the scent of breakfast and wood-smoke.

'It is 'licious,' Sally stated emphatically, with a frown in her direction, as if it was her fault they weren't already eating. 'Papa said we was to fetch you,' she accused and Freya realised it would be no easy task to win over the female so firmly in possession of the cottage and its owner's heart.

'That was kind of him. I am very hungry indeed after missing my luncheon *and* my dinner yesterday,' she said with unfeigned horror.

'Not even any supper?' the little girl asked with a slight softening towards this unwanted guest she had better not take for granted, Freya decided ruefully.

'By then I was too tired to care,' Freya confirmed and could almost see the child brace herself against nodding sympathetically.

'We're not tired and we're very hungry indeed, since Papa had to light a fire in the woods to cook on because we weren't supposed to disturb you,' the boy asserted with a cool stare that accused her of causing a delay he found nigh intolerable.

'And yet you still did so?' she said just as

coolly and met his uncannily direct blue eyes equal to equal.

'I never saw a dead person,' he explained as if that trumped every idea of polite consideration his long-suffering parent had tried to teach him.

'Oddly enough you still have not done so, have you?' she parried.

'No, unless you feel a bit ill?' he suggested as if she might, out of consideration for those who were kind enough to delay their breakfast for her.

'Not in the least,' she said airily and discovered it was true. 'Just a bit sore and my ankle hurts,' she admitted as she hobbled along and even little Sally had to slow down to match her pace.

'It could be worse than you think,' the boy suggested hopefully.

'Why are you so eager to see a dead person?' she asked.

''Cause my mama is one and I can't really remember what she looked like no more,' he said crossly, as if he blamed her for asking, but was still too young to lie.

'I'm very sorry about that. My mama is dead too, and I miss her every day of my life, but at least I remember her. I hadn't realised how lucky I was until I spoke to you, Master Whoever-you-are.'

'That's not my name,' he said, reluctantly impressed she shared his motherless state.

'He's called Hal,' the boy's sister said impatiently, as if everyone ought to know that and she was a very ignorant visitor after all.

'My name is Henry Craven, Master Henry Craven to you.'

'Very well then, Master Henry,' Freya said with the shadow of an elegant curtsy that was all she could manage with her staff clutched in her hand and an ankle that was sure to let her down if she bent any lower.

'Who are you, then?'

'Miss Perdita…' Freya cast about for a suitable alias and found inspiration all around her. 'Rowan,' she finally came out with and decided she might like being Miss Rowan of nowhere in particular, if she wasn't dressed in a bedcover and someone else's underwear whilst hobbling along like a ninety-year-old invalid to eat a breakfast her hosts were personally acquainted with before it became a tasty meal.

'It's a pretty name,' Sally approved with a smile of feminine conspiracy she must have acquired by instinct and years of manipulating her father mercilessly.

'Thank you, and so is yours, Miss Craven.'

'Papa, we found her,' Sally cried as if they had been looking much of the day and Freya tried not to envy her host the confident joy in the little girl's voice at the sight of him.

It would be easy to love the spirited and naughty little girl, Freya decided wistfully. Their father seemed to be raising his children as individuals, not patterns of childhood silence kept strictly away from the adult world her own father had expected children to be. She supposed it was easier to gently teach the realities of life when you lived in a hovel, not a mansion, and dined on what you could grow or raise, like poor Percy the pig.

'Your breakfast, ma'am,' Orlando said with a piratical bow as he handed her a trencher of rough bread topped with bacon, mushrooms from the forest and her share of a kind of omelette he seemed to have made with the addition of herbs and tips of various greens from the large garden he must have hacked out of the forest.

'Thank you, kind sir,' she said as she sank on to the tree stump they had saved for her with as much dignity as she could manage, which wasn't much as she tried to ease herself down without jarring her foot. 'It smells delicious.'

'Your fork, ma'am,' he added with the wicked parody of a liveried and impassive footman that made her wonder anew about his real place in the world.

'What a delightful luxury, Mr Craven,' she said lightly as she took the two-pronged, freshly carved wooden one he must have whittled especially for her.

'Then eat, Miss…' he said, trailing off as he realised she hadn't given her surname last night.

'She's called Miss Rowan, Papa, had you forgot?' his son piped between mouthfuls of food and shook his head at them with such quaint wonder they were bothering with social flummery while their food went cold that Freya was reluctantly enchanted all over again.

'I don't believe Miss Rowan gives her name as easily to grown gentlemen as she did to you, my son. You must have charmed her quite wondrously well.'

'Yes, he did,' Freya insisted in the face of Henry's slightly conscious flush at the memory he had actually demanded it of her rather rudely.

'Eat,' said Orlando Craven as if unable to argue with a lady just now.

Freya had never enjoyed breakfast so much, sitting on a tree stump in a forest clearing miles away from civilisation. Birds sang and Atlas snuffed politely about the edge of the clearing, pretending not to be lurking for leftovers. Every bite of crisp bacon, richly dark mushroom and deliciously herbed egg tasted like ambrosia and as the juices soaked into the bread underneath, it seemed no hardship it wasn't fine and white as she was used to and she pulled pieces off it with the same glee she saw in the children's rapt faces as they ate. Now and again she allowed herself a shy glance at Orlando and noted he ate with neat economy, but somehow the idea of him seeing her naked in his scullery not half an hour ago stopped her saying how she appreciated his cooking and the thoughtfulness that had made him do it outside and not disturb her. Because he had disturbed her, acutely.

'Better?' he asked at last, seeming to wake from some sort of reverie when she sighed and handed Atlas the still-savoury remains of the bread where the crust was too hard to eat without endangering her teeth.

'Much better, thank you,' she said with a

contented sigh. 'Your dog has very fine manners, Mr Craven,' she added as Atlas took the morsel with such polite courtesy she felt no fear as his impressive teeth and powerful jaws closed on it.

'Nice to know I can flatter myself on one success in that area,' he said with a stern eye on his angelic-looking offspring that argued he hadn't forgotten their disobedience.

'I wonder what time it is?' she mused, more to divert him than from an urgent need to know.

'About seven of the clock,' he said without reference to a timepiece and she must have betrayed her disbelief, since Sally piped up,

'Papa *always* knows what time it is.'

'I've learnt the habits of the sun and the creatures around me,' he said with a shrug, as if that wasn't an unusual skill, and Freya felt guiltily at her own ignorance about the busy schedules of those who must toil for a living.

'It must prove very useful,' she said and heard self-consciousness in her voice as she couldn't get the awkwardness of their last encounter out of her head.

'It is,' he said as if he couldn't either.

'Can we go, Papa?' Henry interrupted as if growing tired of adult silliness.

'So long as you stay within earshot,' his father said with a straight look that said he meant it and his son returned it with a solemn nod. Sally gave an exasperated shrug at the sheer contrariness of men that made Freya long to laugh out loud.

'And while my little demons are gone, we need to think about your day, Miss Rowan,' Orlando said without looking directly at her.

'I will try not to get in the way,' she said, Lady Freya's rigid dignity hard in her voice and she regretted the return to her old self more than she would have dreamt she could only yesterday.

'Don't be ridiculous,' he snapped as if she was demanding he devote every minute of it to her comfort.

Now Freya knew what Sally meant to convey with her long-suffering gesture. She must know all too well what it was like to live with two such prickly males. Freya wished she had the faintest idea how to cope with this Craven male and bit back a weary sigh.

'You still need to do whatever it is you do to earn your bread. I cannot see how my offer to let you do so is ridiculous, sir,' she told him with icy dignity.

Hopefully he didn't know how conscious

she was of sitting here with bare shoulders and a rather inept plait of hair hanging down her back. She did her best to stop her impromptu gown showing the length of her right leg to anyone who wanted to see it, even if he already had, along with the rest of her, and she tried hard not to blush at the very idea.

'A day away from it won't hurt me,' he said gruffly as if silently agreeing he was being unreasonable, but unable to stop being so.

'I don't need to be entertained like a fractious child.'

'Good, I already have two of those to cope with,' he said and finally the wry smile that had made her trust him against her will last night broke through his dark mood. 'We need to solve some practicalities before you hoe my peas to the ground or randomly chop down trees,' he told her as if he had as little confidence in her domestic skills as she did herself.

'Even I know this isn't the time of year to fell whatever it is you usually fell.'

'And do you know a pea from a bean?'

'Not unless it's on my plate.'

'So you might as well agree to leave them where they are until I can teach you which is which, might you not?' he said.

She wondered if he really thought Lady

Freya Buckle might dirty her hands and get blisters on her fine soft skin to repay his hospitality, or relieve her boredom in a household without the usual ladylike occupations. Freya nodded regally and wondered what on earth she *was* going to do with herself while she waited to be well enough to walk away.

'It will all work out in the end,' he reassured her as if he knew the reality of her situation had come rushing back as soon as she thought about the day she would have to leave here and go back to finding her way in the wider world.

'I really don't see how,' she argued with a quiet despair that sounded very un-Lady Freya-like in her own ears.

'With life and hope it's remarkable what the human spirit can cope with, Perdita,' he said and she supposed he must know what he was talking about.

'I know and I will try to be more optimistic.'

'And perhaps agree you need to sleep as well?'

'Perhaps.'

'Then why don't you do so while I take the children over to fetch some clothes for you?'

'I don't see why you should put yourself to so much trouble, sir,' she said a little stiffly, wondering where he was to get them and a ludicrous shaft of jealousy bit into her as some likely possibilities leapt into her mind.

Chapter Five

Orlando let his eyes rest on Freya's smooth white shoulders and the swell of her breasts under the tightly knotted cotton, then the hint of a bare calf under her awkwardly shuffled-up draperies and she flushed. If he was one or two of the gentlemen she had met in society, or the two greedy-eyed villains of yesterday, she would shrink from his open masculine scrutiny, but this was Orlando. Part of her she didn't dare to examine too closely was flattered if he thought her desirable and, given the banked-down heat in his eyes, she rather thought he did—whether or not he welcomed the fact was perhaps more open to question.

'It will be no trouble,' he assured her softly.

Freya had no idea if he meant he wanted

her covered up so he didn't have to watch her with too many possibilities in his eyes, or because he knew she was uncomfortable with her bare shoulders and arms so blatantly on show. 'Then I must thank you in advance for your trouble,' she said and let her eyes meet his properly for the first time since he had seen all she was this morning.

'You are welcome, lady,' he said with a version of his son's courtly bow that made her realise where young Henry got his grace and some of his swagger.

It was a bow that said *here is a gentleman of power and leisure who only bends his knee to anyone because he chooses to.* She could imagine him an immaculately dressed beau strutting up St James's long after noon, to meet one of his select band of cronies for whatever elegant dissipation they had planned for the day. Frowning at the idea he might be even more of a mystery than she'd thought, she used the staff to get up and made certain no more of her showed than was inevitable in her state of semi-nakedness. If she had met him in a London drawing room when she first came out, might he have saved her all the petty humiliations of the last few years? He must have been wed and done with the stifling elegance of the London Season by the time she came out, if he'd ever been tame enough for that in the first place, so it was just as well he hadn't been there to confuse her even more.

'Where are the children?' she asked to distract herself from such silly daydreams.

'About somewhere. They usually obey me in their own unique fashion and at least Atlas is with them,' he said as he stood aside for her to precede him.

'Would it not be better if you went ahead? I'm very slow, despite the staff you kindly found for me.'

'Who knows what you might get up to if I leave you to make your own way, Perdita? You might even find a bear to chase you.'

She chuckled at the reference to the most unlikely stage direction in the whole of Shakespeare's mighty canon—'exit, pursued by a bear'—and decided to occupy herself by reading *A Winter's Tale* from the volumes of the great playwright's work from the shelf slotted in next to her box-bed, as he clearly had to use every inch of the small space the cottage allowed.

Rich fought the husky and totally unselfconscious appeal of the right sort of feminine laughter. He vividly recalled the high-pitched titter of the débutantes and their older, freer sisters as they did their best to charm elusive Richard Seaborne, grandson of a Duke and close relative and friend to the wild and deliciously elusive Jack, Duke of Dettingham. Now the difference between those brittle, affected lovelies and his lost princess was so similar to the gulf between his Annabelle and the rest of her kind it should make him wary.

This odd mix of a girl–woman was so different from his love in so many ways the comparison seemed odd. Perdita was naturally arrogant as Annabelle had never been, but she had the same dauntless spirit. She was also much taller, her limbs long and slender and, despite her limp, he knew a little too well how sleek and seemingly endless her legs were under her draperies. That endless moment of wolfish desire in his own scullery had shown him her curves were more pared down than Annabelle's. The thought of Perdita's firm high breasts, with just enough richness to fit easily in a man's palm, sent desire shooting through him in a warm shudder of temptation at the thought of her standing there slim, naked and perfect, and so very shocked by all the possibilities humming between them.

He was a man with huge responsibilities on his shoulders, he reminded himself. A father and protector who thought he'd buried such endlessly demanding urges to sink into a woman's body and glory in her to their mutual satisfaction in his Annabelle's grave. Still the sight of another woman's neat *derrière* outlined by the fine cotton cover his wife had so carefully hemmed into a summer bedcover made his loins leap and his breath shorten and he had to send his thoughts somewhere compelling to stop himself becoming a complete satyr.

What is mad Jack Seaborne doing right now? he quizzed himself and found it didn't help him at all. Knowing his cousin, Rich had little doubt Jack would be making love to his wife at this hour of the morning. He allowed himself a wry smile at the thought of Jack and lovely, determined Jessica Pendle so wrapped up in loving each other they had no time for silly ideas about dynastic marriage so many of their kind suffered from. He knew as soon as he found out who Jack was going to marry it was a love match, despite all Jack's raving against them. Jess would be so good for him, Rich thought, as he plodded behind another decided female and fought the appeal of such a woman to a family cursed to love for life.

Which led him to his mother, who had shared a marriage of true minds with his noble father; better to consider how the other woman in his life might be going about her daily life than battling with the uncomfortable idea he might not be as immune to ladies of character and undeniable attraction as he hoped. His sources told him Lady Henry Seaborne had insisted on retiring to a neat house in Ashbourne village once her nephew Jack, Rich's sister Persephone and his little brother Telemachus wed their own Seaborne obsessions one by one. How he wished he could see his mother again and tell her how much he loved her. Even the thought of her should make Miss so-called Rowan invisible, but the idea of how shocked Lady Henry would be at her eldest son lusting after a waif in need of his protection and not seduction only made her more of a problem.

Relieved they were nearly at his door, he tried to block out the feral fantasy of rushing this female thorn in his side inside the cottage to make hasty love with her on the box-bed. He wondered for a tortuous moment what her children would look like—would she have lion cubs to take on her golden-amber eyes and that rich nut-brown pelt of hair hanging down her back, hers a silken lure he desperately wanted to feel under his stroking hand? Or would those cubs of hers share his green Seaborne gaze as stubbornly as most of his relatives insisted on doing? The potent idea of a mix of both was as utterly ridiculous as it was forbidden to Annabelle's husband and a man who dared not even admit his real name.

'Atlas will stay with you if you prefer not to be alone,' he made himself say coolly, as if he'd been thinking of the state of the nation while they got here at her slow pace.

He watched her consider the idea with her head on one side as he realised she often did when weighing up her options. No need to find that appealing and at the same time worrying. She shouldn't have to consider her next action or word might be reckless or wrong as she appeared to out of ingrained habit. His Seaborne blood rebelled at the idea of a strong woman so confined by her role in life that all spontaneity was drummed out of her.

Perhaps her misadventures had broken the cocoon so many aristocratic young ladies were bound in and he couldn't think it a bad thing, even if she *was* in danger of turning into a siren. An unconscious and unwary one, he reminded himself, but the idea threatened to remind him he was a wolf by nature, not the tame creature of hearth and home he currently appeared to be.

'And miss the chance of a good run? I wouldn't deprive such a truly noble creature of such a simple pleasure,' she replied to his question and he had to rack his brain to remind himself what it was.

'Atlas would see it as his duty,' he remembered with relief.

'I know, but sometimes duty makes us slaves and he takes them too seriously already. He is a true gentleman in dog form, Mr Craven, so where did he come from?'

'He was a half-grown puppy back then and living with a rather gentle elderly lady I met on the Weald of Kent. He had been thrown out to shift for himself, but was too large and lively for her and she begged me to take him on. I brought him home and never regretted it, even when he ate Anna's favourite pair of shoes and chewed Hal's hobby-horse so badly I had to stay up all night to make another in the hope he wouldn't notice.'

'Since I don't see tooth marks everywhere now I assume he got over the habit?' she asked and he realised she was making polite conversation to divert them from their odd situation and the strained atmosphere between them. Could she read the earthy thoughts behind his distraction, or was she too innocent to know he wanted her as he shouldn't want any respectable female, let alone a lady he hadn't even met this time yesterday?

'Aye, he's grown into a sober and responsible gentleman,' he agreed, knowing she was right to try to make things as normal as possible between them.

'Like his master?' she suggested as if it might make him so.

'Would that was so, Miss Rowan,' he replied ruefully.

'A gentleman who brings up his children as well as you appear to have done has to be so, doesn't he, Mr Craven?'

Luckily her touching belief in his integrity and the name he had given Anna and himself in a fit of bitterness at having to hide from their enemies sobered him. He was still a coward to keep his children away from their heritage, but one who would keep on doing so as long as there was any threat claiming it back would endanger them. Until they were grown and able to deal with their foes they must stay hidden, he decided bleakly. Another fifteen years of exile loomed endlessly and reminded him he had nothing to offer a lost vagabond, let alone a lady in distress.

'They make a fine corrective against my more selfish needs and desires,' he admitted as he cast his eyes round the room as he always had when Anna was alive, to reassure himself there was no threat to his lady and his love hiding in a corner.

Best not to even think about that fierce instinct to protect his mate, he ordered himself, as he climbed the stairs to check nothing lurked above. Annoyed to feel the dangerous knife-edge of caring what happened to a vulnerable female while he was absent once more, he told himself nobody could squeeze through the tiny squares of glass he had let into the gable walls of each cramped bedroom and there had been no need to look in the first place.

'All's well. You'll be perfectly safe from intrusions if you bar the door behind us,' he informed his amused guest, who was now sitting on the edge of the bed flicking through his volumes of Shakespeare.

'I shall do very well,' she assured him and, since half her attention seemed on the book, he suddenly felt awkward and in the way.

'Would you like me to light the fire again?'

'I'm not ill,' she said as if the very idea was ridiculous and he concluded she'd been brought up with a host of contrary expectations.

'A good many females would be after such an ordeal.'

'But I am not a fragile flower.'

'Let me hear you bar the door behind me anyway,' he ordered and swung on his heel so he wouldn't have to look at her any more and long to be on the wrong side of that door when she barred it to the rest of the world.

'Yes, Papa,' she said meekly and hopped to the door so she could do exactly what he'd thought he wanted her to and shut him out.

Rich listened to the thud of the stout lock he'd made to fit the equally stout door so he could leave Anna and the baby alone while he went off to sell the furniture and nick-knacks he made from the wood he felled in the forest and 'bodged' together. He stared at the stout oak planks for a long moment, rueing his folly. Time to remember real life, he reminded himself as he whistled Atlas and waited to see which direction the faithful mastiff came from, so he could find his children without having to yell and disturb half the creatures of the forest as well as Miss Rowan. Like the first name he had given her, she certainly hadn't been called by that one before she christened herself today. There, he was thinking about her *again*. Doing his best to slam aside the memory of the slender nymph he'd spied naked at her *toilette* this morning, he greeted his dishevelled children and promised them a piggyback ride by strict rotation as they set out for Keziah's cottage, which lay just far enough away to suit their mutual liking for isolation whenever they weren't feeling sociable.

Melissa Seaborne finally gave up trying to court sleep and padded to the windows in order to draw back the curtains and watch June sunlight flood the mellow landscape outside. She selected a book from the shelf before returning to bed and piling up her pillows behind her to make a comfortable nest. How she wished her Lord Henry was still here to share the easy intimacy of such an early morning, she thought wistfully, smiling regretfully at the thought that there would be little time for reading if only he was.

After six years of widowhood, she still missed him so sorely it could hurt like a knife to the gut at the most unexpected moments.

She let the memory of holding each of her grandchildren and her great-niece in her arms without her beloved Hal at her side to dote on them edge in. Wonderful occasions every one, but not to grow old with her love and her lover, never to share such joy with him again, was an everyday loss that was overwhelming at times like this.

She thought by moving out of Ashburton New Place, and refusing to tenant Seaborne House in the absence of her eldest son, this house would give her a home with no heavy reminders of the husband and father her two then-unwed daughters had lost to sadden them. Her lovely Helen was now blissfully content with a new husband and Penelope a happy and popular young lady who would be introduced to the startled *ton* as a beauty to rival her famously lovely elder sister, Persephone, Countess of Calvercombe, in a few short years. To their mama, all her chicks were extraordinary, but fifteen-year-old Penelope would fight beaux off the instant she came out, if not for the fierce protection of her cousin Jack, brother Telemachus and two brothers-in-law who didn't suffer fools very gladly at all.

'How hard it can be at times to have such fine offspring as ours, Hal,' Melissa murmured and caught herself in her habit of talking to her husband as if he was still here that she knew others would find deeply eccentric or plain mad. 'If I could see our dear Rich again maybe the world would fit together a little better without you, my love,' she added wistfully and caught herself looking out of the window at a fine view of her rose garden and the distant Welsh hills beyond.

Her eldest son could be out there, among those green and lovely hills, or maybe even adrift on the other side of the world and she would never know, she decided gloomily. Little wonder she felt so dismal on this shiningly beautiful morning. As long as he was safe, that was all that mattered, and she knew he must have the best of reasons for staying away. When she had learnt Richard had disappeared at the same time as Lord Calvercombe's young cousin Annabelle, it was a relief to know he'd done it for love, not perversity. If they were happy, she told herself, she would be glad and bide her time until it was safe for them to reappear. Meanwhile, their disappearance brought dear Alex Forthin, Earl of Calvercombe, to look for a clue where his cousin had gone and found a countess in her darling Persephone instead.

Three years ago her nephew Jack had wed his Duchess and her goddaughter, Jessica Pendle. Shortly afterwards Persephone married her love, followed up the aisle three weeks later by Telemachus, her younger son, and his vivid and lovely Antigone. Lady Henry smiled at nothing in particular; Antigone was an endearing mix of fire and resolution and had kept Marcus on his toes and passionately absorbed since the day they'd first met as no freshly pretty débutante could ever have done. Their own son, Thomas Henry Seaborne, was a bright and headstrong Seaborne barely two years old, and he had a plain pair of names that argued she should have insisted on similar ones for her own children.

Lord Henry had loved his Homer and she'd done well to limit him to the more hopeful *Odyssey* and not descend into tragedy with names from the *Iliad*. After she got her own way and managed to name their first child for her beloved grandfather, she hadn't the heart to fight for a more conventional first name for their next one and after Telemachus, Henry came up with such charming suggestions for their daughters she could only agree. Poor Antigone hadn't been so lucky and her mama Electra had suffered an even more unlikely christening, the only time Melissa could feel sorrier for the woman than she did for herself, she concluded wryly. Her exasperation at Telemachus's totally self-absorbed mother-in-law often made her feel guilty. However many blessings life poured on Electra Warrender, they would never be enough and the greatest of them were the ones she valued least—her family.

Melissa hated the idea of growing bitter and demanding like Electra, yet without Rich in his rightful home with his family around him, she always had a stubborn worry at the back of her mind at excited family gatherings. Ordering herself to count the blessings showered on her, she still eyed those distant hills and wondered what Rich was doing as she did every morning and always would until she knew.

Despite her resolution not to sleep, Freya woke from dreams she didn't care to remember and glanced at the solemnly ticking clock. It was nearly two, if the clock was to be relied on and something told her it would be, since Orlando would see no point in a timepiece that lied. He might be able to tell the hour by the passage of the sun, or the flight of the moon or some such nonsense, but he probably liked his genius confirmed by the mechanisms of lesser men as well.

Unfair, she rebuked herself, he struck her as a practical man with a touch of wayward poetry in his soul and the new Freya, who tried to look deeper into her fellow beings' hearts and minds than the old one ever dreamt of doing, would not make shallow judgements or shrug off the rest of the world as unimportant. The constant battle to get her own way among a family determined to go theirs was over, she assured herself and, whatever happened next, she wasn't going back to it. Which was all very well, but it left her sitting in this oddly comfortable bed in a poor man's home in the midst of a forest, with not even a penny-piece to her name and hardly a stitch of clothing on her back. Not much of a start to her wonderful new life, she concluded with a gusty sigh. It was a huge task to remake Lady Freya, now there was going to be more to her life than marrying well.

If one failed Season, a year in mourning and another sitting at Bowland twiddling her thumbs and fending off repellent suitors hadn't ruined her chances of a brilliant match, going missing and taking up with a penniless cottager for the time it took her ankle to heal would certainly do the trick. Even if Bowland's supposedly tame Member of Parliament was still willing to take her, she would rather walk barefoot all the way to her aunt's house than endure such a husband. So, when she was finally whole, she had no money to hire a carriage or buy a ticket for the accommodation coach and if her great-aunt refused to take her in, nowhere to go even if she could get there.

There was nothing to do but wait patiently for her ankle to heal and decide what to do when she could manage more than a slow hop on one leg. Having settled her immediate future, she lay back against the pillows and sighed again. When a flash of the horror at all she could have suffered yesterday shot through her head like some terrifying play she shuddered and thanked God for such a safe and comfortable resting place. She had a healthy and vigorous body, apart from her constantly aching ankle and some sore spots and twinges of stiffness that would soon pass, and a sane mind. Everything could be so much worse that it was silly to bemoan her current lot in life.

It had been wickedly wanton to strip off her bedcover and under-clothing and sleep naked though, she decided, stretching that body sensually against the sheets. Freya yawned neatly as a cat, then let herself think the unthinkable. What would it feel like to wake up beside Orlando and know they had enjoyed each other's vigorously youthful bodies to the full and would shortly do so all over again? The idea should never have entered her head, but somehow her total embarrassment this morning had mutated into a curiosity that seemed to eat at once cherished views and values. When she had come out in society, without any of the diffidence run-of-the-mill débutantes were expected to show, she'd been so sure she would catch a nobleman. Three years on it didn't seem important she hadn't married a title and would go through life with the one bestowed on her by her chilly sire.

If her brother thought the only use for a girl was to acquire more influence or wealth by marrying her off, she pitied his coming child if it dared be female. Perhaps her mother made the misalliance by wedding into the Buckle family, rather than the other way about as Freya had been told all her life and suddenly a revolution came tumbling through her head in the wake of that unthinkable notion.

If every tenet she was supposed to revere was false, what did that make Lady Freya Buckle? A fool, she concluded bleakly, and let the delicious tension of rested limbs stretching on a Freya-warmed bed fade as she lay still and considered twenty-one wasted years trying to be a model aristocrat. She grimaced at the wide boards above her head and wondered how she'd been that fool quite so long. Being a Buckle, she'd taken her own sweet time to see herself as she was, she supposed, and wished she'd realised she might be wrong about what mattered in the world sooner.

Having friends would have been pleasant, she concluded, but so few girls had come up to her family's rigid standards of fit breeding or behaviour that their neighbours' children were declared unsuitable companions and the notion she should go to school unthinkable. To her father the Royal House of Hanover was an upstart race. Freya had a picture of him asking at the gates of Heaven if the inmates were suitable company for the head of his noble house.

Looking at the world from a very different place, Freya could see why even breeding, a substantial dowry and a passably pretty face hadn't caught a noble husband at last. She pictured herself at eighteen years old, convinced she was the finest catch ever to grace the marriage mart, let alone the crop of young ladies called to Ashburton New Place in Hereford-

shire one summer for the dashing Duke of
Dettingham to make his choice of a Duchess,
and flinched. Even then instinct had warned
Freya that something she didn't understand
was growing between Jack Seaborne and the
Honourable Jessica Pendle. Something deadly
to the shining future she herself deserved as
his Duchess. With that unease at the back of
her mind she'd grown more fretful and disagreeable as the month went on, until her
hopes and dreams finally vanished like mi-
rages.

The prospect of outshining her sister-in-law
as Duchess to her mere Countess had probably appealed as strongly as the Duke himself,
Freya saw now. Such a masculine and brilliant
man as a husband would have been a bonus,
of course, but she wouldn't love him. Love,
Mama informed her before Lady Freya was
presented at Court, was for those who knew
no better. Perhaps her mother's disappointed
hopes and dreams had been talking, she decided, and pitied her parent for slamming up
against stony Buckle pride herself. Becoming
the second wife of an Earl when her father was
born the son of an impoverished vicar probably blinded her to the fact she would only

ever be an upstart nabob's daughter to him, never an equal.

Away from Bowland Castle and all the outmoded stuffiness and formality of an age gone by, Freya could see what a house of cards it truly was. Without Mama's substantial dowry the castle would have fallen into ruin long ago. The reduced staff and family retreat to Bowland every summer instead of Brighton—her sister-in-law Winfreda's cheeseparing suddenly looked a necessity, not the refusal to indulge in vulgar show Winfreda insisted it was.

How furious the family must have been when her maternal grandfather had left his fortune to his only grandchild instead of his noble son-in-law. Freya vaguely recalled slammed doors and a new tension in the house after Grandfather died, an ever-widening coldness between the late Earl and Mama. Lady Bowland did her best to conceal it from her one precious chick, Freya decided with a tenderness the lady rarely encouraged when alive. At least Mama had loved her. If her efforts to marry Freya off seemed misguided in hindsight, they were prompted by love.

Chapter Six

Seeing a little too deeply into her former life for comfort, Freya pushed back the bedcovers and reached for her improvised walking cane. At least this time the door was stoutly barred against the world so she could resume her coverings in private. Feeling ashamed of herself for her fascination with how she looked naked to Orlando, she ran a speculative hand down the curve of her slender waist and along the neat symmetry of her feminine hips. She was well enough formed, if a man didn't demand all females be buxom and plump to be desirable.

Perhaps Orlando preferred pocket Venuses to leggy Amazons, though. The woman who originally owned her shift slipped into her mind and rendered her inadequate. His wife had been inches shorter than her, yet her chemise fitted Freya apart from that, which argued she was full-breasted and probably Orlando's ideal woman in every way.

Which was exactly how it should be, Freya assured herself, then was in danger of falling over her own feet as she scrabbled the bedclothes back together in her first effort at bedmaking. He'd married a woman who suited him and his chosen life as neatly as if she'd been made for him. Lady Freya Buckle was clearly not for the likes of Mr Orlando Craven, whoever he might really be, so what did it matter if she was less than his late wife? Perdita Rowan wasn't a noblewoman and, weighed by worldly goods, more of a pauper than her rescuer—the man she depended on for a roof over her head and food in her belly. Never had she felt more dependent and at the same time more free.

Since she wasn't going to make that brilliant marriage, what *was* she going to do with her life, then? It would take years before she could think of going about the world alone and not be considered scandalous. The first thing she needed was a chaperon she could tolerate while she wrested control of her fortune from her half-brother and sister-in-law. The lawyers were sure to make that as difficult as possible for an unwed female, but generations of arrogant aristocrats at her back had to be useful for something, so perhaps she could intimidate them into it.

Which still left the huge question—what was she going to do with the rest of her life? Maybe she could find a husband even now—if he overlooked this adventure and her icy reputation. A man who didn't know or care what society with a capital S thought. A man who suddenly looked very much like Orlando in her fantasy of an ideal life with the perfect husband for Freya, the woman, not Lady Freya, aristocrat.

Ridiculous, she mocked herself—he was a man who chose to hide himself as far as he could get from any society at all. Why on earth would he saddle himself with a wife who would bring attention down on him in cartloads? Particularly when he had already had a wife he'd loved very dearly and mourned to this day. And why would he need her when he was doing such a fine job of raising his children alone? Anything more between them than enforced guest and reluctant host was clearly impossible for Lady Freya and Mr Craven. But must it be so between Orlando and Perdita? The question echoed in her mind and refused to go away, despite the voice of common sense telling her such an unequal relationship was doomed to end in tears, even if he could forget his dead wife long enough to notice Perdita as anything other than a nuisance to be sent on her way as soon as possible.

Trouble had stumped into his life along with Perdita so-called Rowan and trodden all over it with muddy boots, Rich decided crossly. He'd been perfectly content until she came—well, perhaps not *perfectly* so. He missed Anna too much to be that, but he'd done well enough. Striding along in the lead, he heard Sally and Hal chattering like starlings to Keziah and wondered why he was allowing himself to be herded back to the cottage by his friend and mentor because Keziah was eager to judge for herself if the lady he'd stumbled on last night was a fit companion for Sally and Hal and perhaps even for him when the boot ought to be on the other foot.

Why had he prided himself in having his little world under control last night when he ought to know better than that by now? It had been tempting fate, he decided gloomily, wishing he'd put Perdita in his cart and driven to the nearest inn with her as soon as it got light this morning. He frowned at the feeling he'd had as if he'd just run headlong into a wall when he came on his lost princess naked as the day she came into the world.

It was the sweetest disaster to see her in the shadowy light reflected off the forest at this time of year and lending the scullery a watery enchantment. She had looked like every warning legend he ever heard of, with her own enchantment added to remind him sirens were a story and she was real. He'd never seen such a thickly waving hank of hair spilling down a woman's naked back before, the diffuse brightness catching lights and depths in that wild mass of soft nut-brown hair so it was revealed as so much more than merely brown.

Her long, long legs only added to his openmouthed awe, but he'd already seen and felt the blisters and grazes yesterday's rough journey left on the soft-skinned soles and heels of her misused feet. Then he'd wished he could kiss them better like Sally's smaller hurts, but knew if he even tried it she would be horrified. Now he knew he might not be able to stop at comfort and would long to trail hot kisses upwards until... *Until nothing*, he barked at his inner

rake and strode on so fiercely even Keziah protested, so he slowed down and tried to recall he
was a civilised man these days and not an idle
aristocrat.

For a while he managed to keep his attention
on the here and now and off Perdita. He even
managed to smile and nod when Hal pointed
out the darting turquoise flash of a kingfisher
as they passed a summer-tamed stream. Then
Sally marvelled so hard at a brilliantly yellow
Brimstone butterfly that it took fright and flew
away, so she had to be comforted and reassured it was probably nothing personal.

Keziah's thoughtful gaze on him only made
him uneasy and reminded him he wasn't living
the lovely promise of a June day in the forest
as he should do, because he was so busy thinking of a lady who should bring out his protective instincts, not these rough desires. Yet there
had also been something touching as well as
hotly arousing about the sight of Perdita bal-
anced on one leg, intent on washing dust and
grime from every inch of her silky skin.

It would be good to think he'd averted his
gaze and left her to her privacy. Except he
hadn't, and perhaps it was his punishment that
he now couldn't seem to evade memory of
those endless legs leading to the lithe curve

of her *derrière* and up to an impossibly slender waist and breasts so high and perfect he wanted them in his hands or mouth, whichever could first wrap about the cold and shock-tightened amber nipples. No doubt she only remembered the untamed wolf she'd seen in his eyes and shivered at the very memory he was slavering over like a wild beast.

He had subjected her to a lecherous, eager survey no gently bred female should expect to endure outside marriage. When he finally raised his eyes from her creamy-skinned and lovely form her averted cheek was flushed with shame and her full bottom lip caught by pearly teeth as she bit back a gasp of shocked dismay. Knowing she was controlling an urge to scream or rage at him because his children were a hair's breadth away from discovering what a satyr they had for a father, he had muttered a brusque apology and left her standing frozen in that haunting sylvan light like an artist's wildest fantasy.

How his Anna would have raged at him for being such a boor, he reflected, as he felt the thunder and lightning of wanting Perdita released in him threaten to turn him rigid and painfully aroused all over again, if he didn't get back to his workshop and work himself into the ground to tame it. Had his wife been here he wouldn't be without a woman and three years of denying his basic nature to honour Anna's memory began to look like a sad mistake. His driven urge for a lady he shouldn't want would never have sprung into infernal life the second he held Perdita in his arms if Anna was here.

His love had welcomed her husband's amorous attentions and revelled in their passion for each other. Annabelle would be the first to condemn him for subjecting a lone female to his lecherous stare if she could see him now. Yet the idea of slaking his animal lusts on a woman paid to endure them had about as much appeal as a rotten egg. Once he might have seen it as merely sating a need healthy males felt with varying degrees of urgency. After he met Annabelle and discovered how to love as well as need a woman, anything less seemed insulting.

Only a romantic would fall in love with a woman at first sight, he accused himself, particularly when she was little more than a schoolgirl and obviously with child by another man. He remembered the shock and awe of that unlikely moment in the hope it would push the memory of a naked Perdita out of his head.

Annoyed when it didn't, he strode on until he outstripped his children and Keziah and stormed along the forest track as if he'd a kingdom to defend at the other end of it.

Impossible to love again with every impulse and instinct he had, he assured himself. Not even a fool like Richard Seaborne loved headlong and without boundaries twice in a lifetime, certainly not with Perdita Rowan, lady of the woods. This was lust, brought on by a misguided belief he could never want another woman as he wanted Anna, urgently and completely and, he recalled with an un-Seaborne-like blush, somewhat insatiably for a sober married man with another man's widow in his bed, big with his posthumous child.

When Keziah delivered Annabelle's precious son he fell completely in love for the second time in his life. Hal was his as if he'd been at the heart and source of his conception, instead of the boy who hadn't even lived long enough to know his young wife was carrying his child. Jealousy that Annabelle met and loved the lad before she was struck by the same thunderbolt that felled him threatened. He made himself remember Annabelle saying her first marriage came out of their mutual desperation to get away from home, not a passionate love at first glance like theirs.

He smiled at the memory of her bold and brazen admission that she wanted him as urgently as he did her. If she'd come to him as pure and virginal as she had to her marriage bed with Colton Martagon, they might never have wanted each other so hotly. He'd loved her lustily and deeply and promised to try to live well without her. His mouth twisted as he recalled her extracting that promise out of him once they knew she couldn't survive the struggle to push Sally into the world. These last three years he'd found grief had no boundaries and men did cry, but now he wondered what his Annabelle would make of Miss Perdita Rowan. Would she see his hot need of another woman as him beginning to keep that promise, or a shameful abuse of his duty as a host?

Now he was back where he started, hankering after a female he couldn't have with any trace of honour. So why had he rushed ahead as if he needed to get to her all the quicker? Even now he'd realised what he was doing, he couldn't seem to wait for Sally and Hal and Keziah's presence to remind him that Perdita was as unattainable to Orlando Craven as a royal princess.

* * *

A heavy knock on what she could call *her* door if she wasn't careful made Freya jump and threaten to drop the kettle she had so laboriously filled and tried to set on the fire she had finally managed to light after only an hour of strenuous effort.

'Who is it?' she shouted through the heavy oak planks, although she knew perfectly well it was Orlando.

'Me,' he bellowed back and she could almost feel his impatience as she put down her sooty burden to turn the key with both hands and draw back the bolts she'd shot home.

The instant the door was open they froze as if examining each other for changes. It was odd, but yesterday his face seemed a stronger, more defined version of features she'd seen on young men all her life. Today they were his alone. Was that because he'd seen her as no man had since the doctor announced the bad news she was a girl? Or because Orlando was a man and he'd wanted her hotly for a fleeting moment this morning, before he turned away from her as if the idea poisoned the air between them?

'I was worried about you,' he said gruffly and disarmed her completely.

'It might be better if you worry about your house next time,' she told him ruefully, standing aside and waving a grubby hand at the dying fire.

'That's easy enough to mend. People need more care and attention,' he said, sounding almost cheerful as he bent to see to her sulky bird's nest of a fire. 'Next time add to it little by little until it's well alight, then you can put on the larger pieces. You overwhelmed it.'

She tried to listen and learn, but seeing his large hands so deft and skilful set her senses reeling all over again. He was pretending he wouldn't dream of seeing her naked, so she only had herself to blame for wishing those broad-palmed hands were busy about her body and not building a fire. It wouldn't even matter they were sooty and smelt faintly of woodsmoke and dry lichen. It might even add to the wonderment as she watched the shadow of his exploration form on her body; a map that said Orlando was here, and here, and here...

'I thought I should like tea, if you don't mind?' she said hastily.

'Of course not, but I doubt our version will match your usual one,' he said to the fire, as if he might get more sense out of it.

'So long as it's wet and warm. I sometimes share the gardeners' tea when nobody is likely to catch us hobnobbing,' she heard herself say. He didn't need to know her family employed gardeners in the plural. Although it was her money that paid for such luxuries as pleasure gardens and Freya hoped her friends wouldn't lose their jobs now she'd escaped Bowland Castle for good or ill. 'I like gardening,' she said, admitting the secret vice her brother found so deplorable that he called her a peasant brat when he caught her sneaking in through the garden door to wash dirt off her hands or change her muddy shoes.

'Good,' he said with a wry grin. 'Once you're well enough you can help with mine and let me worry about keeping house.'

'Doesn't that set the natural order of things on its head?'

'The one that says Adam gardened whilst Eve span? If Eve was the better gardener, Adam should have learnt to spin,' he replied and Freya wondered if he might be a radical after all.

'Perhaps we should try a little of both if we want to improve?'

'Aye, but first you must want to achieve such wonders, Perdita.'

'True,' she said sagely. Unwed daughters of

Earls did not dirty their hands with work and first her mother, then her sister-in-law ran the household, so Lady Freya Buckle had little to do and long hours of relentless boredom to do it in.

'And here come my little neither gardeners nor spinners, unless I've mistaken a herd of wild horses for my sweet offspring,' he said, as if she needed telling.

'Papa, Papa, Keziah says there are soldiers in town,' Hal shouted eagerly.

'There are always soldiers in town, lad,' his father told him as he hefted the kettle over the merrily burning fire.

'But these are dragons, Papa,' Sally said earnestly, pushing her big brother aside so she could nod at her father to emphasise the truth of her statement.

'Not dragons, silly baby, dragoons,' Henry told her scornfully and yelped when Sally's carved dog hit him amidships, as it seemed to do with such regularity he ought to provoke his sister from a distance, if he must do so at all.

'I'm not a baby,' Sally wailed ominously.

'Of course you're not, my duck,' a rather harsh female voice interrupted their quarrel.

'I'm not a duck neither,' Sally insisted sulkily, as if she'd been looking forward to a nice refreshing drama.

'I'm not a duck *either,*' her father corrected her with a quack-quack motion of a duck's beak with his hands as he launched into a strutting walk, as if he was about to paddle about on the nearest pond. His nonsense distracted Sally so she joined in, and soon all three Cravens were lined up in a row, quacking happily like foraging mallards. Freya watched them with wide eyes and the newcomer shook her head and shrugged.

'Mad as hatters the lot of 'em,' the older woman said.

'So I see,' Freya replied and smiled shyly at the tiny little nut-brown woman, who looked as if a breath of wind might blow her away, although something told Freya not even an earthquake would dislodge her unless she wanted to go.

'I *am* a duck, Kezzie. I really am,' Sally insisted now, delight brilliant in her green eyes as she launched herself at her big brother's back and he caught her mid-flight into a piggyback and tore outside as Freya finally realised the boy doted on his little sister.

Orlando stood and watched his still-quacking offspring dash towards the nearest pond with resigned amusement, nodding a signal at faithful Atlas to go with them and keep the enterprising pair out of harm's way.

'It's only two feet deep in the middle,' he excused himself as if they might upbraid him for letting his children run so freely into danger, 'and they can both swim.'

'I wish I could,' Freya said wistfully and wondered why so many useful things were forbidden to Earls' daughters when being able to swim to safety might save their lives.

She sensed it on the tip of his tongue for a moment, the offer to teach her in rather more than two feet of water. Her disappointment when he bit it back made her remember she wasn't here to enjoy herself, or learn useful accomplishments; she was here because she had nowhere else to go and he was too kind not to make her go away again.

'Can't see why, m'dear, nasty wet stuff is water. I wouldn't swim in it if I was the Queen herself,' the older lady told her with a twinkle in her bright brown eyes that told Freya she hadn't missed her shameful fascination with her host and thought it quite normal for any woman to be dazed by Orlando's manly charms.

'Just as well. Neptune would take one look,

then carry you off to be *his* Queen,' Orlando teased.

'You do like to talk daft, Master Craven,' she told him, but the impish light in her shrewd eyes and merry, gap-toothed smile told Freya she'd once lured in more males than she quite knew what to do with and Neptune would have to queue.

'But you love me anyway?'

'Of course I don't—why would I waste good honest love on a rogue like you?'

'Good question,' Orlando said with a wry smile that spoke of many sins he was half-ashamed of committing. 'But I haven't introduced you to the belle of Longborough Forest yet, Perdita. Mrs Keziah Brooks, this is Miss Perdita Rowan; Miss Rowan, Mrs Brooks,' he said as if they were about to take tea in the drawing room.

'It's a pleasure to meet you, Mrs Brooks,' Freya said sincerely and they bobbed heads towards each other as equals.

'And it's good to have another woman within shouting distance again, Miss Rowan, or who-ever you really are.'

'I'm just a lone female who got waylaid, then ran off and got lost,' Freya claimed.

'From what Master Orlando says you went

through a lot more than that yesterday. So you sit yourself down and heal, missy. Even little Sally could tell those hands ain't made for toil. You'll burn yourself if you don't stop trying to learn all there's to know about running a house inside a day.'

'Little chance of that,' Freya said and sat on the stool Orlando thrust at her, as if she was sadly in the way and making work for others to walk round.

'I'll have a look at that ankle of yours as soon as we've had this tea the young master promised us,' Keziah said and Freya tried not to flinch at the idea of anyone even touching her sore foot.

'All in good time,' Orlando said with an affectionate smile at the older woman. Freya tried not to envy her while he made tea in a fat brown pot the current Countess of Bowland wouldn't even allow in her lord's kitchen.

'We're honoured today, ain't we?' Keziah asked as he produced two fine china cups and saucers from the cupboard on the opposite side from the one the kindling and the cooking vessels were kept in. 'Your missus would be proud of you today, lad,' she said with a nod Freya couldn't interpret.

'Would she now?' he responded as if he wasn't so sure.

'And she'd be the last one to want to see you stay so sad and lonely because she ain't here no more.'

'I could hardly call myself alone when I've got my two imps of Satan to keep me company, but don't make me out to be better than I am, Keziah,' he said seriously and Freya had the oddest impulse to smooth his wildly curling hair out of his eyes and gaze into them with a tender smile in her own and had to clench her hands in her lap before they began the project on their own.

Chapter Seven

'You don't care a whit about me or the baby, Francis Martagon,' Philomena, Marchioness of Lundy, said mournfully, rubbing a white hand over her swollen belly as if her unborn child reproached him too. 'If you did, you would find the brat who could beggar us and dispose of him, as you should have done before our first child was born.'

'What a wasted effort that would have been,' her lord replied disdainfully, 'since you only whelped me a girl.'

'My father's first grandchild, my lord. Don't forget who holds the purse strings,' the silvery-blonde and supposedly delicate Lady Lundy reminded her middle-aged husband with a steely glint in her blue eyes that would astonish her admirers and those less impressed by her lovely face and avaricious nature, which she managed to hide most of the time.

'Or who has the title you love so dearly,' Francis Martagon replied.

'Imagine how little I will love you if you lose it, my lord,' she said silkily and if he had any illusions about his lady they evaporated under her chilly gaze.

'It's only a name,' he said wearily.

'Why were you willing to murder that wretched female and her unborn child to keep it, then?' she taunted as if she wasn't the one who'd needled and nagged him into that appalling act in the first place.

'Because you refused to bear me any sort of child and would have done your best to win an annulment of the marriage through the courts if I didn't. Even I am astonished at what you'll do for a title, my dear, and I thought you'd taught me not to be surprised at anything an ambitious and venal woman will do to get her way.'

'Why? What point would there have been in wedding you without one?'

'Who knows?' he said.

'That boy ahead of you in the succession died and you were heir to a marquisate. Did you expect to stay a fusty old bachelor absorbed in your books and letters after that? You're a simpleton if you did, Francis Martagon.'

'Less of a one now than I was when I wed you.'

'I put steel in your backbone. You would have meekly handed your lands and titles over to a puling infant without a murmur if I hadn't been here to stop you. You were nothing more than a sheep looking for the most peaceful field to chew cud in before you met me.'

'I'm man enough to get you with child then and now,' he muttered and Philomena saw the mulish set of his mouth and sighed. She hadn't bargained for this when she lured him into marriage with the promises of a delightful young body in his bed and a pretty blonde wife his peers would envy him.

'Find the brat and kill him. My son can't be born a commoner,' she said brusquely.

'Like his mama was, you mean?' Lord Lundy asked bitterly.

'I may have been born without a title, but so were you. The only useful thing you ever did was make me a Marchioness and you couldn't even do that properly,' she taunted, then smiled with satisfaction at the impressive parkland round Martagon Court for once when her husband strode furiously out of the room and slammed the door behind him.

'You drive him too hard,' a harsh voice even chillier than her own informed her as the owner of it emerged from the shadows of my lady's private closet.

'He's spineless and idle; it's the only way to goad him into action, Papa,' Philomena argued impatiently.

'Push too relentlessly and he'll run the other way to spite you.'

'Would I could be sure this baby was a boy, then we could make sure Francis went the same way as this phantom heir he can't seem to find and destroy without your help.'

'No, we'll keep the fool alive even if this child's born male. A boy could die and then where would we be if you don't have a spare?'

'Well, I'd be Dowager Lady Lundy with a huge dowry to catch a Duke with,' Philomena replied practically.

'No, you'll be a penniless commoner's widow if you dare cross me, my girl,' Lady Lundy's doting papa informed her coldly.

'How could you threaten me with such a terrible thing, Papa?' she objected half-heartedly, aware she might as well talk to the splendidly moulded and plastered state-room walls for all the good it did her.

'I don't threaten—I do.'

'Then find this wretched upstart brat Colton Martagon got on the giggling schoolgirl he ran off with and kill him for me.'

'Nobody will rob my boy of anything he wants or needs, least of all the cursed brat that fool Seaborne's hidden away so well you'd think it was his own,' Jonas Strider asserted and even Philomena had the sense to shudder at the prospect as her father lived up to his name and strode out of the room to put his words into action.

Rich decided Perdita looked even more out of place decked in the colourful garb Keziah's daughter had left at her mother's house last time she drifted back there, with or without her Romani husband. Lucky that Cleo had inherited her *gorgio* father's height as well as her mother's fine looks, so her skirts only showed his waif's ankles and one of them was unglamorously bandaged. Yet he still caught himself watching her like a fascinated boy. Her skin was beginning to turn golden from the sun now she spent her days outside playing with his children or trying to tend his fruit and vegetables, despite her injury. She had even begun to reclaim Annabelle's flower and herb gardens from the weeds and he wondered if he was man enough to let her go when she was strong enough to walk away.

No question about that; he had to. He still wanted her mercilessly, so he avoided her as often as he could, but in a cramped cottage in the middle of nowhere that wasn't nearly often enough. So he'd shut himself in his workshop and barked at anyone who tried to interrupt him. He must work anyway in order to buy what he couldn't make, like cooking pots and sheets—both of which were under threat thanks to Perdita's best efforts. Yet he didn't recognise the besotted fool in Rich Seaborne's battered working boots. He'd known what it was to burn for a woman—what spotty youth full of fascinated curiosity about the opposite sex did not at a certain stage of his life? Yet since he had grown to manhood and learnt to satisfy a lover extravagantly he had never felt like this—as if his very skin was burningly sensitive with sheer, driven need of Perdita Rowan as his lover.

He'd wanted Annabelle with all of him as well, but he'd known from the moment they met that they would spend their lives together—once he found out the man who put her babe in her belly wasn't alive any more to object. There had been no restraint between them, before or after the brief marriage ceremony in a quiet city parish, far from the haunts of the *haut ton*. Yet there could be no such hasty and headlong coupling for him and Perdita. Even if he wanted a wife, he could never ask a high-born lady to live this far from civilisation and attend to the day-to-day needs of another woman's children and her gruff and lust-ridden widower. Annabelle's occasional fits of the dismals had rasped his conscience and she had as potent a reason to endure the solitude as he had himself.

And he was a Seaborne, for goodness' sake. He owed it to his clan not to hopelessly crave the first pretty girl to stumble at his feet. Still he woke every morning in a rigid fever of desire and had to exhaust himself to ignore it all day. Then he had to lie in bed at night and fight his baser urges, knowing Perdita was downstairs in her box-bed and he yearned for her like a lovesick boy.

'Damn woman,' he muttered grumpily and gasped as he unwarily ran his chisel into his thumb because he wasn't concentrating on what he was doing.

He'd been too busy watching Perdita labour in the garden even from here to pay attention and he looked down at his battered hands with a sigh. Every new mark and graze spoke of another daydream about her. Perdita wasn't to blame, but try as he might to tell himself this was animal lust, she revived a tenderness in him that he'd made himself forget when agony at Annabelle's death made him lock part of himself away in order to go on without her.

While he was busy growling and raging at the devil for torturing him so inventively, somehow Perdita coped with his house and his children and it only made him more cross-grained and driven. She even seemed to admire Hal's natural arrogance and Sally's determination to be her own person, whatever society and her brother had to say about a girl's place in the world. Rich wondered what sort of childhood his lady of the woods had endured while he watched her laugh and attempt to run, as if such simple delights were usually denied her. Cursing as he caught himself thinking of Perdita in his life for more than the few more days it would take her to heal, he threw down the chisel in disgust and made himself consider her dispassionately.

She was pretty enough—her features evenly

made, although her nose was pert. Her eyes were the colour of sun-washed amber and might be her best feature, if he wasn't so fascinated by her generous mouth. The sun was turning her creamy skin golden and her face clearly wouldn't do much good in overcoming this obsession, so maybe her hair would turn the trick. Lucky it was brown, then, not Titian, angelically blonde or sable dark. Yet it curled in soft waves down her back, now she had given up on hairpins and wore it tied in a glossy tail or a loose plait. Glowing highlights shone in it where the sun seemed to linger in the soft curls that escaped to kiss her brow and tickle her nose as she worked.

He thought of her flicking impatiently at those stray wisps of fine curls and a tender smile quirked his lip at the trail of dirt often left across her cheek or nose. Idiot! He was supposed to cure himself of this obsession, not make the spell stronger. She was clearly an impractical woman to weather the life he lived now, but her dainty-looking hands and fine-boned wrists held far more muscle and sinew than he would have dreamt of at his first sight of her as a defeated waif lost in the wilds.

No use trying to lie to himself she wasn't desirable then, but she still wasn't for him. He couldn't seduce her or ask her to stay as either his woman or a wife. Unthinkable only a week ago, when he was arrogantly sure he would never consider putting another woman in Annabelle's unique place. No, he had to send the confounded female back to live in the luxury he knew she was used to, from the look and sound and fineness of her.

His Annabelle had been the present Earl of Calvercombe's first cousin and a DeMorbaraye by birth, but she had loved him passionately. He saw curiosity and feminine interest in Perdita's eyes whenever she let them dwell on him for an unwary moment, but he couldn't ask her to live like this. No lady would sacrifice so much for a boy who wasn't even his son, let alone her own. Sometimes Rich thought it best the world forgot all about Hal for ever, but his boy was the rightful Marquis of Lundy. One day he might choose to reclaim his inheritance and then Annabelle's son would need all the power of the Seabornes at his back, yet Rich had no legal claim on him. If he stepped into the light, Hal would be given into the 'care' of his nearest living relative—Francis Martagon—the man who had tried to kill him while he was still in his mother's womb.

Rich hoped the worm was constantly afraid

of him and Hal riding up to Martagon Court to claim it from him; he deserved to suffer agonies whenever an unexpected carriage drove up or a knock hammered on the door. He had set out to murder a pregnant girl, his Annabelle and her son both, so Rich savagely hoped the rat looked over his shoulder every day and wondered if today was the day he would lose every acre, stone and penny he'd stolen off an unborn baby.

That was it, then—the brake on his need for a woman who would never have crossed his path if the gods were kinder to Rich Seaborne. The life they might have had, if he met her in an elegant drawing room or they danced at an overcrowded country ball, could never be. Yet never had he so badly misread his headlong Seaborne nature as the day he swore to his dead love he would never yearn for another woman. If he hadn't been such a fool, he would have slaked his wilder passions with a female he could please and leave, but instead he met Perdita in a state of hibernation he hadn't the sense to realise was as false as spring in December, until she dropped into his life like a wondrous gift from a contrary god.

Turning from the sight of his enforced guest weeding salad greens and laughing at his daughter stealing strawberries, Rich bit back a howl of frustrated bitterness and thumped his powerful fist into the rough-hewn planks of his workshop wall. *Fool, you damned fool!* The unspoken condemnation echoed in his head as he sank on to his clenched fists and burned all over again.

No, he'd been wrong just now; nothing could put a brake on his endless need for this contrary jumble of a woman he hardly knew. A wry smile lifted his mouth for a moment as he acknowledged she didn't know herself very well either. So much about her new life was a revelation to her. Her surprise at talents and qualities she never suspected she had charmed him. No, he couldn't afford to be charmed by her; there were places, even round here, where a man could go when he needed a woman. Unfortunately he knew only this one would do and he had to get away from her until he had the madness walked off and self-control firmly back in place.

'Sally, you stay here with Hal and Atlas and Miss Perdita. I need some green wood. If you need me, shout and I'll hear you, Miss Rowan,' he barked at her before striding away without giving them time to question or demand to come too.

* * *

Freya watched him go, then turned to re-assure Sally all was well and check Hal was nearby. Did Orlando feel the tension strung between them too? Shaking her head at that very silly idea while trying to ignore a shiver of excited curiosity, she stood up and stretched cramped limbs. Making sure she could see both the children out of the corner of her eye at all times wasn't likely to help her garden-ing efforts, so she sent Hal a questioning look.

'It's about noon, Miss Perdita,' he said with a manly grin that told her his belly was empty and whatever time it was, it *should* be noon, so he could fill it up again.

'Then I might as well find out if the milk has kept nice and cool in the scullery. It would never do if it turned before you two could drink it all.'

Sally followed Freya back to the house hap-pily enough and only Atlas cast longing looks after his master. Freya hoped she concealed her obsession better than he could, or Orlando must know by now that she was on pins when-ever he was nearby and about as shamelessly eager for his attention as his devoted hound.

'I was nearly right,' Hal said once they had the door open and their eyes were used to the shadowy light within so they could actually see the time.

'Only an hour here or there,' Freya agreed straight faced as she removed the netted cover from the earthenware milk jug. 'Just half a mug now,' she insisted and Hal grimaced, 'you will get a full one with your luncheon and not an hour before it, young man.'

'Can we have one of your bakestone cakes as well then, for we're both very, very hungry,' he said with the mournful expression of a sad bloodhound to back up his assertion.

'That might be possible, given the right words in the right order.'

'Please may we have a cake, dearest Perdita?'

'You may, Master Craven, but I shall decide who is to have which one. Sally and I don't think the smallest of everything should always be her lot in life.'

Sally nodded emphatically and Hal threatened to sulk for a moment, but shrugged and accepted the equal-sized flat scones she handed them. Freya was proud of her latest efforts, since the little cakes were not even burnt, once she let the bakestone heat up exactly the way it said in a neatly written receipt in the commonplace book she'd found in the scullery. It was full of the observations Orlando's late wife had made on daily life. The odd clever sketch and that lady's notes about plants of the forest were enlivened with a sense of wonder.

Freya sensed this young woman had had to feel her way with the domestic arts just as she was doing. Mrs Craven must have been a lady, accustomed to others doing the housework and cooking as well. Freya liked her rueful recording of minor success and failures and it felt odd that the one woman who could understand her deepest dilemmas if she was alive was also the last person she would ever confide them to.

How could she confess to a woman of character she thought she was falling in love with her husband? Unthinkable for Lady Freya to love a woodsman; beyond ridiculous to fall under his gruff spell if there was a Mrs Craven to make it a bigger sin to want him so much it made her ache with yearning. So why must Orlando, out of all the men she could have chosen to secretly desire, have to be the one who made her heart beat faster? It wasn't as if he flattered her or set out to charm her. His sharply critical green eyes had cut through Lady Freya Buckle's thorny pride to the vulnerable creature beneath from the first moment they laid eyes on each other and she wasn't at all sure she liked being an open book to a man who guarded his own inner self so fiercely.

He was still a mystery to her and that made her fume, so she put all she knew of him together and told herself it made him less than her adoring inner idiot thought him. He was abrupt and rude as well as short-tempered. She doubted he could fit politely into a great lady's drawing room or trim his impatience to the mannered politeness of the *haut ton*. On the other hand, she couldn't imagine him enjoying the snobbery and petty amusements of bored society beaux and sophisticated young matrons either. She only had to imagine his impatience with the pretence and flattery of a night at Al-mack's Club or the grand balls of the London Season to catch herself grinning at nothing.

No, this was doing her no good. She was just losing herself in daydreams again and where were her supposed charges while her thoughts were on their complex sire? Forgetting the absurd notion of Orlando making his début in high society, she hobbled outside to find Hal and Sally. Relieved to find them playing with the hobby-horses their father had made, she sat down on a convenient tree stump and let herself wonder what it would feel like if they were her children. For that to be so, Orlando would have to be her husband and she told herself not to be a fool as a warm shudder racked her. No need to steel herself to face the marriage bed with this man who made her pulse race and an odd feeling of sharp heat clench her loins at the very thought.

Her heart raced for a very different reason as Sally waved happily at Freya, as if she was part of her young life. She waved back and smiled even as tears stung her eyes at the idea of waving goodbye to them when her ankle was properly healed. How she wished she *had* been born to a country squire and his comfortable lady. At least then stumbling on Orlando hiding in the woods with his children wouldn't be the disaster it was threatening to become for my Lady Freya, lately of Bowland Castle.

As it was, sitting brooding over a life Orlando didn't want to share with her was only silly, so she got up to begin hauling enough water in to fill the improvised copper so they could have a bath of sorts tonight. Orlando would do it if she asked, but she didn't want to ask. Better not to see much of him, so she could live without him better when she went back to real life.

* * *

Two days later Freya was still wondering how to do that. Now she could manage without her stick for short trips to the well or the wood-pile and had even managed a week's baking with Keziah's amused assistance and Mrs Craven's invaluable book. There was no Orlando handy to carry pots and pans, wield the long rakes and paddles to get rid of the fire, then push first the bread into the oven, then pies and cakes for her, though. Thanks to Keziah's help in putting the list of ingredients together and judging the heat of the oven at least most of it had been edible, even if she was forced to bathe in the stream to rid herself of the sweat and grime of her labours afterwards.

Whatever would society make of Lady Freya not only working for her daily bread, but making it as well? she wondered ruefully. From here Lady Freya looked like a haughty and rather useless luxury to Perdita Rowan, so was it any wonder even her own family had judged her so harshly once upon a time? Probably not, she conceded, and felt her heart sink into her borrowed shoes at all the silly waste and misunderstandings that had blighted her old life.

She had been looking for a different future

when she left Bowland and had certainly found that, but how could she stay here when reality was waiting outside the forest? She felt more at home here than she ever had in the echoing splendours of Bowland Castle, but how could she stay here as Perdita when Orlando clearly didn't want her to?

It was as well Keziah came striding through the forest just then to say her daughter and son-in-law were back and distract her from her own woes. Keziah spoke so little about her daughter Freya sensed anxiety under her front of pleasure at having company again. At least someone else's problems made a change from her own and Freya felt ashamed of herself for using Keziah's family difficulties to mask her own. She was on the edge of loving Orlando while he did his best to avoid her, but Keziah's Cleopatra and her husband Reuben were back in Longborough Forest and the world ticked relentlessly on.

It did so even more determinedly when she met Cleo's hostile dark eyes and noted how they flickered across and lingered possessively on Orlando's powerful shoulders and strong masculine features. This sensuously lovely creature might as well pin a notice on him, despite the handsome husband most women would have been very content to call their own. 'Mine,' it would smugly insist. 'My lover.' Freya might accept Orlando wanted her gone, but she couldn't let herself believe he would seduce another man's wife when he could have Freya instead if he only chose to ask.

Heat scorched her cheeks at that shocking conclusion and she informed herself she was worth more—had always been worth more. The contrasts between her latest suitors and Orlando were stark, but she'd let herself believe she might wed the Duke of Dettingham once upon a time and nobody could accuse him of being less than masculine. Watching Cleo flirt and play up for Orlando's attention, Freya kept her distance and wondered what made Orlando so potently attractive to her own sex and how she could stop herself following in this wayward beauty's footsteps by making it a little too clear she would welcome him in her bed.

He was so real, she decided at last. Which was odd when she was sure Orlando wasn't his real name. In disguise or not, maybe he'd buried his heart with his wife, the mother of his children, but why would he love Freya even if he hadn't? She was an impostor nobody but her mother and nabob grandfather had ever found lovable. So that settled that, she decided, and did her best to forget their impossible sire and protect Hal and Sally from the dislike they seemed to rouse in Cleopatra for some strange reason.

Rich left his workbench as graciously as he had it in him to do anything at the moment, which meant so gruffly he won a speculative look from Reuben and an arch smile from Cleo. Now why was she little more than an annoying fly buzzing in the background compared to his sharp awareness of Perdita's every move? Only a fool could think Perdita more beautiful when Cleo seemed born to embody a man's most unlikely fantasies, yet her sloe-eyed beauty left him cold.

If a man's ears could be attuned to a voice his were on Perdita's. His eyes wanted to watch slavishly as she went about this odd life of his with a leaven of wry humour. There were scratches on her tender skin, a battle scar from the hot oven door and the odd blister and broken nail marred her once-immaculate hands. He didn't want to admire or need her and couldn't help doing both. There were times when he lay in bed and felt as if he could smash through walls and floors between them because he wanted to be in the box-bed with her so badly.

He caught himself trying to gauge her re-action to Reuben Summer and glared at the mocking devil, then reminded himself the man was as close to a friend as he got these days. Lucky they both knew he wouldn't lay a finger on Cleo, since the witchy female was doing her best to flirt with both men and ignore Perdita, his children and Keziah. He exerted himself to play genial host, despite Cleo's worst efforts, and ended up sitting next to Perdita while they drank his weakest cider and ate cake and pre-tended for a while all was exactly as it should be in Longborough Forest.

Chapter Eight

Feeling his body react to the feel and scent and touch of Perdita next to him with Cleo's dark eyes sharp and accusing on both of them for no good reason, Rich tried to pretend he was somewhere else. He felt Perdita stiffen at his side, then hold a little aloof from him as if she sensed his unease at Cleo's silent malice and thought she was the source of it. Rich wondered gloomily how a lady in her early twenties could be so naïve about the workings of the male body as to think she repulsed him. Whoever was in charge of the upbringing of well-born young ladies had an awful lot to answer for, he decided, as he burned on the rack of forever wanting her and not being able to even kiss her.

'You're a martyr, my friend,' Reuben Summer murmured as they exchanged handshakes before parting. 'Why not take her to your bed?'

The urge to hit someone bit so strongly Rich's fists knotted before he could remind himself part of him was wondering the same thing. He made himself relax before he ruined his friendship with the wily rogue beyond mending.

'She can't stay here and I can't go with her,' he reminded himself bleakly.

'Why not, *veshengro*?' Reuben asked with a shrug that said his forester friend was an idiot for not taking his woman to his bed, whether it was for an hour, a week or for ever.

As he had clearly thought Cleo was his for life when he married her, Rich didn't think Reuben was particularly expert on affairs of the heart. No, this was merely a physical need a mature male ought to be able to endure as the side-effect of having a young and pretty woman in his house and not sharing her bed.

'She doesn't belong here, Reuben, and I can't leave.'

'You're a fool, Orlando.'

'There's a lot of it about,' Rich made himself say lazily, as if parting from Perdita as soon as she was well enough would be a gnat bite to him and no more.

'At least I'm a satisfied one, Englishman.'

'Lucky you, Gypsy,' he mocked back and sighed with relief when Reuben laughed, nodded and made a lewd gesture Rich hoped nobody else saw.

That evening Rich lit the lamps he used to work by during long winter evenings and shut himself away in his workshop. Reuben's idea—that he could keep Perdita at his side, living as he must for the sake of Anna's beloved son—had made his attention drift until he cursed colourfully and threw his latest attempt to block out a chair seat under the bench to be remade as something lesser when he wasn't so distracted. A picture of Perdita wearing his wedding band, dreamy eyed and contented as she watched his children grow and laugh, while another little Craven grew and kicked in her belly, nearly doubled him up with longing. He smashed his fist into the wall to mask some of his frustration with a different pain.

Never—he simply couldn't do that to her. He couldn't take her innocence and snare her into a life of unrelenting work and constantly looking over her shoulder for the enemy who wanted Hal dead so badly he would seize any advantage to make sure he got his way. The thought of Perdita in Martagon's hands—held as hostage against his beloved son—made him shake and go so cold he wondered if he was about to faint.

The moment she could put her foot to the ground without pain, Perdita simply had to leave. Meanwhile hard physical labour would have to blot out the image of Perdita naked in his bed, with only her silken skin and that luxurious hank of softly waving nut-brown hair to cover her. He nearly threw the unformed block of elm in his hand at the wall and despaired, but he was a Seaborne and he was going to beat this. Miss Perdita Rowan would walk out of the forest a maid. A lonely one, whose family had already failed her, the siren voice in his head argued; his fist clenched again at the thought of the terrible danger she'd run from the day she tumbled into his life. No, it was self-serving rubbish to tell himself she was better off with him; he must let her go.

He managed to focus on the task in hand at last and only stopped work when the dawn chorus informed him he'd made it through another night without trying to seduce Perdita. Returning home with the dawn, he tried to ignore her asleep in the chair by the cold hearth. He crept up the narrow stairs, shut his door and sprawled face down on the bed, then slept as if he'd returned from a war and not been able to relax during a whole campaign.

Freya awoke with protesting limbs and all sorts of strange dreams fogging her heavy head. She stretched, then groaned at the stiffness in her neck and shoulders, cricks in her back and the raw nag of pain from her injured foot. Last night she had waited for Orlando to come in, but it seemed that he'd crept in whilst she was asleep. 'Drat the man,' she muttered crossly to herself, then looked about her temporary domain and sighed. She raked out the fire, re-laid it and reached for the tinder box. It was a fine June morning, but she was shivering with cold.

Orlando was out of reach and she was a fool to dream he was wrapped in this chair with her, holding her on his lap as he soothed and caressed and mesmerised her to sleep in his arms. Not that her body dwelt much on the idea of sleep when she thought of being in his arms. The detail of how a man and a woman made love were still a bit blurred, but instinct told her there was more to it than simply mating as the animals did, then sleeping in a man's arms. Even falling asleep feeling him breathe so close would be warming and intimate, but it was only a pipe dream. So Freya lit her fire and sat soaking up the warmth and comfort of it until the children stirred and it was time to begin another day as the guest in Orlando's house he couldn't wait to be rid of.

When he finally awoke, nearer to midday than morning, Freya soon wished Orlando had stayed upstairs and slept off his ill humour. For a while he stumped about the place with a forbidding frown that hardly let up even for his children, who soon decided they preferred her company until his dark mood lifted and gave him a wide berth.

'Take the children to Keziah, Perdita, and stay with them there,' he ordered abruptly at last. 'I shall be gone all day and most of the night and she will keep them safe for me.'

As if she wouldn't, or couldn't, when she would fight with her last breath to keep his children from harm. Determined not to betray her hurt that he didn't trust her to care for his children by herself while he was away,

Freya gave him a regal nod. 'Very well,' she said stiffly.

'Papa?' Sally faltered.

'I'll be back by morning, darling. You stay with Perdita and Kezzie and be a good girl,' he managed more gently for his beloved daughter. Then he whistled Atlas, ordered him to stay with the children and walked away.

'And goodbye to you too,' Freya muttered at his retreating back and rolled her eyes at Sally to make her laugh and Hal thaw from his offended man-of-the-house pose, since she didn't think she could cope with two grumpy Craven males today.

As their father had been so busy and distracted of late the children hardly seemed to miss him once they settled down to eat their luncheon, then play at knights and dragons. Freya sat close by to mend their clean clothes with neatly meticulous stitches she blessed learning from her embroidery, a skill all the world knew was suitably ladylike, she reflected ruefully. So maybe her once being a lady had its uses after all and at least her task kept her from thinking too hard about Orlando and she could keep an eye on the children. Once it was done and they were happily ensconced in the low-branched oak tree nearby pretending to be King Charles the Second hiding from the Roundheads, there was nothing to stop her thoughts racing straight back to the wretched man.

However hard she tried to tell herself he didn't matter to her, she was wrong. Which left the problem of what to do about him stark in her mind; she could walk, or limp, away and resume her old life as if she'd never discovered what it was like to truly live. Or she could employ a chaperon respectable enough to outfox Bowland and set herself up as an eccentric but independent lady. How odd that neither idea appealed and she only wanted to stay here in the woods with Orlando and his children, although he was a widower who had adored his late wife and probably always would.

He had so little to offer her she wondered at herself for yearning for him every waking moment, as well as a few sleeping ones when he managed to creep into her dreams. She hoped she didn't moan his name out loud with the sensual longing those fantasies unleashed in her sleeping mind. When sensible Freya was no longer awake to resist the masculine spell of this man her inner siren wanted her imagination blossomed and informed her she was a passionate woman. So that left one last sce-

nario she hardly dared let herself fully explore.
Freya let the book she had taken from his shelf
of them drop into her lap as she pondered it at
last. She could take a lover.

Since there would only ever be one, wasn't
it as well he should be skilful, tender and passionate? Impossible to know why she believed
Orlando would be all three and that there
would be nothing cold and calculating about
his loving, but somehow she still did. This new
Freya decided she wanted to be reckless and
bold for once in her life. After years of seeing
marriage as a way to make her family realise
her value, as a mere girl, she was awake at last
and so glad fate hadn't let her wed a Duke of
any description. What a relief to cast off the
hollow idea of outranking her father and half-
brother and showing them she could be every
bit as good as them. Her mother was dead and
Bowland thought more of his pet dog than his
half-sister, so there was no doting relative pulling her back to endure the narrow life she'd
fooled herself was enough for her for so long
the waste seemed almost criminal.

She would leave the *haut ton* behind without a pang and her heartbeat thundered as another possibility tugged at her imagination.
If Orlando got her with child she could bear

it under another name, then keep it and Lady Freya could disappear for ever. How would it feel to be reborn as a grieving young widow left to bear his posthumous child alone? *Dangerous*, her more cautious self informed her. *Wondrous*, Perdita argued serenely. Something told her she would mourn Orlando as her one and only lover for ever, but at least she would have a heart and purpose to her life. More of that than if she made a suitable marriage and bore a troop of proper ladies and gentlemen; one bastard with Orlando sounded a life of hope compared to watching her impeccably bred family take after their very dull father and turn away from her as well.

Why she knew he wouldn't let her stay was something of a mystery to her, like the rest of his secret life in the hidden house deep in these woods. Part of her knew him better than she had any other being and yet they had only met days ago. She remembered the way Jack Seaborne and his Jessica had been together during that house party at Ashburton and finally knew why passion and love and yearning drew them so inevitably together that even the arrogant daughter of an arrogant Earl couldn't shine through as the ideal wife for a Duke in search of a Duchess. A wry smile twisted her mouth at the thought of herself then, believing she only had to be Lady Freya for the highest in the land to want to marry her. Jack and Jessica had known each other for years before they finally let love in, so wasn't she more privileged to feel the certainty of it so much more quickly?

She chuckled at the thought of her proud ladyship of three years ago even admitting she could fall in love with a man who earned his own bread with hard physical labour, who lived in a two-up, two-down cottage in the midst of a forest miles away from civilisation and was still abidingly in love with his late wife. Had she picked out the ideal man *not* to fall in love with, that man would surely be Orlando Craven; a man who couldn't, or wouldn't, share his true name with her, let alone the secrets of his formidably guarded heart.

'What are you laughing at, Prudie?' Sally scrambled down from her tree to ask, having grown bored with lying still along a broad branch so Cromwell's long-dead troops couldn't find her, or the self-proclaimed King Hal on the next one up.

'You, my princess,' she lied and gave the lichen stains and liberal smudges of dirt about the royal person a rueful look. 'As well I've finished mending your other skirt, your high-ness, since that one will have to be washed and mended again before it's fit to be seen.'

'Papa's not half as good at mending as you, Prudie,' Hal told her, using his sister's nick-name for their uninvited guest as easily as if he'd always known her.

It sounded as if he thought tending their clothes and feeding them at regular inter-vals was her given task in the wide scheme of Henry Craven's life. Freya realised how in-fatuated she was with all three Cravens when that seemed a treasured compliment, not the insult it should be to a lady of birth and for-tune. How her heart would reel and contract when she had to leave these two not very an-gelic children behind as well as their sire. She swallowed a weak desire to weep at the very thought and told herself to treasure what she had now instead of mourning what she might not have tomorrow.

'So you've turned up at last, have you?' the Duke of Dettingham greeted his friend and cousin-in-law, Alexander Forthin, Earl of Cal-vercombe. 'I was about to send for you.'

Alex raised one arrogant black brow and

refused to ask why even a Seaborne thought he could summon my Lord Calvercombe as if he was a tame lackey.

'I think Rich is in trouble,' Jack Seaborne confided in a low murmur to avoid even the acute hearing of their wives, who were greeting one another only yards away.

'Any particular kind?' Alex asked warily, knowing a wife's ears were attuned to her husband's secret thoughts, let alone anything he was rash enough to say aloud.

'No, but I always knew when he was in a black mood. Not long after Jess and I married, he was in despair for some reason and there's something wrong now.'

'I thought only twins felt each other's thoughts, but I'll believe you. You two always were more like brothers than cousins. Indeed, it must be hard for you to have that resty devil forever in your head, but we'll talk about it later,' Alex said, since they didn't want their ladies wound up in Rich's troubles.

'I hope you're not thinking of dragging my lord into some rackety misadventure?' Jack's cousin Persephone remarked as she kissed him and eyed him distrustfully.

'You know very well by now that Alex Forthin never goes anywhere he doesn't want to, Coz,' Jack countered lightly.

'Now *I'm* suspicious,' his own wife asserted and he met Jess's clever dark eyes as innocently as he could, while cursing the instincts of women and more especially wives.

'Me too,' Antigone Seaborne informed them as she crossed the famous marble hall to greet Alex and Persephone, now the host and hostess had been hugged and it was her turn.

'Outvoted and outmanoeuvred by a trio of mere women.' Marcus met his wife's angry glare with provocation and pride in her brightness in his green Seaborne eyes.

'I'll give you *mere* women, Telemachus Seaborne,' Antigone threatened.

'Yes, please,' he replied irrepressibly and she laughed as she did so often nowadays, reluctantly perhaps, but she still laughed and he still loved her with all the passionate delight of a Seaborne male who has found his true mate and never intends letting her go.

'Before you two set the curtains on fire with one of your lover's tiffs, perhaps we should adjourn to the drawing room and find out what our husbands are conspiring about?' Jessica suggested and three Seaborne ladies looked expectantly at their husbands, who did their

best to pretend a six-way council of war would
suit them very well.

The three ladies exchanged glances that
said, *Who would have thought these three
could enjoy marriage definitely not à la mode,
yet still be their fierce barbarian lovers in
breeches and topboots underneath it all?* Marriage was a wondrous adventure for each of
them and perhaps only they could know how
glorious it felt to have the love of your life concentrating his sensuous experience on pleasing one woman. It was a bond that would unite
them if they weren't also the best of friends
and they badly wanted to meet Annabelle De-
Morbaraye and compare notes on her lion, if
Rich would only allow her out of his lair along
with their cubs long enough to do so.

It had been a very long day. And utterly useless for the task Rich had set himself. Today
had been supposed to help him get Perdita out
of his head once and for all. He'd done his best
to exhaust himself by striding about the forest like an escaped wolf all day, and half the
night, then finally decided he might as well
go home, since she was at Keziah's with the
children. Now instead of a refuge and a brief
respite from wanting her mercilessly, this was

another disaster. Perdita was here and what folly to feel betrayed by that fact. Nevertheless she was here and should be at least a mile away from the beast she'd made of him. The dratted female had made him dangerous and that felt almost unforgivable.

'What the devil are you doing here?' Rich growled when the stoutly barred door was open at last, since he'd thundered on it furiously when his key wouldn't let him in and he realised why, instead of standing there glaring at it like a slow-top.

'And a good evening to you too, Mr Craven,' Perdita said stiffly as Rich tried to clamp manners over raw fury and failed.

'Good evening,' he said shortly, 'what the deuce are you doing here?'

'Wishing I had somewhere else to go,' she said with wounded dignity that cut like a knife and made him feel guilty and angry and a finely masculine mess all rolled into one.

'It's not that I don't want you here,' he muttered gruffly, although he desperately wanted her gone and all this endless temptation and soul-searching along with her.

'Really? You have the oddest ways of making a guest welcome in your house, then,' Perdita replied coolly as she stepped back to let him in. When she stayed as far away from him as she could without standing in the scullery, he told himself that was what he wanted.

'Where are the children?' he asked, giving up on politeness since rudeness made her wary and by heaven she needed to be.

'I sold them to the rag man,' she ventured recklessly and one of the chains he'd clamped on wanting her outrageously snapped.

Rich felt the world skew as his inner beast roared for the contrary female and she didn't have sense to realise it. 'Tell me!' he gritted and she flinched.

'Keziah has them,' she said, as if he shouldn't have to ask and he had no real doubt she would make sure they were safe before she worried about herself, but somehow even that made it all worse.

He tried to remind himself she didn't know the terror he always lived with: that Hal could be seized by his enemies and disposed of like an unwanted kitten. He trusted Keziah as he would his own mother, but Cleo was as tricky as a badly primed firework. He'd done his best to ignore her languorous looks in his direction, but he knew it was wise to be wary of a woman scorned, particularly when that woman seemed to have very few scruples and a devious mind behind all the surface charm. For tonight Atlas was with them and Reuben would be there to keep a check on Cleo's wilder impulses, so she was quite right and Hal and Sally were safe—would he could say as much for Perdita.

'Then why are *you* here?' he asked grumpily and locked the door behind him from habit more than good sense.

'Cleopatra insisted there was no room with the children, Atlas and three adults crammed into a tiny cottage.'

'And the real reason?'

'Apparently I'm after her man,' Perdita admitted with such a look of contempt Rich almost laughed.

'And are you?' he growled instead.

'Mr Summer is a married man,' she snapped and sought the only sanctuary this room allowed her by reaching for the curtains about the box-bed, so she could shut herself away and make it very clear what she thought of his monstrous allegation.

Contrarily, he refused to let her put that fragile barrier between them and swung her back to face him again. 'He's still a handsome devil though, isn't he?' he muttered as if some other idiot had control of his tongue and immediately shook his head. 'I'm sorry, that insults both of you,' he admitted curtly.

Rich looked down at his calloused workman's hands on her slender yet rounded arm and told himself to break the contact. The start of awareness she gave when he held her, her refusal to shrink away and the sweetness of their contact, after so many days wanting her, was too heady to resist.

'Cleo made you walk back alone?' he asked and another thread of control broke at the very idea of her wandering about the forest alone and unprotected once more.

'Reuben went to check his traps and Keziah was upstairs with the children, so she had the chance to make it clear as day I wasn't welcome under the same roof. Your Mrs Summer wants me so frightened I'll meekly scuttle back to whichever stone she thinks I emerged from under so she won't have to guard her territory any more.'

'She's not *my* Mrs Summer and Cleopatra has a husband. I can assure you that I'm not her territory and never will be after this.'

'Then you might have been otherwise?'

'No, I never wanted her—that's all in her head. She's just Keziah's wayward daughter and Reuben's restless wife to me and nothing more.'

'I don't think she realises that,' Perdita replied with a cold snap in her voice.

Somehow the sight of her composed as a pale society lady, who ought to be dressed in finest silk and lace fashioned by an exclusive *modiste*, instead of faded cotton and a lightly tanned countrywoman's skin, undid the last slender thread that tethered him to sanity. His inward beast roared so loudly for the contrary female he couldn't beat it back into its cage.

'The only woman I want is you,' he admitted bitterly.

'And *I* only want *you*,' she replied as if he was a fool for dreaming otherwise.

'It can't work.'

'No, but why should that stop us?' she whispered with such painful honesty his heart lurched uncomfortably, even as the beast roared with possession and triumph inside him.

'I can't kiss you and step away. I won't be able to stop myself once I start loving you, Perdita Rowan. You'll be spoilt goods as far as the marriage mart goes if you encourage me *not* to walk over to Keziah's house and fetch my children and dog back here to chaperon us right now,' he warned.

'How do you know I'm not already fully a woman?'

'Don't be more of a fool than nature made you,' he snapped, knowing it from the bold bravery with which she met his eyes.

Even his certainty reminded him he'd once been a rake and knew far too much about women for a simple countryman. She was far too good for him in every way he could think of, even if he had his old self back and could offer her so much more than a cottage in the woods and a life of toil and obscurity. And now he couldn't even offer her that for much longer, he reminded himself bitterly.

'I'm a realist, not a fool, Orlando,' she said softly and how could he *not* want her?

His Perdita, with no illusions about a future of loving endlessly—this woman he had no right to want. Her breath stuttered as if *not* being his would hurt her in some drastic fashion and he finally kissed her with a curse that shuddered through him and into her as something broke.

She was tangled round every sense and scruple Rich had. He raised his head to look at her at last, a desperate question in his eyes and hers shone deep gold with expectation and an answer he shouldn't ask for and she shouldn't give. For an arrested moment he wanted to know every thought and desire in her amber gaze, delve every hope and wonder in her deepest heart and make himself part of her life for ever. As their gazes heated and promised so much to one another he told himself that now would have to do, but, oh, how he yearned for the freedom to love her endlessly and enduringly.

Chapter Nine

From the moment she had met Orlando Craven in the darkness that first time, her wayward inner Freya had longed for the touch of his mouth on hers and now she wasn't even ashamed of herself for wanting him. She'd tried so hard to pretend such nonsense didn't happen to Lady Freya Buckle back then, but knew deep down that all the bluster and pride in the world couldn't stop this force of nature flaming into an unstoppable thing between them.

Dismissing all the possible futures that might haunt her and spoil the moment, she savoured every second instead, imprinted every racing heartbeat on her memory, so that she could recall it in vivid detail afterwards. When she left, she would be able to remember that she'd once been wanted so badly her powerful lover's hands shook with need. Then she could relive this in vivid colour, not a monochrome sketch drawn by an impatient hand that grew fainter year by year as light and life faded from the quick line of a mere impression Orlando might leave behind. If she didn't love him.

Perdita knew what she wanted and could live with consequences, because Lady Freya had lived without hopes and dreams for so long. A few days with Orlando would outshine a lifetime with the noble husband she'd once wanted and she thanked her stars he had never come to pass. Even now Orlando seemed to need a little sly encouragement to make her his and forget the future they couldn't have, so she wriggled delightedly under his exploring hands.

She gave vent to a breathy little moan and slid her hands up to caress his impressively muscled neck and winnow her fingers through his shaggy locks, then tug his head lower with frank impatience. Now she'd find out what it felt like to get closer than she'd ever been to a man in her adult life. It felt wonderful. He groaned and fed on her mouth as if he was starving and she learnt avidly from every hungry invasion into her willing mouth, then echoed it to drive him beyond the noble scruples she sensed hovering at the back of his conscience.

Cleopatra's flowing skirt and loose blouse lent her some of the swagger and sauce the older woman possessed and how she'd hate to know that. Freya was certain Keziah's daughter would be horrified if she knew her old clothes were helping her enemy seduce a man she wanted herself.

'Go warm your own man's bed and stay away from mine,' the sulky beauty ordered as soon as Keziah mentioned she was to stay the night.

Freya wondered if Cleo knew she had the gift of prophecy, for she fully intended to spend a whole night warming her man's bed rather than holding out for another Duke. *To the devil with Cleo and with Dukes and all the lesser aristocrats who didn't want to marry me either*, she told herself and excitement rushed through her like a lightning flash when he finally moaned as if he couldn't help himself, then pulled her even closer into his hard body and took over their kiss.

She moaned in her turn and he took ruthless advantage to explore her mouth with his wickedly probing tongue. If his mouth on hers could give such pleasure, her very toes tingled in anticipation of what more and deeper might feel like. She leaned up on her tiptoes and imitated him with a greed that made him gasp and want even more.

My, but he was mighty, she concluded gleefully; his shoulders were heavy with work-honed muscles and the ones over his ribs and belly were corded and toned so intriguingly she wanted the leisure to explore them intimately. The thought of being here to watch him fell and fashion timber come winter made her knees wobble with hotly sharp desire. Who would have thought the very idea of witnessing hard physical labour in her man would leave Lady Freya almost sweating with need to see him just so, then make love on the forest floor before the glow of all that manly effort expired?

'Stop!' he ordered frantically, as she let her hand drift lower and he pulled away to trap it, then bring it back to his face and neck despite her mewl of frustration. 'I can't endure your touch down there and not be unmanned by it, Perdita,' he whispered into her eager ear and she shivered with the delightful tension of longing for him so badly it almost hurt.

'I want you so much,' she said on a whispered sigh and hardly recognised her own voice, so husky with it maybe words were unnecessary. 'I need you,' she added, just in case she was wrong.

'And you have no idea what you're doing to me,' he protested almost incoherently as he abandoned words and decided to show her.

Deliciously, he showed her how it felt to have her lover kiss the length of her throat while she let her head fall back as if there wasn't strength left in her bones to hold it upright. He untied the cord that held the low neck of her simple blouse and cupped her eager breasts so he could display them for his sensual inspection and heat leapt higher in his green gaze until she knew what emerald fire looked like. At last he seized one of her aching breasts in his mouth to suckle and caress the stingingly hot and tight nipple at the centre of so much wanting and she moaned with hot satisfaction, wanting more of whatever came next as urgently as he did, despite not knowing what it actually was she needed so badly.

Heated shocks of longing seemed to arc from those brazenly stimulated nipples of hers to her deep feminine core and she let out a stuttering sigh at the unknown want it set off inside her. She shared this with him; knew he longed as deeply and had a hunger to match hers, even if he did know what came next. He didn't love her now, but he wanted her, oh, how ardently he wanted. She fought back the thought it wasn't enough, because if this was all there was between them, it was better than not knowing this glory as urgency and hot need flared between them like the strongest magic.

She wriggled enough to make the blouse fall off her shoulders and gape open shamelessly, so he could take the hint and bare her all the way to the waist of her full skirt and the underskirt beneath that she had found so unfamiliar at first and now gloried in. Orlando must have observed a great deal about Cleopatra's mode of dress, although he claimed not to want her, as he found the button and tie that held the skirts in place with a sure ease that sent both whispering to the floor and left her standing in her incongruous lady's day shoes. Kicking them off, she stepped out of the circle of downed plumage and stood proudly before him as nature intended only her lover and her maid ever to see her. Working in the garden had firmed her own muscles and tanned her skin so there were darker lines where the scooped neckline of her blouse stopped, but she felt no shame in the unladylike gilding on her skin.

Since he gasped at the sight of her, then began working his mouth fanatically along the sun-kissed line where tanned Freya met a paler creamy-skinned version of herself, she enjoyed every kiss and touch with him. How changed she was, she mused, as his mouth sent shivers of delight through her needy body. Distracted by wanting more, she let her fingers explore his wild dark-gold curls and noble head as his mouth feasted lower and he wove a potent spell round the upper slopes of her eager breasts and she wanted more and yet more until she was all hunger. The feel of his hair under her fingers was soft, yet springy, and she crooned nonsense in his ears as he settled his mouth on a begging nipple and she keened an inarticulate protest that nothing seemed to salve the hot desperation at her centre where she roared for more, luxurious and fiery as this was.

'Do you know—?' he began to ask, but she stopped his mouth with a kiss so desperate he gave up on words.

Smoothing his hands over her slender rib-cage and down to her narrow waist so he could hold her far enough away to shrug off his outer garments in a hasty, practised hurry told her he had plenty of experience of urgent lovings with his wife. No, she would stall in her tracks if she let the reality that he still loved his wife back in. Then he let his hot green gaze skim the long and lovely sweep of her hip and thigh and admire the lithe length of her legs and this was for them alone once again. He wanted her, so urgently even she knew his sex was many times mightier than it would be unstirred by newly wanton Perdita Rowan.

Sheltered as she had been from an early age, Freya knew the differences between man and woman, but had never been so starkly certain they would be wonderful somehow put together. She felt her breath come short and let her eyes explore the difference of him to her, then licked her lips and nodded in what she hoped was intelligible as acceptance of all they could be together. With a great marriage in her head and her mother's, she had never thought to have this precious moment of urgent consent to be ravished by someone special like this.

Orlando was awaiting some sign she would take him as her lover, if she could blast through his over-gallant hesitation at the thought of her virginity being broken by a man who wouldn't marry her. Resolute, she ran a wondering hand up his muscular thigh and intriguingly narrow manly hips and let an impudent finger whirl into the springy curls at the root of his starkly aroused manhood. She actually felt him quiver like a greyhound at the sight of a hare and watched fascinated as his member grew even larger. It felt powerful and wonderful as well as a bit terrifying and she raised her eyes to meet the molten emerald glow in his by the last fading tatters of daylight and let all she wanted show.

He saw and seized and plundered, a golden-skinned barbarian lit by the last warm shard of a June sunset coming through unshuttered windows. Swept backwards as he lifted her, then strode to the waiting box-bed, she rode her lover's mighty body and wound her legs about his narrow waist, feeling the butt of his sex against her nether cheeks with a sensuous sway of her hips that won her a half-playful, half-serious tap of reproach on her buttocks.

'Behave yourself, unless you want to be left wondering how a woman could ever enjoy bedding her man, Perdita mine,' he growled as he tumbled her on to the bed.

'And I've quite liked it so far,' she claimed with a pert smile.

'You'll more than "like" it if you keep still

and let someone who knows how to drive us in tandem gallop to our destination.'

'You talks so pretty, Mr Orlando,' she said in such a perfect mockery of Cleo Summer in full-siren mode that he gruffed a surprised bark of laughter she felt in every inch of her roused body and decided amusing him in bed would be enjoyable indeed, if only she was lying here already pleasured instead of wound tight with wanting him.

'We're not here to talk,' he declared in perfect tune with her thoughts and set about racking her body to such a state of fraught tension she felt she might break into small pieces of need if he didn't do something urgent about it very soon.

'Sorry, Perdita,' he muttered at last, as his own control seemed about to shatter and he bucked under her unwary hand when she smoothed it over his shaft and found it silky smooth and yet fascinatingly rigid under her fine touch. 'Can't wait any longer,' he gasped as he gave up exploring the fascinating curlicues of her inner sex and the hot wetness the fire inside her that wanted him with a leaping blaze of need had unleashed.

By instinct and the incendiary touch of his hands on her while he tried to prepare her for him with such heart-stopping care, she fully knew now that his sex belonged somewhere inside hers and parted her legs for him in complete faith this was what they both wanted. Still he held himself back and she felt his entire body quiver with the effort to be gentle while the blunt head of his erection met the frantic heat of her unplumbed depths at long last.

'It will hurt a little at first,' he warned, deep voice gravelly and eyes wild and desperate for her to trust him that it would only be a fleeting hurt.

'I want everything,' she explained and let herself fully open to him in a way that seemed to allow him into her very soul, let alone her body.

So he surged into her and at first she felt alien to herself as she felt the intrusion of this rigidly desperate man into her most private inner self. Reminding herself he was going to be her one and only lover, so she might as well enjoy every minute of mutual seduction, she let herself feel the power and rightness of that broad and lengthy sex of his as it stretched and stimulated hers, until she gave a quiver of delight at the fact of him inside her and gasped out loud. She felt and saw him driven to another level of needing she hadn't dared suspect he could feel for her. It constantly surprised her, this endless need—whenever her dearest hopes seemed about to be satisfied, another layer would engulf her and every one surpassed the last. Now she wanted him all the way inside her and, if taking her maidenhead hurt, it would be worth it to have all of him in her so they could be fully joined in the ultimate intimacy between man and woman.

'Everything,' she reminded him, her eyes open and steady on his, even as her breath stuttered in her lungs and every inch of her concentrated on where they joined together and all the pleasure of his body so hard and driven and the new and heady feel of it inside hers.

'Everything,' he replied as if it truly might be. She wouldn't think about the forbidden possibility of it now, when paradise might be beckoning round the corner and at least they could have that much of it, for now.

Then he plundered on through that fragile last link to her innocence and she felt a momentary pang of hurt, as much mental as physical as Freya the girl became Freya the woman. He had made her ready for him; the welcome of slick need he'd woven for both of them made it only a hair's breadth of hesitation for her before the pain was almost forgotten in the new satisfaction of having him fully seated within her, every stretching and novel inch of his manhood exactly where he should be, in her. She kept her eyes open on his while he rocked in the cradle of her feminine hips and the very suggestion of a rhythm triggered an instinctive response that made her wonder if she was born to be an Orlando-fascinated sensualist.

Her amateurish attempts to set the pace of lovers seemed to release another tether of restraint and he took it up instead, riding her until she began to feel the rock of it in her very bones and eagerly rode back, until he settled them into an exquisite trot to extreme pleasure that soon became an urgent gallop. Glad they were alone, she keened under the sheer exquisite sensation of his body and hers in perfect accord and heard her own gasps for air harmonise with his harsher ones as speed gathered and everything but him within and without her blurred and faded away. His pace seemed to change of a sudden and his thrusts went harder and deeper. She felt an even harder flush of colour scorch across her cheeks, then wash over her whole body as something wonderful dashed headlong into view and she still didn't know what it was or whether she would ever get there. Head thrashing from side to side, she whimpered with the promises a whisper away, a frustrating shadow away from reality.

'Hold on, lover, and trust me,' he managed to grate before he seized her striving face with cupped hands, even as his body drove even more frantically into hers, and their eyes met and meshed as he plunged into her as if his very survival depended on it and suddenly they had both got there at once. Together; blissfully, infinitely together.

Wild convulsions of the most unimaginable pleasure rocked through her as his body convulsed and raced into hers and took her with him into an uncharted glory. She heard herself gasp a triumphant moan that went on and on as joy surged through her in long waves of unimaginable delight. He ended his own long groan of satisfaction on a husky chuckle at the sound of it, then he kissed her what felt like endlessly as they swam together through an endless drift of passion and absolute pleasure locked into each other's rapture.

Her body still soaring with ecstasy, she felt as if she was being deluged with sensual satisfaction, truly joined with her lover in a private paradise where nobody else could ever reach or touch them again. She held his gaze as his kiss went on and on and hung on to his striving shoulders when the rigid, pleasured joy finally went out of them and he collapsed for a long lovely moment on top of her. Revelling in the ultimate luxury of her spent lover's body resting on and in hers, she let her senses satiate themselves in him before he had his way and separated from her before rolling over on to his back with her sprawled like the wanton she felt now at his side and loving every inch of bare skin on bared skin.

'Was that enough?' he asked at last and she adored the husky timbre of his voice as he seemed as lost in the moment as she was.

'Enough of what?' she managed and heard the same hoarseness in her own softer voice and wondered if this was the true intimacy of lovers, this mutual and joyous experience of each other that made them somehow bonded for ever, however far apart they might be fated to become if he had his way.

'Everything,' he pointed out helpfully.

'It will do for now,' she told him with a secretive smile he chose to trace with a calloused finger as moonlight drifted over their skin. His touch made her shiver with heat she had thought faded, until next time he wanted an amateur houri like her in his bed.

The thought this might be the only night they would ever have to lie satiated and content in each other's arms occurred to her, but she thrust it aside and refused to dwell on the lonely future when she was royally satisfied in the powerful arms of her lover.

'It will have to, for you will be sore,' he told her gently, as if he now knew her body better than she did. She flexed her newly discovered internal muscles and considered whether he might be right and whether she cared even if he was.

'Will there be another time?' she let herself ask and there seemed no point pretending she didn't want it when he had every reason to know it would be untrue. Her enthusiasm for him *and* his lithe and sleekly muscled body and magnificently rampant manhood was so obvious there seemed no point trying to pretend otherwise when their time together would be so short.

'Aye,' he breathed on a long sigh, as if he had almost hoped this conflagration of the senses would cure him of her, but the cure had turned into a new and virulent disease.

Wishing it could be different between them,

she muffled her own sigh and nestled her face into his still-fast-breathing chest to nuzzle the fire and gold curls that she knew shadowed a fine haze over the mightiest muscles of his powerful torso by daylight. She breathed in sweat and salt and arousal with that edge of mossy wood-smoke she now associated with him and would for ever have to avoid if she wasn't going to turn into a watering pot every time she smelt it in future and he was nowhere near. Shifting restlessly at the very thought of the parting to come, she felt an unexpected ruck of scar tissue under her sensitive cheek and raised her head to peer up at him with a question in her wide eyes that he seemed tempted to ignore for a moment, before he grimaced and decided to let her in that far.

'I was stabbed one night many years ago, when I wasn't quite as wary of stealthy villains and dark corners as I am now,' he told her.

'Because?' she insisted, despite the attempt he was making to shut down the intimacy of his glittering eyes holding hers in the silvery moonlight. Now their heat was fading, he seemed to be already locking his essential self away from her again.

'Because I was a fool and let an enemy creep up on us.'

'Us?'

'I was with my wife at the time,' he said tersely and turned his head aside as if he couldn't talk about his lost love without cutting himself off from the woman he'd carelessly taken to his bed in her absence.

'She must have been terrified,' she made herself say, as if they were talking of strangers, not a man who wouldn't be here to take her to ecstasy if his enemy had had his way back then.

'Not she—my Anna laid about the rogue with her parasol and made such a commotion it shamed the fashionable throng who would have passed by into coming to our rescue. She saved my life and I fell completely in love with her, as she always swore she did with me.'

'How romantic for you both,' she said as generously as she could and was suddenly glad he'd turned away.

If not, he might see the death of the unlikely hopes and dreams she'd clung to, despite the voice of common sense telling her he only wanted her and didn't intend to love anyone but his lost wife. Now they shattered like ice on a winter puddle under a child's gleeful heel. He sighed as if it was agony to love so deeply, then lose his Anna, and Freya wondered how a mistress should behave when she became an embarrassment in her lover's bed.

'I can't be the man I was when I met my wife for you, Perdita, any more than you can ever be a virgin again.'

'Do you regret I am not, Orlando?' she asked coolly, considering the desolation that urged her to run outside and rage uselessly at the moon.

'Do you?'

She pretended to think about his question when the negative sprang straight into her head and whispered *liar*.

'No,' she admitted at last.

'Then neither do I,' he told her, eyes full on her again and as honest as he could make them. He levered himself upright and draped a shawl Keziah had lent her about his waist to try to protect her from what she now knew so intimately about him.

'Clearly not,' she said, refusing to let the fact he wanted her again pass politely by.

'Be wary of me, Perdita,' he warned half-seriously. 'I'm a wolf in wolves' clothing, so don't mistake me for an honourable gentleman. We only have a brief spell out of our lives to give each other before we part.'

'Do you think I don't know that?'

'I think all women hope for more from their lover than I can offer you.'

'You're unwilling to take more than that brief spell of you and me. I accepted that you don't have enough for me as well as your family when I took you as my lover, Mr Craven. Don't paint me other than as I am to make yourself feel better.'

'My children must always come first for me, Miss Rowan: before my selfish wants and needs, even before you.'

'I envy them that love, Orlando,' she said truthfully, for her own father had never felt even an iota of that emotion for his unworthy daughter. 'I'm sure you love them enough to do whatever is needed to keep them safe and help them grow up strong and true,' she said as sincerely as she could. How deeply she wanted to love his tempestuous little girl and endearingly manly little boy for the rest of her life would have to remain her secret.

They had accepted her so matter of factly that it tugged at her heart strings for the lack of a mother in their lives. She recalled her own mother's love for her as a spoilt yet uncertain little girl and hoped Orlando wouldn't make the mistake of putting his own hopes and dreams on to his children like that.

He didn't seem likely to, but something held him back from fulfilling his true role as piratical protector of anyone who needed him. Love was the only thing she could imagine stopping him seizing the day and everything that went with it and, if only he loved her, she would have eagerly joined his bargain with fate and joyously forgotten Lady Freya Buckle in Mrs Perdita Craven, but Perdita didn't really exist and now she never would.

'I do—I have to,' he said softly in reply to her implication he always had to think very hard about what his children needed most and it wasn't her.

She finally shook off the ghost of the cherished lover she might have been and believed him. 'Then we'll seize the day and please each other for a time, Orlando. You can't love me and I refuse to love a man who won't love me back,' she lied without a blush, 'so we can enjoy each other and part friends.'

'I might get you with child,' he warned and, given the driven passion they roused in each other, he could be right.

'That will be my problem and not yours.'

'I won't have any babe of mine put out for the wolves to bring up,' he made a half-hearted try at joking, although she could see he found it as poor an attempt as she did.

'Neither will I,' she said quietly and he nodded as if acknowledging that with her as a mother, a child would never need a fiercer protector.

'I will endeavour to control myself,' he promised shortly and she knew he was embarrassed by the fact he had wanted her so badly he hadn't done so this time.

'And I shall make sure you don't,' she vowed and meant it, for she longed for that child more fiercely than she could have believed possible, considering it would come into the world a nameless bastard in the eyes of the world, if it came at all.

Chapter Ten

Despite the unspoken competition between them to exert control on one side and over-bear it with headlong passion on the other, as Orlando and Perdita they managed to fit a lot of loving into the bare week they agreed to take from real life for wanting, and having, each other. Freya discovered the heady power of a touch or a look to tease her lover into such a stew of frustrated need that, by the end of a long day's work, he was incoherent with passion for her by the time the children were safely abed and asleep.

She learnt how it felt to be so urgently wanted there was no question of refined couplings in the chastely curtained box-bed when he dragged her outside into his workshop, after a long and particularly fretful evening, to be hastily kissed and urgently taken on the workbench he padded with his discarded jacket with only slightly muffled enjoyment out here for the sake of not waking his children. Even that had hardly taken the edge off his appetite for her, she decided with the assurance of satisfaction to come when he tugged her back inside and met her eyes with a heavy-lidded gaze that promised her there was no need to look outside for the moon and stars tonight.

'Trust me?' he whispered when she had already done so with everything she was and had and might be.

Nodding her head silently and wondering what was to come, she would have gasped her astonishment all the same when he deftly gagged her with his clean neckerchief and lured her back to the bed. He confounded her by lying full length on it and beckoning her to do as she pleased with his prone body, so she did, with sensuous thoroughness and rode them both to a climax that would have made her one long scream of satisfaction, if she had been able to utter more than a muffled moan to tell him what she'd learnt about loving that night to add to the precious others they'd enjoyed to the hilt.

'This is our last night, isn't it?' she said as soon as she had breath enough to spare and could keep the sadness out of her whisper when he removed that now-mangled binding.

'Aye, it has to be,' he told her with plenty of it in his own voice and knowing he would miss her warmed the ache of letting go inside her a little as she knelt over him, still braced across his narrow hips and naked in the faint light of the dying fire.

Impossible not to feel bitter and forsaken at such a moment, she decided, and set out to make him pay dear for his rejection of all Perdita Rowan could be to him in her own special way. Let him forget her when she was gone after this, she raged to herself as she found undreamt-of depths of sensual witchery in her until-now untapped imagination. Using his kerchief to draw him along with her, she led him to the fire and stoked it, despite the June heat, so they could love naked by the golden light of it. If he could let the image of her bathed in firelight and staring open eyed with every inch of her aware of every inch of him, inside her, around her and for ever in her head as she bucked and bowed on the rug beneath him slip out of his head when she was gone, he was beyond cold and well on the way to heartless.

She might not have his love, but she had his passion and it stirred for her again and again as they wore out the night with each other, driven by the ever-present goad that this was all they would ever have of each other, the only pleasure she would ever have with a man because there couldn't be another after him. He had the experience of a loving marriage behind him and, she suspected, a good few years of untrammelled bachelor freedom before that. He would find another woman to slake his passions on and maybe that woman would take her pleasure of such a mighty and driven lover then move on as easily as he could.

Astonished by her own lack of inhibition as he had shown her ways of coupling she would never have dreamt there even were, as if he was trying to pack a lifetime of loving into one night as well, she greeted the dawn with dread and revulsion that it was becoming ever harder to conceal.

'Keziah will be here soon and I must light the copper ready,' he told her at last, his eyes as weary and flat as hers felt at the idea of what was to come, as well as the sudden fatigue their lack of even a moment's sleep made out of their last night together.

'Why?'

'So you can have a bath. It's high time you had that wild and witchy hair tamed and dressed as befits a lady again,' he informed her, as if she had been slacking from the high standards of a fine lady for the last few days out of sheer laziness and needed goading to reclaim even some of her former perfection.

'Considering my gown is in shreds and my cloak not a lot better, I don't quite know how I'm to pretend I walked out of the forest as fresh as if I was dressed out of a bandbox,' she said grumpily.

'You underestimate us,' he told her with a tolerant smile for her bad temper that made her want to hit him.

'Do I?' she said disagreeably.

She saw him flinch at her implied criticism of a lover so determined not to give his heart to a woman twice in his life. Good, he was making her leave him in the face of every desire she had to stay with the man who had stolen her heart and taken her love as if it was a candy twist, to be consumed for its sweetness, then forgotten when the next treat presented itself to him to be enjoyed. She might go, because Perdita had her own pride and it wouldn't let her stay unless he needed her as unendingly as she did him, but she wouldn't let him dismiss her as if she was a pretty little nothing.

'Keziah, then,' he qualified shortly and went to do as he had promised the older woman he would and get the makings of a bath ready while Freya sat on the stool by the now-cold fireside to comb out her tousled locks with the wide-toothed wooden comb he'd made for her so she could tease the tangles from it more easily.

It had been too easy to part with Perdita and yet so hard he wondered his teeth weren't ground to a powder he'd had to clench them so many times in order to beg her not to go, Rich decided, as he drove the hired horse and cart back to Reuben Summer's taciturn friend and walked off in the opposite direction to the one he needed to take for home. Far too easy to leave her at the nearest inn where the accommodation coaches halted and far too hard to force himself to drive away and not go back before she was gone for good.

Keziah would care for the children while he made his long and aimless wandering way through country lanes and heathland tracks before finally turning for home, so nobody could follow him back. Not even Reuben's people would take time or trouble to stay on the trail of a person who seemed without wealth or purpose. Just as well, considering his head was far too full of stubborn, gallant Perdita Rowan and the tearing fear possessing him that he'd let half his life drive away on the swaying accommodation coach and would never be whole again without her.

Not inclined to allow her to be so important, he tried to fill his thoughts with Annabelle and their children instead. Love for his vital and courageous wife hadn't fallen away, but the awful suspicion a man might love deeply and abidingly twice in one lifetime was beginning to creep up and make him feel an abject fool. Not a fool to perhaps find love again, but one to let all the hope and glory of it go without the trace of a fight.

Too late, echoed about his head like the knell of doom as he let himself realise what he'd known in his heart every step of their wretched journey this morning. Once Perdita got into that coach and he watched it move off from his hiding place nearby, she had vanished out of his life as if he'd imagined her. How he could imagine such a wondrous conundrum as his lost princess he had no idea, but Miss Rowan was no more real than Mr Orlando Craven and it would be hell's own job to track her down under her real identity.

Impossible to trace a shadow and how many brown-eyed, brown-haired ladies of quality were there on this racing island of theirs? Far too many to track this special one, even if he dared, he told himself as he halted his march to nowhere in particular and almost turned back. A fast horse might catch up with the ponderous stage even now, but what would he say to her once he'd attracted more attention than Rich Seaborne had dared draw to himself in six long years of hiding in Longborough Forest?

Come live with me and be my love and slave in the forest with me, isolated from your kind and limited to the narrow little life that is all I can offer you? He forced himself onwards with the harsh thought his lost lady was better off without him echoing round his head like knife blades clanking in the wind. The sneaky suspicion he must change to deserve her still ate away at his certainty he was doing the right thing, but a cowardly impulse to ignore it made him walk on. Hal was the rightful

heir to a grand title—no, he was the rightful
Marquis of Lundy right now and had been
ever since he was born. How could Rich bring
up a Marquis to care for his lands and people
as he should while Annabelle's son continued
to run wild about Longborough Forest like a
wild cottager's boy, with no more to take on
one day than a narrow patch of land and his
father's trade to live by?

Then there was his mischievous little daughter, uniquely herself from the instant she was
placed in his arms when she was born. Even
though her coming took Annabelle from him,
he could never have resented their perfect little daughter or wished her dead instead. Sally
bore the stamp of the Seabornes on every feature and had fire and determination running
through her from both sides of the family. Rich
wondered if he was selfish to hide his children from the world, then remembered what
the so-called Marquis of Lundy had to lose
by Hal's very existence and knew he'd been
right to conceal the true Martagon heir for so
long. Small and vulnerable to a corrupt nurse
or a physician paid to treat the boy so direly
he would no longer be an obstacle in Francis Martagon's path, Hal had been too easy a
mark when he was a baby and then a toddler.

Now his son was five years old and the first to declare himself independent, Rich was beginning to realise his days as an isolated forest dweller could be almost over. Or they definitely would be if he managed to expose Hal's venal cousin as the murderous rogue he was. Then Richard Seaborne could openly search for his amber-eyed lady with her nut-brown hair and wood-nymph's body and offer her all he was too much of a coward to risk laying before her today. Yet after he let her leave without confessing he'd miss her for ever and a day, he'd made it all too unlikely Perdita would accept him if he grovelled for her hand in marriage on bended knee for a month.

Damnation take it, but he was the biggest fool this side of poor mad King George, who at least had bouts of painfully aware sanity among his humiliating interludes of lunacy. Rich slashed moodily at a clump of nettles with the stout stick he carried. It would be a risk the most protective side of him would fight furiously, but somehow he must move against the usurper of the Lundy marquisate and secure his son and daughter's future, then hope it wasn't too late to find one of his own with his lady of the woods.

Rich frowned fiercely as he strode heedlessly on his way and brooded about the dangers ahead. He wasn't the boy's real father; he couldn't claim guardianship of Annabelle's son unless he managed to prove Francis Martagon the villain Rich knew him to be. To take the risk of establishing Hal's identity in front of the law and his peers, Rich would have to be sure there was no chance he would ever leave his precious son vulnerable to the very cousin who wanted him dead.

Revulsion at the idea almost made him change his mind and revert to his intention of hiding away until Hal was of age. By then his Sally should be plenty old enough to make her come out in polite society, if she hadn't already run off with one of Reuben Summer's handsome cousins, or decided to launch herself on an unsuspecting world in a wild Seaborne fashion it made him shudder to even contemplate. Both his children needed family and feminine influence and they would need civilising if they were to shoulder the responsibilities of their true place in the world one day and not make the same sort of mistakes both Hal's fathers made in their wild youth.

So, if he could hunt Francis Martagon down and neutralise the threat to Hal's very existence, if he could render himself a gentleman once more and a suitable mate for a proud and finicky lady, then he might somehow find Perdita and convince her he wanted to marry her. So many ifs and not a guarantee among them he could find her again and beg her to accept him in every way a woman could accept a man this time around when he'd made it insultingly clear to her up to now that there could be no future for them, no second marriage for Orlando Craven.

Yet what a life it would be if only he could persuade her to forgive him. She would make him a queenly yet hospitable lady and who better to grace the lovely home his parents had made of Seaborne House and the position of Lady of the Manor Perdita could have been born for? If she would take a man with wide business interests and a very adventurous past, he knew she was equal to anything his past and present lives would throw up. The courage and truth of her reflected exact opposite qualities in him, but Rich longed for a chance to prove worthy of a good woman's love for the second time in his life now he'd finally let himself see past that ridiculous promise he'd made Anna that he would never love or wed another woman.

* * *

Miss Carolina Bradstock tapped a thoughtful finger on the breakfast table and stared at her guest of six weeks with a directness her family had always found disconcerting. So much about the girl across the table was still a mystery, but she was now certain that Lady Freya Buckle was in even more trouble than she had admitted to her great-aunt when she turned up at her quiet house in the country with only the clothes she stood up in and a battered purse with a few pennies left in it.

If the girl hadn't borne the stamp of her parentage as clearly as if the Earl and his Countess had branded her, Miss Bradstock might have doubted this pale, quiet and perfectly polite girl was the notoriously proud Lady Freya Buckle of legend. From the letters and rumours that reached her from old friends and one or two acquaintances who couldn't resist gloating at how her niece had made herself a laughing stock by regarding the Duke of Dettingham as her personal property, this Freya was very different from the one her fellow aristocrats now regarded as something of a joke. Apparently the girl had carelessly lost her Duke to a lame spinster, but apparently it was rumoured she was such a cold piece no red-blooded male wanted to marry her for anything but her grandfather's plump fortune.

Either this picture of the perfect daughter to the Earl of Bowland, whom Miss Bradstock had considered a deplorable choice of husband for her unlucky niece, was false or Lady Freya had changed beyond recognition. She suspected the latter, for how could any child grow up into a normal being under the blight of the late Lord Bowland's overblown pride and belief he was the greatest aristocrat ever to waste his rent rolls and his wife's dowry on useless pomp and puffery?

It wasn't in Miss Bradstock's nature to pry into the business of others, or at least so she told herself when the urge became so strong she was nigh bursting with curiosity about where her niece had been before she turned up on her doorstep one fine morning. Prying or not, she hadn't been able to resist listening at the door when Lady Freya's pompous brother turned up to find out what had really happened to her. Although she hated to agree with the dull and unadventurous young idiot, Bowland was right to suspect there was more to his half-sister's tale of being waylaid and taken in by kindly strangers than she intended to admit. Even such poor and simple folk would have got a message to Bowland that his sister was safe and recovering from an attack that would have left most females broken in mind and body.

The dilemma of not wanting to argue with a tale the girl might have invented to hide her dishonour and the disgrace the world would heap on her meant Miss Bradstock watched her guest with unusual discretion after Bowland's visit. Even an ageing spinster had an idea of the shock and horror such an attack would have on even the strongest-minded female, but she saw none of the giveaway signs of flinching away from male company or nervously starting at shadows. Some mornings she thought the girl *had* been weeping, but it had gradually dawned on her that there could be a very good reason for it if she had.

'Hmm,' she said now, with a long and challenging look at her ashen-faced guest. 'You don't seem to have even the trace of an appetite this morning, so never mind pecking at your breakfast like an invalid. We'll adjourn to my private sitting room where we will be undisturbed at this hour of the day and then you can tell me all about it.'

Freya managed to swallow the nausea that threatened to send her bolting from the room and sipped her tea very slowly, then met Great-Aunt Carolina's sharp dark eyes.

'Very well, Aunt,' she said with at least some of the Buckle arrogance she now found so hard to deploy even when she wanted to.

She owed the lady honesty, she decided with a gusty sigh, little doubting she would shortly be setting out on another journey as a consequence. Who knew where it would take her this time? she mused, as she followed the bustling little lady upstairs and through her bedchamber to the room beyond. Miss Bradstock locked the bedchamber door behind them and as there was no other access to this room but through the larger one beyond at least she knew they could be assured of privacy for their most important conversation so far.

'Well, my girl, and what a fine pickle you got yourself into during your wanderings about the countryside, did you not?' Miss Bradstock said as soon as they were settled and Freya felt the greasy weight of sickness lift once more and let stark reality back in.

'So it would seem,' she admitted carefully, bracing her shoulders for the inevitable tirade that must meet such an admission.

'Did those villains ravish you?' her great-aunt asked the question Bowland hadn't been able to make himself say outright and offered her a coward's way out of her dilemma that Freya refused to take.

'No, I spoke the truth when I told my brother I managed to run fast and far enough to shake them off when they would have done so,' she said, all her best Lady-Freya defences in place now she had revealed her 'pickle' had very different origins from the rape she found the idea of so repulsive she shuddered and felt the acid bite of nausea threaten once again.

'Here,' Miss Bradstock said impatiently, holding out one of the very plain dry biscuits she had ordered cook to make to settle an imaginary stomach upset of her own, since she dare not let the woman put two and two together and admit they were for her niece instead. 'My sister swore by these when she was *enceinte*. Eat one very slowly and you'll soon be well enough to explain how the kindly strangers you met on your travels left you with a child in your belly, despite preserving you from arrant rogues and would-be ravishers of innocence.'

'I don't know if I can explain all that,' Freya said with a rueful shrug as she did as she was bid and found her rather fierce relative was quite right when her stomach settled at last.

'Don't you think I was ever young, girl?' Miss Bradstock demanded with a hard challenge in her fathomless eyes that made Freya take a second look at her hostess and decide, yes, she had clearly been very much a woman in her time. 'I was handsome,' the lady claimed without a trace of false modesty. 'Not beautiful, but decidedly handsome. The family considered me fast, which is probably why I ended up having so little to do with them.'

'Were you really fast, or were they so stuffy you couldn't bear to live as they wanted you to?' Freya couldn't help asking, although she should be worried her own dark secret was out instead of wondering how many Miss Bradstock's fearsomely respectable appearance concealed.

'I was a disgrace to the Bradstock *and* the Buckle name,' the lady said proudly.

'Were you really, ma'am? I never heard so much of a whisper of it from either side of the family.'

'You don't think they would advertise it, do you, girl? You're more naïve than you have any right to be if you did, given what you must have been up to lately.'

'I suspect you weren't anything like as black

a sheep as I am about to become,' Freya admitted ruefully.

'He was married,' Miss Bradstock replied baldly, and Freya recognised the pain of loss in her eyes, since it was a twin of the desolation she saw in her own when she looked in the mirror nowadays. 'Yours?' her aunt asked.

'Widowed,' she admitted matter of factly.

'Then why didn't he marry you? Never mind differences of rank and fortune,' her aunt said impatiently, as if convinced such things mattered to the daughter of an Earl, when Freya had found over the last few weeks that nothing mattered much beside missing Orlando every second of every day she woke up without him and the world was still grey, whatever the weather outside had to say to the contrary.

'I would have walked barefoot round the world in his footsteps if he'd only asked me to,' she admitted gloomily.

'He's a fool, then,' Miss Bradstock declared and Freya was tempted to agree.

'He had his reasons. I would never have left if I didn't consider them valid.'

'Then you're a fool as well. There's nothing more important than love when you have a bastard in your belly to prove it.'

Freya smoothed a protective hand over her

still-flat stomach and wanted to rage and argue, but it was the honest truth of how her baby would enter the world and she had come so close to retracing her steps these last few weeks. Remembering how she had taken the risk of such an outcome, she refused to go back on her word. Anyway, it was better for her baby to have a loving mother and a much-regretted and falsely dead father than one who would resent its coming for tying him to a woman he couldn't love. Which was all very well, but now she needed her fortune and some native cunning to bring that false future about.

Anyway, Orlando was no more real than Perdita Rowan and from the moment he told her to call him Orlando, she knew it wasn't his true name. Nobody else questioned his alias and the deepest parts of the forest were a refuge for those who wanted to hide from the world for their own particular reasons. Orlando and Keziah's reasons must be good, as they were good people, but how could she take her own unborn child back to live a lie when its father couldn't even tell them what his true name was or bestow it on them? What little he had left to give had been enough for Perdita for that magical week they spent loving outside reality, but it wasn't enough for her precious child.

Lucky for her that she had chanced on an honourable outlaw, she supposed, and couldn't resist a tender smile at the thought of him torn and troubled and rampant for so many days before he gave in to temptation and her eagerness to be ruined and made her his lover. Even now she refused to see anything sordid in their coupling and deeply regretted the lifetime of loving they would never have. Whether she would admit it to his face if he stood in front of her now was another matter. Whoever he turned out to be, could Lady Freya forgive the bungling idiot his lack of faith in her? Probably, she admitted to herself with a gusty sigh.

'This bastard is more important to me than anyone else now,' she said, meeting her relative's eyes steadily, trying to make her determination to protect her child plain without abusing her hostess's hospitality more than she already had.

'So we'll just have to make plans for a new life and inform Bowland he can't and won't get us to change them at his bidding.'

'I certainly must. If you feel able to back me whilst I do so, despite everything you know about me now, I shall be most grateful for your support, Aunt Carolina,' Freya managed to say steadily, although she was tempted to sob like a child at such stalwart support when she had been dreading another rejection from her family and after she had got to like and respect this member of it more than she did any others.

'The fortune your grandfather left you gives you more power than you realise, my dear. It's time it was used for a better purpose than keeping Bowland's wife in unbecoming silk gowns for the rest of her life.'

'I doubt I could spend it all if I tried, so my brother is welcome to most of it.'

'Nonsense. You will need to be rich and eccentric to get away with the plan I have in mind and I have no mind to live in penury while you nobly support everyone in comfort but yourself and your child. It's very clear to me you need me, my girl, and the babe you're brooding even more so, if you're not to make a complete shambles of the whole business as you have everything else since your mama insisted on bringing you out when you were far too young to leave the schoolroom.'

'But I can't stay here,' Freya said, puzzled that her most unusual relative could think that possible when she was known here as the lady's noble, but very single, niece.

'Of course not, but dull respectability has grown devilish tedious.'

'So I imagine,' Freya replied faintly as the possibility she would have some sort of family around her, apart from her coming child, slotted into her mind and got comfortable there.

'Even surrounded with a pack of fools as I am, we only have a few weeks to be done with this place before you start to show and everyone knows what you've been up to, my girl. There's no time to lose, so we'd best get busy if we're to depart on a protracted visit to our Irish relatives in a hurry we won't deign to explain to the British ones.'

'And are we?'

'Are we what?'

'Going to visit our relatives in Ireland?'

'Of course we ain't—whatever would be the point in that? Misdirection is the secret of a sound campaign.'

'This love of yours, was he a military man by any chance?'

'Navy. I don't hold with the military, far too light minded as well as full of idle blockheads and time-servers.'

'I dare say,' Freya said faintly and listened

intently to the scheme Miss Bradstock had
thought out with a thoroughness that would
awe most admirals.

Chapter Eleven

'Are you certain it was my cousin Richard who wrote to you and not a crafty fraudster?' the Duke of Dettingham demanded of the quiet gentleman who'd been admitted to his study so late in the day most of his household were already fast asleep.

'Yes, your Grace,' Mr Frederick Peters asserted quietly.

'So, after six years of silence, I'm expected to believe my cousin would write to a complete stranger and not to me?'

'Perhaps he believes your correspondence could be intercepted more easily than mine, your Grace.'

'With the enemies you must have gained over the years in your profession, I can't help but question your logic, Peters. How do you know for certain this isn't a hoax?'

'I know Mr Seaborne's hand too well for that, your Grace.'

'For heaven's sake, stop "your Gracing" me. We both know you don't respect me because of the bed I was born in.'

'Perhaps I respect you despite it, your Grace,' Mr Peters suggested with such a straight face the Duke shot him a very suspicious look indeed.

'Calvercombe and I have retained you to find my cousin and Miss DeMorbaraye these last three years and I can't help but think you knew more about either of them than you're willing to admit even now. Given all that, I hope you can see why it looks more like contempt from where I'm sitting?' he said in such a coldly silken tone that the temperature in the comfortable room seemed to drop about ten degrees.

'Nevertheless it is not so, but I'm afraid I made some solemn promises to your cousin that must trump my duty to yourself and the Earl,' Mr Peters admitted uncomfortably.

'And what would those promises be?'

'Not to tell anyone I knew him well enough to make one in the first place. As for the others, I still feel bound by them and cannot reveal their nature. The safety of others depends on my discretion and one day I hope you'll understand why I had to keep silent until he gave me permission to say even as much as I can now.'

'And you expect me to believe he's suddenly changed his mind about trusting me with even this little of his secret life and decided he wants to come back into the fold? I can't help but find that very hard to believe.'

'So does he, if I read him rightly,' Frederick Peters replied with a frown.

'Then you've seen him recently if you talk of reading him aright?'

'He finds me now and again,' Peters explained. 'Never where I might expect him to and not in the same place twice.'

'He always was good at being someone else,' Jack said cynically.

'And I wonder if he knows what a challenge awaits him here, besides the obvious one of needing to beat off his enemies before he returns home,' Peters stated.

'My cousin never used to care whom he offended,' Jack mused, staring at the massive family portrait the Seabornes sat for last summer, with the space where Richard Seaborne should be that they all pretended not to notice, but had felt so acutely at the time.

'It's not his own safety Mr Seaborne is desperate to secure,' his uncomfortable visitor admitted as if divulging a state secret.

'D'you think I hadn't worked that out myself, man? No doubt he's with Lord Calvercombe's cousin Annabelle and any little Seabornes they've made between them. It's a good match and both their families would be more than happy with it if they would only come home.'

'The situation is complex, your Grace.'

'Then are you going to tell me what it is, or keep me guessing for another six years?'

'Perhaps we should wait for Lord Calvercombe so I can tell the tale only once and there's less risk of being overheard?'

'And maybe you should get on and tell me which tiger my cousin has by the tail this time, since I've been employing you to find what you already knew but didn't deign to tell me for so long.'

'I wanted to, but Mr Seaborne insisted nobody must know about our acquaintance. I suspect he believes it safer for you and the rest of his family not to know where he is.'

'Since neither Lord Calvercombe nor I are

puling infants or aged breakdowns, I speak for us both when I tell you we're prepared to take that risk.'

'I can't reveal where he is or the name he uses now, but Mr Seaborne gave me permission to tell you why he's determined to hide away until he's certain it's safe to resume his true identity.'

So Frederick Peters told the Duke of Dettingham the full horror of Annabelle DeMorbaraye's plight one dark evening in the Strand when Mr Richard Seaborne rounded a dark corner into a little-used court to find a young woman at bay as a pair of thugs tried to beat her insensible and kill her unborn babe.

'Luckily the desperate fight that ensued between Mr Seaborne and two of the most dangerous villains in London was as noisy as it was deadly and I heard the commotion on my way back from visiting a client. The lady recovered enough of her strength and considerable will-power to shout for help and between us we managed to scare the villains off, although I suspect one was mortally wounded during the scuffle with your cousin. Unfortunately Mr Seaborne took a knife wound to his ribs, so the lady insisted we go back to her lodging to make sure it was properly cleaned and a physician sent for. They were married a month later and I was a witness and after the wedding they left London for I know not where.

'Mr Seaborne has found me about once every six months ever since to gather news of his late wife's enemies and hear what's happening in his family, but he made me promise never to reveal our meetings to anyone or let it be known I had even met him. Given the attack and rumours I heard of them being harried further while they remained in London, it seemed a wise promise to give. Nobody suspected a connection between a humble lawyer and Mr Seaborne, so I've been safe enough from the villain behind it all.'

'Does my cousin know who the reprobate is, then? And, if so, why hasn't he brought the coward to book long ago?'

'This is a far darker business than it appears and the stakes are very high indeed—'

'Hold a moment,' Jack interrupted again. 'You just said Rich's *late* wife?'

'I am sorry, your Grace, but Mrs Richard Seaborne died three years ago in childbed.'

'Poor Rich, is he a father as well as stepfather to his wife's child, then?

Mr Peters nodded his assent.

'By marrying her when the girl was already big with child, I suppose the gallant idiot meant to claim paternity?'

'I warned them it would complicate matters, but Mr Seaborne insisted it was the only way to protect her from further attacks.'

'He always was a hot-headed fool, despite his dark and dangerous reputation.'

'You knew that Mr Richard Seaborne far better than I did, although I have to admit he is resolute to the point of stubbornness. Despite his insistence on muddying the waters, I have managed to unearth proof your cousin was out of the country on one of his many so-called business trips to the Continent during the entire term of the late Mrs Seaborne's elopement and first marriage. Her first husband's paternity of the boy cannot be in doubt under the law, despite their best efforts.'

'At least Rich found a purpose in life with Annabelle DeMorbaraye, babe and all.'

'Indeed, the late Mrs Seaborne was a truly exceptional lady.'

'So why has he decided to break his silence now, three years after she died? Why did he really agree to let you tell us this tale at long last, Peters? And please don't try to hoodwink me it's mere chance he'd decided to emerge from the shadows at long last.'

'I have no idea, which is always a difficult thing for a man in my profession to admit. Mr Seaborne seems to have finally come to the conclusion he cannot hide himself and his family much longer, but why he made that decision now and not last month or in a year's time is beyond me. He seemed preoccupied, but that could be because he fears for the late Mrs Seaborne's son. He looks on himself as the boy's father, even if that was beyond even a Seaborne to achieve.'

'Why so fearful, then?' Jack Seaborne demanded with a look that told his visitor it was high time he explained the power and resources of the boy's enemies and when he'd finished not even Jack could argue his cousin had been wrong to disappear in the face of such odds.

In a very different world from Cousin Jack's wide domain, Rich stared moodily into the fire the dog days of summer had made it intolerable to light inside the house he and his family would have to sleep in tonight. So he was in the clearing where they had all sat eating their breakfast that first morning Perdita walked in his life, watching his woodsman's fire and brooding on his own stupidity and cowardice. If he wasn't such an idiot Perdita might be next to him right now, content to be with each other and never mind anything else. Browned by the sun and replete with loving as she struggled to mend the children's oft-snagged clothes, or badgered him to tell her stories of his fanciful adventures, with Hal and Sally eagerly listening in, they would have whiled away the summer—loving when they could and living well the rest of the time.

Most of those tall tales were true and he looked back to his days of smuggling spies into France and trading wine and secrets wherever the best deals in both were to be done without regret. His sporadic disappearances from polite society had gone almost unnoticed since he made no secret of his boredom and took a close interest in lovely women. The latter made the gossips shake their heads and wonder which beauty he'd lured into some silken den of iniquity to be pleasured until he was tired of her this time.

He was hardly likely to tell Perdita or his children about that and perhaps it was as well they didn't know what an idle gentleman Richard Seaborne once was. Bonaparte's Continental System had edged his shady deals out of the reckoning even before he met Annabelle, but he supposed living a secret life was second nature by then. Anyway, he'd been Orlando Craven for so long now the thought of going back to the duties and responsibilities of his real life made him wonder if he truly wanted to be Rich Seaborne again after all.

'Idiot,' he chided himself, shifting the skewered fish he was cooking over the fire so it wouldn't burn.

Missing Perdita was the heaviest load to bear of all and he missed her every moment of the day. Indeed, he couldn't imagine a morning ever dawning when he *didn't* wake up needing her almost unbearably. He was so gruff with the loss of her that even his children avoided him whenever they could and ran off to find Keziah. The spectre of Keziah's daughter Cleopatra lingered at the edges of his life like nagging toothache and nothing seemed as secure as it had a few short months ago. Letting Perdita go was the act of a blind fool. The loss of her finally showed him he was a lonely man without even the courage to fight for what was dearest to him, then defy the world to ever take it from him. It was high time he found a way to keep his children safe, then went after Perdita, for all their sakes.

And suppose he'd got her with child? He felt sick with revulsion at himself for risking such a calamity, then pushing her out of his life as if she didn't matter. He threw half his fish to patiently waiting Atlas and felt ill at the idea of Perdita facing life pregnant and alone. His hands knotted into fists and an urge to drink himself into oblivion almost overcame him at last. Impossible for a man with two children depending on him for everything to lose himself in the bottom of a bottle.

He was torn between taking them to his mother or Persephone, so he could go and find his lover, and the knowledge he would make Hal a target the instant he walked out of the forest as Rich Seaborne. Even if he found her, Perdita probably wouldn't want him in her life now if he came wrapped in gold leaf and pouring diamonds and pearls into her lap by way of an apology. He couldn't risk exposing his son to danger when Martagon sat in Hal's house with all those ancient titles at his fingertips and the power of the Lundy title to awe and bully others into doing his evil bidding for him.

The idea of Jack's blistering contempt when he heard what Rich had done to a lady who came to him in desperate straits made him squirm as well. Rich found himself guilty of being the craven he'd christened himself when he wed his first love and hid, instead of facing her enemies and risking more than he could bring himself to lose. Love was the devil, he decided, as he counted the sleepless nights and haunted days he'd endured since he packed Perdita up like an unwanted parcel and sent her on her way. He'd loved Annabelle: instantly, passionately and for life. So when Perdita Rowan stumbled into his life, he'd told himself wanting wasn't loving. All the excuses he could make for taking her innocence so he could slake his frantic need of her rang in his head and mocked him now—all straw in the wind now it was too late to admit he loved her too.

He felt so tired and heavy with missing her he could almost see his dead wife shaking her head at him, the reproach in the vivid silver-blue eyes she'd passed on to her son making her a ghost he didn't want to meet, after he'd longed so bitterly for her to haunt him for three long years. He should have seen the gallant spirit and ardent nature of the waif who stumbled out of the night as the mate whom loving Annabelle should have taught him to recognise.

Thinking of the cool lady his Perdita had been at first, uncertain of her own attractions and thinking herself unlovable, made him feel more of a villain. She had been so lost that first night with her slender ankle puffing with injury and her poor, scratched, filthy and painfully raw feet battered by her trek through the forest. His heart turned over at the very idea of what she'd escaped that day and the fragile fact of her elegantly made limbs under his exploring hands came back to him, as if he only had to close his eyes and she would be there. He let out another sigh and wondered how she'd react to his pleas to let him back into her life if he did manage to find her.

Knowing her, she would send him her best haughty look, pleat her fine brows with a faint look of puzzlement as she tried to recall who he was and say no until even he gave up and went away. But even though he knew it would be a battle to woo her back if he did track her down, his heart ached for her; his body yearned at the memory of her wrapped up in learning all she could about loving for the brief, ill-mannered snatch of time he'd allowed them. Life here had once felt so simple, the limits of it a welcome sacrifice. Now it was the rack he must stretch on until Jack and Alex Forthin could tease out the lies and villainies of Francis Martagon, supposed Marquis of Lundy, despite his attempts to hold fast to power with both hands, then take it off him and restore Hal to his rightful place in life.

If he'd entrusted the task to lesser men than his cousin, brother-in-law and true-as-steel Fred Peters he would have to laugh at himself for putting so much faith in the actions of others. As it was he trusted each one of them to battle on Hal's behalf until justice was done at long last and hoped they would believe him when he told them one day that sitting here waiting and doing nothing was an even harder job than the one he'd set them all when he asked Fred to finally ask more than he had any right to ask of them for the sake of Annabelle's beloved son.

'Hurry up, missy,' Miss Bradstock demanded as her great-niece took a last look at the neat house they were about to leave for good.

'Best if you learn *not* to call me that in future, Mama-in-law dearest,' she teased as she gave Aunt Carolina her newest role in their charade to christen the parts they were about to play, 'but won't you miss this place dearly?'

'No, it was high time to leave it and the idiot who thinks living here will make him into a great poet by some miraculous transformation is welcome to it.'

'Then you really were bored and looking for a new life?' Freya asked as she turned to follow her great-aunt into the carriage, hoping her favourite relative wasn't telling her comfortable lies to make her feel better about the huge upheaval she was causing.

The groom shut the door behind them and their hired coachman whipped up the horses until Birch House was lost to view and Freya said goodbye to another home—after parting from so many these last few months it threatened to make her head spin.

'I was always more of an adventuress than a proper lady,' Miss Bradstock said and, even though Freya knew she was trying to divert her from the challenges ahead, the details of her aunt's scandalous life intrigued her mightily. 'Much to the disgust of our stuffy families I never really fitted in to their expectations of a single lady of comfortable enough means, my dear, and life has been deadly dull these last few years,' Aunt Carolina insisted and Freya decided to believe her, since there really did seem to be a new sparkle in the lady's bright eyes and a spring in her step many a younger lady would envy her.

'Then I suppose we were very lucky to find such an eager buyer for Birch House so we could leave it before I publically disgraced you,' Freya observed with a shrug and a smile for the changes her interlude with Orlando had wrought on her own life.

After almost three months getting used to the loss of her lover and the gain of his child, Freya felt as if the isolated and arrogant Lady Freya Buckle might as well have died the day she gave in to impulse for once in her life. She had few regrets for the life she might have lived, if she'd never fled Bowland Castle what now seemed more like three years ago than a short summer season. Lady Freya might have married some dull friend of Bowland's out of sheer desperation and dutifully presented her husband with a couple of sons and the odd accident of a daughter. She would never have known love under the stars with a man who made every fiery inch of her shout for joy as they rose to ecstasy together.

She let her eyes haze over with sensual memories of mating with a man who made her feel as if the very air itself had a new vitality and glow as it kissed their naked skin and lent them the whole of a summer night to revel in each other. Her Orlando was taut with muscle from the routine toil of his life, his hands calloused and strong from his craft and yet he'd been as tender with her as the endless urgency of their need allowed. She never felt less than his equal as she learnt to give pleasure as well as receive. He wanted more, took and gave more and made her feel it was a joy to be female, not a disappointment to be tolerated with difficulty as her father and half-brother always regarded her.

'I doubt my brother will ever forgive me for this wild start, as he calls our insistence on complete independence from him and the life we could live in Bowland Dower House with him and Winfreda so close by,' she mused as the horses settled into their stride.

'Ridiculous made-up name—she's Winifred whether she likes it or not,' Miss Bradstock insisted.

'I can hardly blame her for not doing so, even if she was smug about being named after a good Saxon saint whenever Bowland complained about my heathenish name.'

'At least your namesake was a strong-minded female.'

'Perhaps that's what my grandfather intended when he suggested it, given how poorly my birth was received by the rest of the family.'

'What a shame he didn't live longer and see you weren't bullied into living such a dull life with Bowland and his tedious Winifred. At least you have managed to frustrate Bowland's scheme to keep you single, or allow one of his political cronies a fraction of your fortune as a dower.'

'Do you think that's why it was impossible to go to town for the Season last year?'

'Of course, they couldn't risk you finding a husband of your own choosing. Winifred must have hated having to stay at Bowland until they could push you into a convenient marriage, so no wonder she was cross as crabs at having to live in the country all year round. It must have been deadly dull for you though, my dear.'

'At least I could hobnob with the gardeners and poor pensioners Winifred detested having to visit every now and again. She was so relieved not to have to do so it didn't seem to occur to her that I enjoyed their company.'

'Very likely, but it was still no life for a young woman of any character at all. I can't applaud what you've done, my dear, it will have too many hard consequences in the years to come for me to do that, but I do understand it. In your shoes I would have rebelled a lot sooner and more publically. At least you have the tact to leave society before it discovers what you got up to when you were lost in that wretched forest.'

'That will become clear very soon,' Freya acknowledged as the carriage lurched over a pothole and reminded her stomach it had only recently begun to settle.

'Then we'd best make you look like as respectable a widow as we can contrive before it does so,' Miss Bradstock said bracingly.

Wondering if she deserved respectability when she had embraced ruin so eagerly, Freya sat back against the squabs and hoped they could discuss their plans swiftly, then open the small window on her side of the coach and let in some much-needed air.

'I have him at last, my dear,' Mr Jonas Strider informed his daughter when he found her staring gloomily out of the long windows of Martagon Court counting down the days she must spend in the country before she could leave her newborn daughter with the elder one and launch herself back into polite society.

'Do you, Papa, and who might he be?' she asked absently, wondering why her father was looking at her as if he couldn't imagine where she came from yet again. He seemed to do a lot of that since she gave birth to her second daughter and disappointed him once more.

'The whelp, of course,' he said, as if she was even more of a fool than he'd let himself think possible.

'That horrid little Martagon creature?' she asked with awakening interest. She might not enjoy being a Marchioness as much as she believed she must before she married Francis, but the idea of being stripped of that title made her shudder with distress.

'Aye, why would I care about any other puling brat your husband's family left about the place? Of course I mean the boy.'

'I'm not stupid, Papa.'

'You're nowhere near as clever as you think you are and you had a lucky escape when the brat in Lundy's nursery was born female, my girl. Land back in that particular bed before you give Martagon an heir and I'll give him evidence you've been cuckolding him myself.'

'Disgrace me and you'll lose any hope your grandson will be Marquis of Lundy one day.'

'Keep whelping girls and I won't need to

wait on your disgrace to lose all that,' he told
her with an edge of temper that made her sigh
even louder as she cast her eyes back to the
view of distant cornfields falling relentlessly
under the gathering sickles of massed harvest-
ers and no town or assembly room on offer for
miles and miles.

'I will endure him in my bed so he can get
another brat on me,' she agreed bleakly and,
if Mr Jonas Strider was sensitive to the hopes
and fears of others, he might wonder if his
daughter's happiness was too high a price to
pay for a titled grandson.

Since he only regarded her as a means to an
end, he believed he put up with the caprices
and weaknesses the girl inherited from her
mother very well. He decided he'd achieved his
purpose of keeping the fickle wench faithful
to the noble idiot he'd manipulated into marrying her. Now he could forget her while he
secured the future for the grandson she must
produce for her spindleshanked lord at her
third attempt.

Chapter Twelve

Rich tried to shake himself free of the black cloud hanging over him since the day he sent Perdita away. Another month had dragged on without her and soon autumn would be scorching through the forest, scattering fiery red and gold in its wake until the leaves fell and winter truly set in. At this time of year there was far too much to do for him to lean on his workbench like an idler and feel sorry for himself all day, but he still wasn't doing very much of it.

'Orlando! Orlando! Where are you, my lad?' Keziah's urgent voice broke into his reverie and the high tone of voice and her obvious breathlessness made him start forwards to meet her, senses alert for the trouble his thumping heart told him had come at last.

'Here,' he yelled back and ran to meet her, seeing with a hollowing in his belly that threatened to fell him in his tracks how much older she looked without the vital spark of merriment and joy in life that she usually gave off like a force of nature.

'They've been took from us, my boy. The babes are gone and my Cleo too.'

'Gone?' he heard himself echo numbly, as if the real Rich was hearing all this horror from a huge distance away and these two shocked creatures exchanging nightmares were marionettes in a puppet show.

'Stolen out of the forest and away, my poor lamb,' she said so tonelessly he knew it was true although it seemed impossible to take in.

'No,' he bellowed as if shouting it loudly enough could drown her words and make them untrue. 'No,' he whispered desperately.

Since the day Hal was born and he had fallen so hard in love with another man's child, he'd dreaded this moment. He could hardly take in the agony of knowing his children were in Cleo's careless hands and he wasn't there to protect them.

His Sally would be cross and defiant at

being dragged away from all she knew. Rich flinched as if a rough slap from a jealous and impatient woman's hand had thrust a knife into his heart, rather than the smack across his precious little girl's rosy cheek he knew the woman was capable of landing on a three-year-old child without a qualm. Hal would poker up and defend his sister from anyone's wrath but his own and Rich felt his fists clench and his heart plummet, then race on in a panicked tattoo as he hoped against hope Cleo hadn't yet handed them to Francis Martagon or his brute of a father-in-law and sauntered on her way as if she'd been delivering a pair of spring lambs to the slaughter.

'My Cleo took them,' Keziah said. 'I love them, Orlando. God help me, but they're more to me than my own child after what she's done,' she added sadly.

'I know you love them and we all love you, now and always,' he reassured her, 'but now I have to get them back, so do you know where Reuben is?'

Reuben had scolded Cleo for sending Perdita back to his cottage that night alone and Rich wondered if Cleo realised she'd pushed him and Perdita together that night instead of scaring her away and this was her twisted revenge on them all. Yet how could the loss of a man who'd never wanted her drive her to kidnap his children and sell them to his enemies?

Who knew with a she-cat like that one, but he must contain his fury and think. Martagon wouldn't dirty his hands with any more of this than he could help, so every second he spent wondering why and what to do next was a second wasted.

'Cleo waited 'til Reuben was away over to Longborough and I should never have left them with her while I let the boar in with my pigs,' Keziah reproached herself.

'My fault that they didn't want to come back to me, Kezzie, not yours.'

'Well, you never ought to have let that pretty young miss of yours go and that's the truth,' Keziah said with some of her old spirit.

'I can't hold what isn't mine,' he said hollowly, but this wasn't the time for self-reproaches. 'I must find Reuben, since he knows her haunts.'

'I can find him quicker than you. Now get ready to bring them two little imps back to old Keziah and I'll never take my eyes off them again, I promise.'

'I'm not sure they can be safe here now, but that's to worry about once I've got them safe and sound, Keziah.'

'Aye, everything but that will keep,' she agreed and how Rich wished he could agree with her.

Dealing with Francis Martagon and his villainous father-in-law as they deserved couldn't wait any longer than the moment he had Hal and Sally back. In that minute those worthless jackals would find they couldn't goad a Seaborne wolf, then escape his furious revenge. Plotting the sweetest form it could take would distract him from his terror while he chased down Cleo and his belligerent cubs and hoped they were giving her hell.

Freya was deeply thankful her great-aunt decreed a day of rest and recovery when she noted her niece's pale-green complexion the day before and insisted they stay in Gloucester where the stage broke its journey. After the first day they had dismissed the hired carriage and took to a less luxurious and conspicuous form of travel, but after two days of enduring the lumbering coach Freya began to think even walking to their destination might feel better. Now she could rise late and take her ease for a whole blissful day. Ever practical, Aunt Carolina had handed her two of her blessed dry biscuits before they went to bed last night and gradually the sickness that had almost ceased to plague Freya until this journey began receded and her interest in the world revived.

She was so lucky, Freya decided. Without her aunt's stalwart support this whole business of escaping Bowland and starting a new life would be a nightmare. With Miss Bradstock's help she hoped her imposture of an anxious young wife awaiting news of her fictional soldier husband, while she sat out her pregnancy in safety, looked convincing. Using Sir John Moore's Peninsular Army for her own ends lay heavy on her conscience, but to give her child respectability she would lie, cheat and do whatever it took, short of actual murder.

The fierce protectiveness she felt for a tiny being that hadn't even quickened in her belly yet continually surprised her. She splayed her hand where her waistline was beginning to thicken and marvelled she still looked almost the same as the Lady Freya Buckle who last travelled this way three years ago. Then she had been with her mother and travelling in ponderous style in her ladyship's own coach. The Countess insisted on long stops for rest at quiet country inns, so they would arrive at Ashburton New Place, the Duke of Dettingham's country seat, looking fresh and fashionable as humanly possible.

Freya shuddered at the arrogant aristocrat she was back then and wondered why she'd ever been so eager to wear a Duchess's coronet. The shameful fact was that she would have accepted Jack Seaborne if he'd been decades older and dull as ditchwater, if he had asked her. Blushing at the thought of herself greedily eyeing the man up as if she owned him, Freya plumped down on the softly cushioned window seat and stared rather gloomily out of the leaded casement window as late afternoon sun slanted into her comfortable bedchamber as if trying to draw her out to play.

She didn't dare go out and explore the cathedral and close for fear of being recognised as Lady Freya Buckle when she needed to be anonymous. So she must spend a day drifting about her room and the private parlour Aunt Carolina had procured for them. Inevitably Freya's daydreams turned to Orlando and the day when she would finally get to meet the end result of their passionate encounters so deep in the woods it felt outside time and the world.

In so many ways she'd been a fool. She had trusted him with her truest self, given her heart to a man who belonged to his lost wife three years after she was laid in her grave. Most of all, she'd risked making this precious child with him—recklessly taken every kiss and caress and hasty, driven coupling she could have with its father that she could hoard against an endless, empty future without him. Who would think shallow and self-obsessed Lady Freya Buckle could grow into such a lovelorn and passion-betrayed lunatic? Now she was beginning another life with her supposed husband's posthumous child, or at least she would be next time there was a battle bloody enough to excuse killing off a man who didn't exist.

Freya rubbed a tender hand over her belly to reassure her unborn child it was deeply wanted. The boy or girl she birthed in six months' time might never know its father, but she could love it devotedly for both of them. A mere fortnight of knowing Orlando and his son and daughter had taught her so much about what really mattered in life, and she'd learnt yet more from the week of desperate loving they stole from real life.

She stubbornly loved Orlando Craven, but assured herself loving their child would outgrow even that in time. At least she hoped so, because if it didn't this constant yearning for him was with her for life. Anyway, Mrs Rosalind Oaks had now replaced Lady Freya, who could drift into the annals of forgotten spinsters unmourned. She wondered how Bowland would excuse her disappearance; no doubt her supposed stay with Irish relatives would extend to months, then years, until everyone forgot to wonder.

Feeling sorry for her friendless and unloved old self, Freya tried to count her current blessings. She had her forthright and unconventional aunt, the wondrous blessing of her coming child when she would never love another man. It was a very different existence, she decided, her drifting gaze catching a furtive movement outside and distracting her from the changes her unborn child was making to her life.

Freya blinked and opened her eyes wide to make certain she'd just seen what they insisted she had. Orlando would never leave his children to wander in a strange place alone, even in the relative peace and safety of Gloucester Cathedral. She might accuse him of many things when she missed him so bitterly, but he would never neglect his children. Yet a small boy and girl very much like Master Henry and Mistress Sally Craven had just dashed towards the huge old minster alone.

She couldn't let the leap her heart gave at the sight of them be caused by joy since their father might be nearby if they really were here. Being with him for ever wasn't a hope she could indulge in and now she had those children to worry about. Orlando was both old and selfish enough to look after himself.

Never mind being recognised now, she didn't pause to snatch her shawl from the bed before running downstairs and into the street. Hurrying without actually running and risking a crowd on her tail, she sped across the road and followed in their footsteps even while she told herself it couldn't possibly be the little Cravens she had just watched dart towards the grand old church. At last she scurried breathlessly into the ancient porch and paused to allow a quick prayer Hal and Sally were safe in the forest, not playing hide and seek in a city where awful things could happen to two lone tots so far from home.

The side door was partly open and a stern-looking verger stood just inside staring intently into the hushed depths of the cathedral. Freya gave a soft harrumph and called up all her one-time arrogance to look the man up and down severely when he finally turned to meet the eyes of yet another intruder.

'Sorry, madam, but I can't let you in until we've caught the urchins who just barged in here as if they had every right,' he told her in a tone promising terrible retribution to any children who slipped into his vast domain.

Freya decided it didn't matter if Hal and Sally were the miscreants or not, she wasn't going to leave any small child to the mercy of this servant of the church. 'I *beg* your pardon?' she asked as if she couldn't imagine she was hearing what her ladylike ears were telling her.

'Two of them there were. They dashed in here a moment ago as if they had every right to invade the House of God. They will find out their mistake once the sexton's apprentice gets hold of them, I assure you, ma'am.'

'I'm prepared to admit they're spirited and impulsive, but my children are certainly not urchins and don't you remember what Jesus had to say on the subject?'

'Honour thy father and thy mother?' he offered superciliously, inclined to bluster now he realised a high-born lady was looking daggers at him, not the middling sort of woman he'd mistaken her for from her modest travelling costume.

He might intimidate a lesser being into flustered guilt over her supposed children, but he could hardly order the wife of an important man to be silent and get out of the way. Freya decided he was a bully as well as a hypocrite and watched him with such fastidious distaste he shuffled his feet self-consciously.

'The one that says, "Suffer the little children to come unto me, and forbid them not,"' she quoted quietly.

'They didn't look like respectable little children to me,' he argued and she wondered how he'd bluffed his way to his present role with no compassion in his soul.

'They set out neat and tidy this morning, if that's any of your business,' Freya informed him coldly. 'My husband will be most displeased you consider our children unfit to view the cathedral and Sir Ferdinand dotes upon our children, clean or not.'

Freya blessed the fact Aunt Carolina insisted she wear the late Mrs Bradstock's wedding ring from a short and fruitless first marriage from the moment they left the hired coach behind in Marlborough. Doing her best to make it clear a lady of her standing could go about without her gloves on a fine late summer day if she chose to, she felt his eyes linger on the heavy gold band and he pursed his lips as if facing a deep dilemma.

'I won't allow you or some ignorant boy to frighten my darlings and you'll answer to Sir Ferdinand if you lay a finger on either of them, now kindly let me pass,' she demanded and stepped into the huge space, the impression of mellow silvery stone soaring mighty and sheltering above and the stalwart walls all around were impressive even before the height and space and sheer beauty of the place stole her breath for an awed moment.

Bowing her head in respect of the builders who raised this great place to the glory of God as well as her maker, she begged Him to forgive her for searching this coolly serene building for the boy and girl she'd come to rescue, although surely they couldn't possibly be Orlando's beloved children out in the world alone. For a moment she thought they had darted out of some side door and away, then she let out pent-up breath in a sigh as she heard the sounds of a muffled disturbance in one of the side chapels and sped towards the unholy stir as fast as she could go without actually running.

'Stop that this instant!' she snapped at the spotty youth who held poor Hal's left ear in his bony grasp even though Sally was ruthlessly kicking the stripling and pummelling any part of him she could reach with her be-loved carved dog.

'Why should I?' the youth sneered, as if he was enjoying the feel of someone else's ear between his thumb and forefinger instead of being the victim of violence for once.

'Because he is easily ten years younger than you are, as well as being my son,' she made herself say as fiercely as if she really had birthed and mothered these battling young urchins and was proud of the fact. 'How have you got in such a state since this morning since I let you visit the shops with Nanny, Henry?' she pretended to chide her 'son' with an air of genteel disappointment.

She saw Henry struggle with the idea she was claiming to be his mother while he did his best to take in the fact she was here to rescue them. It was a lot to ask, but she pleaded silently with him to go along with her tall story until they were safely away from here and out of earshot of his current enemies.

'It was boring,' he managed sulkily at last and Freya could have cheered.

Her mood switched to dread as his agreement caused his little sister to stop her frantic attack on the youth who had her beloved brother in captivity and gape at her instead.

Sensing all the questions the little girl was about to ask, Freya decided on evasive action. Winking at the child to let her know it was a game, she shook her head sorrowfully at her supposed daughter and wagged an admonishing finger.

'As for you, young lady,' she said in a voice that said she despaired of turning this belligerent virago into any such thing, 'I really don't know what your papa will say when he hears what you and your big brother have been up to.'

'I *want* my papa,' the little mite immediately wailed and Freya supposed unfeigned distress at the thought of Orlando must have done the trick of convincing the spotty youth and the verger she would deal with the hell-born brats, so they didn't have to.

'The best I can do is get you back to him as soon as may be, then. Papa will know how to deal with two such naughty scamps,' she said firmly and picked Sally up, as if she knew from experience it was the only way they would get out of this otherwise hushed place before she caused a riot, which was pretty close to the truth.

'Come, my love,' she urged Henry, holding out her unoccupied hand to him once she had shifted Sally so she could support her on one hip. The warm weight of the little girl as she snuffled disconsolately and burrowed deeper into Freya's embrace made her want to hug and cuddle the pair of them until all three of them felt better, but they had a dignified retreat to accomplish first.

'They shouldn't have been here in the first place,' the verger told her disappearing back as if he couldn't resist the last word. Freya turned and stared coolly at him, then averted her eyes as if he was so far beneath her notice her ears couldn't believe he'd spoken.

'Hold still one moment longer, my little love,' she urged Sally softly as she managed to walk out of the refuge Henry had evidently chosen for them as if she spent most of her life retrieving her children from the trouble they got into as soon as her back was turned.

She could feel the tremor in the hot little hand gripping hers so determinedly, even as Hal tried to pretend he wasn't terrified of the alien world he suddenly found himself in. Whatever had brought them so far from home, she was beginning to doubt Orlando had anything to do with it. Now she had the conundrum of what on earth she was to do with the two little fugitives once they were safely back at the inn to solve as well, but at least there the children could be fed and reassured, even if she doubted their troubles were now over.

It was best if as few people as possible knew she'd come back to the inn with a pair of children she hadn't left it with, so Freya made a game of creeping upstairs so Sally stopped looking as if a storm of overwrought tears was on the horizon and let herself be fascinated instead.

'This is a nice room,' Hal pronounced once he'd taken a long and wary look round the large oak-panelled chamber with its wide window seat and spotlessly clean furniture. 'We didn't like anywhere Cleo took us and we don't like her either,' he said as if expecting to be told off for disrespect.

'Did she take you away from the forest?' she asked as calmly as she could.

He thought for a moment and seemed to be confused about the whole business when he was usually so sharp and aware of all that went on around him. Already horrified by the idea Cleopatra could steal the two most precious people in Orlando's life away from his protection, Freya saw something in the little boy's baffled expression that told her the unscrupulous trollop must have drugged them to get them away without the whole forest being aware and probably carried on dosing them with the evil stuff to keep them quiet on the way to wherever she was going even after that.

'Yes, days and nights ago,' he finally came up with and Sally nodded furiously, then frowned and looked round in terror, as if expecting Cleo to appear and drag her away at any moment.

'Then it's high time we found you some food and thought about a bath and change of clothes for you both, don't you think?' she forced herself to ask calmly.

'We are *very* hungry,' Hal told her seriously, although he looked more doubtful about the good dunking Freya thought they needed almost as badly as food and comfort.

'Yes, we're *very* hungry, Prudie,' Sally imitated her big brother earnestly and Freya smiled at the little girl's version of her alias and it warmed her heart that she hadn't been entirely forgotten.

'Will you trust me to find you some food and not go off and leave you?'

Henry exchanged looks with his little sister that spoke too much of the distrust they had learnt and nodded as if he couldn't bring himself to use it on her.

'Then why don't you two play hide and seek while I'm gone, then find somewhere you can surprise me from when I get back? I bet I'll know exactly where you are—hide as well as you can from me.'

'I bet you won't, as long as Sally doesn't squeak like she usually does and spoil it,' Hal said with a very old-fashioned look at his sister that made her stick out her bottom lip and glare back at him.

'Will not so,' she told him crossly and Freya heard the tot scramble under the bed before she had the door properly shut behind her and hoped the game would protect them if the maids or the innkeeper's wife entered her room for any reason.

Knowing their interest would only hold for a few minutes, she hurried down to the coffee room and whispered a request in her aunt's ear before whisking back upstairs and trusting Miss Bradstock to carry it out as swiftly as possible. Making as much noise as she could to warn her co-conspirators she was coming back, she detected a muffled giggle and a soft scuffle when she opened the door as Henry and his sister competed for the best hiding place. She looked in all the ridiculous places she could think of, once inside, and, serenaded by a descant of excited giggles and breathless shushing, Freya had just finished inspecting every piece of ancient Delft pottery the room rejoiced in for impossibly small children when a knock came on the door at last.

'Quiet as mice, now,' she warned softly before cracking the door open far enough to see her aunt outside with a tray groaning with bread, cheese and cold meat, a plate of delicate little cakes and a pot of tea.

Chapter Thirteen

'Thank you,' Freya gasped with heartfelt relief, stood aside for Miss Bradstock to enter, then swiftly shut the door after a quick look down the corridor to make sure nobody could see or hear them and wonder what they were up to.

As the pregnant young wife of a gallant soldier she was allowed peace and quiet and now Freya blessed her aunt for spreading the story when the landlady remarked on the pallor of her supposed daughter-in-law last night.

'What's to do this time?' Aunt Carolina demanded when Freya's attention wandered to her unexpected guests.

'It's safe to come out now,' Freya said as soothingly as she could manage, but there was only a squeak and the sound of two little bodies squirming even further under the vast tester bed. 'This is my aunt Carolina and she really is a lot like Keziah,' she told thin air.

'Cleo's a lot like her and look what she did,' Henry's voice eventually argued through the heavy skirts of the bedcover and Freya felt a simmering fury at the heartless creature for all the distrust they'd learnt at her hands.

'Cleopatra might look like Keziah, but your Kezzie would never hurt you, now would she?' she asked and trusted the years of love and care Keziah had poured into two motherless tots to remind them there were good people in the world as well as bad.

'No!' Sally said as she burst out from under the bed to defy the world and even her brother to say anything bad about her beloved Kezzie.

'Good gracious me, whoever is this monster?' Aunt Carolina said, hand on heart and an expression of extreme shock on her face that made Sally giggle joyfully.

'I a monster,' Sally cried in her usual exuberant fashion and began menacing the pretend-horrified lady, who didn't look very much like Kezzie, in her opinion, but had the same sort of mischief in her youthful grey eyes as her beloved friend.

'You gave us away,' her brother accused as he crawled out of his hiding place looking a lot more suspicious than his ebullient little sister.

Sally huffed and puffed so hard she forgot what she had been through and clearly felt safe with Freya and Aunt Carolina. Hal would take longer to put their ordeal behind him with his extra two years of living and what he thought his duty to look after his little sister. Freya sat down at the neat table set out with two chairs to facilitate a husband and wife taking their breakfast in private and refused to think about such intimacy at the moment. Considering the largesse in front of her as if it demanded all her concentration, she took one little sponge cake and nibbled delicately, giving an artistic moan as the sweet treat gave up its flavours.

'This ham looks delicious, don't you think?' she said to nobody in particular and felt Hal draw nearer as hunger such as he'd probably never experienced in his life until now gnawed at his little belly.

She broke off a hunk of fresh bread and buttered it, popped succulent pink ham on top and silently passed it to him. He took it and drew back a couple of feet to survey Miss Bradstock suspiciously while he ate with the ravenous hunger of a growing boy denied good food for too long. Since that could mean the boy in question had eaten half an hour ago or not touched food for a day, Freya decided to reserve judgement on Cleo's provisions for her captives, if on nothing else about this shameful abduction.

'Cake,' Sally demanded hopefully when she realised being a monster was causing her to miss out on something crucial to her sense of well-being.

'In polite circles one says "Cake, please", Miss Craven. First you eat some ham or cheese, then you ask nicely for a cake,' Freya said firmly and the little girl decided it wasn't worth wasting her energy on a grand scene and took her bread and ham with regal delicacy, but shook her head at the cheese.

'Don't like cheese,' she muttered, then fell on her food with an eager lack of refinement her father would be appalled to witness.

'You used to like it,' Freya said and felt her aunt's shrewd gaze on her as it became obvious these weren't chance-met waifs she had rescued on impulse.

'Cleo made us eat bad cheese and stale bread,' Henry explained before he grabbed his next mouthful and his papa's strict insistence on good table manners had paid off with him.

'And milk that tasted nasty,' Sally agreed breathlessly before tearing into her next slice of bread and ham as if she hadn't eaten properly in a week.

'Naughty Cleo,' Freya couldn't help muttering as she concluded that proved how she kept these two quiet and docile and so far from their father and their home in the woods.

All she needed to know now was where the wretched woman had been taking them. Getting them to the nearest place of safety had to be her first concern though, since Cleo could have gone to find whoever wanted Orlando's children so they could track them down and try to snatch them back. Freya would fight to make sure they never laid a finger on them again, but since she wasn't a warrior or a magician they needed sanctuary while she let Orlando know his children were out of Cleo's careless hands and among friends. Whatever came next would have to come and she would have to live with it, because these two were more important than her reputation and his isolation.

'What we need now is lots of hot water,' Miss Bradstock declared bravely when their meal was nothing but a few crumbs and a happy memory. 'I dare say my poor daughter-in-law will be feeling so much better now she's eaten not for two but half a dozen that she would like a bath to complete the cure before we set out for home.'

'I dare say,' Freya responded rather hollowly, glad Hal and his little sister were too absorbed in wrestling happily on the huge old bed to pick up that veiled reference to her condition and puzzle over it.

'You had best retire to my room with our unexpected guests while your bath is carried upstairs and filled, then,' her aunt continued relentlessly. 'I'll say you're lying down on my bed until it's ready and, as long as our money is the right colour, I don't suppose anyone will argue with my coddling you as if you're fragile as bone china.'

'Particularly since I'm carrying the heir to your kingdom?' Freya whispered with a severe stare at her relative for speaking too freely in front of Orlando's children.

'Indeed, and when these two scamps are asleep, we have a great deal to talk about,' Miss Bradstock murmured back unrepentantly.

'I might have to be asleep as well, then.'

'I can be a very patient woman and there's always tomorrow.'

'And to think I was feeling so grateful to you not more than an hour ago.'

'Only goes to show, don't it?' Aunt Carolina said as if she was happier to be an irritant than a benefactor and bustled them out of the room.

Freya decided to leave clothing two enterprising imps to Miss Bradstock and managed to keep them quiet until the bath was ready for her to have a quick dip before Sally and Hal gleefully bathed after losing their claim they weren't dirty and didn't need a bath in the least.

'Ah well, it's a good preparation for the future, I suppose,' Aunt Carolina said with a sigh once the children were finally dry. 'Into bed with you and I'll send down for supper. The innkeeper will be so glad to be rid of us come morning I hope he'll be happy to find us the fastest team and best coachman in the whole city.'

'Where're we going then, Aunt Lina?' Sally asked sleepily and Freya smiled at her aunt, who was acquiring relatives so fast her head should be spinning.

'Somewhere safe, my love,' Miss Bradstock said with a soothing smile and suddenly Freya couldn't wait for the children to go to sleep so she could find out what was going on in her scheming relative's head this time.

Her aunt was very preoccupied with the washing and mending of two sets of children's clothes whenever she tried to raise the subject, so Freya gave up and went to bed to sleep as much as her two lively bedfellows allowed her to, then woke up with the dawn, only to find her aunt already up and busy.

'How on earth did Cleo meet with my enemies out in the middle of nowhere?' Rich asked Reuben Summer when he finally managed to find him.

'She sneaks off to a tavern in Longborough and dances for money when she decides she has to have something I won't give her,' Reuben admitted with a sad shake of the head for such a contrary woman. 'Lords and gentlemen don't visit places like that, so this Marquis of yours has a go-between, no doubt?' Reuben asked, contempt for his kind almost humbling Rich. Since he worked hard for his living, Reuben decided he was the exception that proved how idle and useless English gentlemen were and shrugged. 'You know more than I do about this so-noble kinsman of your boy. Has he men to send where he couldn't go himself?'

Rich thought hard about Francis Martagon and realised Reuben was thinking more clearly than he just now. Doing his best to force his fear and fury to one side, he made himself run through the alternatives Martagon had available and came up with his ruthless father-in-law. Fred Peters had described a man of middling height and icy-grey eyes being responsible for Telemachus's abduction, when it was safely over and done with and Rich couldn't dash to the rescue as the black-hearted rogue had apparently wanted him to.

No point rehashing old grievances against Fred Peters, who had proved a subtle and steadfast friend to him and Annabelle when they needed one so badly. The man had to be granted a little leeway as a consequence and he had been protecting him and Henry at the cost of a huge personal dilemma. When Rich measured Jonas Strider against the ruthless pursuit of him and his, the fit was suddenly perfect. He wondered why he hadn't thought of him as the even more ruthless enemy behind Francis Martagon before now and wondered where his famous wits had gone begging off to these last six years and more.

'Aye, one of the hardiest villains I ever came across stands behind him and very likely runs

Martagon, not the other way about,' Rich replied grimly.

'Then he'll have made my woman an offer the greedy little cat can't resist,' Reuben said with a bitter resignation showing he knew Cleo better than she wanted him to.

'And she's taking my children further away with every moment we delay,' Rich said harshly.

'Why did you let your woman go if you're so clever? Perdita would protect your children when Keziah wasn't about, if you had kept her as a sane man would in your shoes. My woman's heart is stone for all her beauty, but you had one any man would envy and you made her walk away—now which of us is the biggest fool, Orlando?

'Me, but you come a close second. Now let's find this tavern and look for a clue to where your Cleo's gone with my children.'

'I'll talk—you keep your mouth shut. They'll expect me to be looking for my wife.'

'Then make sure they haven't got a tale spun ready to fool you with.'

'You forget my people are experts in the art, friend,' Reuben admitted with a grin that reminded Rich how much he liked the rogue.

Rich used the ride to Longborough to wonder how he could contact Frederick Peters without alerting Jack or my Lord Calvercombe and bringing down another set of conundrums on his head while he was busy trying to recover his children.

'But we can't go to Ashburton,' Freya protested as the swiftest coach for hire in Gloucestershire turned on to the open road and sped away from the city and towards the Duke of Dettingham's country seat as if the fate of nations depended on it.

'Why not?' Miss Bradstock asked as if it was a perfectly reasonable idea.

'Because we just can't,' Freya replied limply.

'I'm sorry you don't like the idea, but it's the only place I can think of within easy reach where they will take us in and keep these little devils safe from whoever might want to kidnap them again for some mad reason I can't fathom, since they're more trouble than a nest of hornets.'

The analogy sparked off an attack of buzzing and happy bickering about who would sting their enemies hardest. Luckily the notion of being stolen away again went over their heads, but Freya cast her aunt a reproachful look and brooded on the implacability of aunts and her own inability to think of another refuge sure to keep the children safe.

Knowing the powerful Seaborne clan would protect any child under threat, Freya could hardly argue this was a mistake, but wondered what the chances of a horse casting a shoe or the coachman being inflicted with cramp were as they sped towards the last place she wanted to visit. Useless to argue she'd made a fool of herself there when they needed a safe haven for Orlando's children until he could reclaim them.

Their original plan was to travel to Worcester, then into Shropshire and a pleasant sort of obscurity in the Marches. They would become a gently bred lady of means and her grieving daughter-in-law, looking for a new life without the late, lamented Lieutenant Oaks haunting them at every turn. Since a modest country life would set them apart from the Seabornes, Freya hadn't troubled that the two counties shared a border. Humble Mrs Oaks wouldn't move in the circles the Seabornes glorified and none of them would believe she was that obscure country lady if they saw her in the street by some unlucky chance.

Now she would have to greet them as Lady Freya again and the thought terrified her. Her

pregnancy would begin to show soon and Jack
Seaborne's piercing green eyes missed very little even if the physical fact of her child didn't
betray her. Anything *he* missed his clever wife
would probably pick up. Her wonderful new
life was looking as fragile as a block of ice
left in mid-summer sunshine as memory of
how badly she behaved the last time she was
at Ashburton New Place made her squirm.
Freya wished they could just hand over the
children, then turn the coach about and carry
on their journey, but she loved them too well
to thrust them into a puzzling new world and
merrily drive away, as if dropping off misdi-
rected groceries.

The horses sped on at a rate she would normally find exhilarating and dread made her
stomach churn so hard she was soon the interesting shade of pale green she had been when
the stage swayed ponderously into Gloucester
the day before yesterday.

'Children, I knew we would need these,'
Aunt Carolina said, rolling her eyes at her new
friends and passing out the rugs she'd pur-
chased from a sleepy shopkeeper this morning.
'We can't afford to stop, so keep the window
down, my girl, and hope we don't all freeze
before you feel better,' she informed her niece

firmly and thrust the window down before
Freya had time to protest she wasn't feeling
ill at all.

'Damn it all, Summers, where the devil are
they this time?' Rich shouted to his equally
villainous-looking and unshaven companion
as he grew impatient with waiting and rode
into the broken-down, and deserted, stable
yard.

Apparently Cleo had a lover who might
hide her here and Rich tried not to think of
the humiliations the woman piled on her husband as they trailed her and his precious children through the West Country and found how
many of those she had. Reuben was too proud
to want pity and Rich too plagued by desperate anxiety that they were too late to offer it
to him.

'She was here, but your children managed to
escape from her somehow. The idle fool who
owns this place is off searching with Cleo and
he's welcome to her. I want no more of her.'

'I don't blame you, but do they know where
she is?'

'Gloucester—some lout was in the tap last
night complaining that two urchins broke into

his cathedral and were chased out, along with a woman claiming to be their mother.'

Rich cursed long and inventively as he realised how close he'd been to finding Hal and Sally and wondered desperately who had them this time.

'Time for action, not cursing,' Reuben said brusquely. 'If we ride hard, we can catch this woman before they come to harm. We're overdue some luck, my friend, even if you don't deserve it for sending a far better woman than mine could ever be away like that.'

Rich gave a grim shake of his head at his own stupidity. 'I've regretted doing so every moment of every day since she left, if that makes you feel any better.'

'A little, my friend,' Reuben mocked and Rich hadn't the heart to point out Cleo was the cause of all this, not his treatment of Perdita.

'Never mind the rights and wrongs, we need good horses, a meal and a shave if the good folk of Gloucester are to realise we're not beggars or rogues and answer our questions.'

'Time for all that when we've a better idea where your babes are, Orlando,' Reuben goaded him and Rich did his best to shake the tiredness from his bewildered brain as he turned his weary horse towards the best post-ing house in the city and prayed his children were safe.

'Some unexpected guests appear to be ar-riving in a great hurry, your Grace,' the butler at Ashburton informed Jessica Seaborne im-passively later the same day.

Jess concluded Hughes was as close to being shocked as he ever betrayed from small hints she'd learnt to pick up since becoming Duch-ess of Dettingham.

'Invite them to join me as soon as possi-ble then, if you please, Hughes. I don't feel like stirring from here unless it happens to be the King or Queen come to call on us un-expectedly,' she replied calmly enough while she wondered why these visitors seemed to be in such a hurry they couldn't slow down and stop shocking her butler.

'I can see from here that it's not their Majes-ties, your Grace, although some would say one thinks herself almost as important,' Hughes muttered as he watched the visitors descend hastily and went to invite them to enter the family sitting room, so Jessica concluded they were respectable and not here to steal the plate and her personal jewellery.

The coming addition to the ducal nurseries might have kept her home twiddling her thumbs while her husband and Alex Forthin were off cousin hunting again, but they weren't the only ones having adventures after all. She brightened at the idea of company, however pompous, and levered herself off the sofa, smoothed her delicately sprigged muslin gown over her rapidly expanding baby bump and hoped whoever it was didn't require a curtsy, since it seemed unlikely she would ever get up again.

'Good Heaven's above—Lady Freya!' she exclaimed as one of her least-favourite young ladies entered the room looking unhappy to be here, as well as very pale indeed. 'Do come and sit down. I'm sure Hughes will bring us refreshments,' she said, since the girl looked sorely in need of a seat, although she turned even whiter at the mention of food.

'Thank you, your Grace,' Lady Freya said with un-Buckle-like gratitude and beckoned to her companions into the room so the Duchess of Dettingham could meet them.

Jessica only just stopped her mouth gaping open when two almost-angelic children crept into the room clinging to the dark skirts of a lively looking elderly lady she was certain she

had never met. Disarmed by two sets of child-
ish eyes round as saucers at the splendour of
Ashburton's gilded halls, she smiled and did
her best to make them feel welcome in what
was actually quite a modest room in her husband's grand Tudor mansion.

'May I introduce my aunt, Miss Bradstock,
Master Craven and Miss Craven to you, your
Grace?' Lady Freya asked with a warmly en-
couraging smile for the little ones that astonished Jessica.

'Now you'll have to let go of me long
enough to make your bow, young man,' Miss
Bradstock told the boy with the right amount
of sternness to remind him he was five years
old and mature enough to meet a Duchess
without acting as if she ate little boys for
breakfast.

'Good afternoon, Master Craven,' Jessica
said solemnly, dipping just low enough for all
of them to feel she'd made the effort and no
lower, given her current centre of gravity and
permanently wobbly ankle.

'Good day, your Grace,' the boy managed with quiet dignity that argued he'd been
trained to know his own value as well as that
of others. His bow had such a flourish to it that
Jessica's gaze sharpened on him as she decided

he reminded her of someone—she just wasn't sure exactly who at the moment and wondered if Hughes might know.

'Come out from behind me now your brother's remembered his manners and stop pretending to be shy, young missy,' Miss Bradstock ordered the little girl clinging so determinedly to her skirts the lady couldn't curtsy to Jessica without more risk of toppling over than she ran herself.

Engaging little Miss Craven giggled and put a small hand over her mouth as she finally let go and wobbled precariously, before losing her balance completely and plopping down on to the floor in a welter of meticulously mended cotton skirts.

Lady Freya laughed, raised the child to her feet, then smiled as she met green eyes dancing with mischief as if she might join in at any moment. Jessica blinked and could hardly believe this was the stiff and insufferably proud young woman who so blighted the summer house party Jack had held here to select his Duchess from the fairest and finest young ladies of the *ton* three summer ago and picked the least likely of them all as his bride.

'One day you'll get it right,' Freya promised her charge, then set her on her feet as Jessica's gaze sharpened on the little girl now and finally took in her distinctive features and mass of fine dark-gold curls before she met Miss Bradstock's shrewd gaze and received a faint nod as if to confirm her wildest suspicions.

Chapter Fourteen

'And here comes Hughes with our tea,' Jessica remarked calmly while she struggled with all sorts of unlikely conclusions under the calm of an expert hostess. 'Oh, and cake as well, I see. What a clever man to know how very much I should like one right now,' she said with a sidelong look at her little visitors as they obeyed the chiding look Lady Freya shot them and clasped their hands behind their backs as if they hadn't been about to grab one off the plate the butler ordered the footman to place on the low table next to her Grace's sofa.

Stifling her laughter as the endearing little girl did her best to look so appealingly hungry she couldn't possibly *not* deserve cake, Jessica solemnly offered her older guests tea and waited for Lady Freya to prove once again how radically she'd changed by sending her hostess an appealing glance to remind her how good the wayward Miss Craven was being and she surely deserved a treat. Now who would have thought such a tender heart beat under Lady Freya Buckle's conviction she was one of the most important ladies in the land? Jessica smiled at the two apparent angels and invited them to take a plate and eat their cakes and drink the milk Hughes had brought in especially for them, while their elders sipped their tea and chatted about nothing in particular.

'This is the very best sort of milk, my love. You need not worry it will taste bad,' Lady Freya told the girl, who looked about to pull a face and refuse, thirsty though she clearly was.

'See, Sal, I'm drinking mine and it's not nasty at all. It's almost as nice as milk from Kezzie's brown cow,' her big brother encouraged and Jessica thought the closeness between the two very touching.

Being from a large family herself, Jessica had no difficulty seeing they were *not* two angelic beings who lived in idyllic harmony. She decided they had been very well brought up by someone though, and the possible identity of that someone was exhilarating. Finally they might discover where Rich Seaborne had been all these years. The weight of anxiety that would lift off Jack's shoulders would be enough to make her heart sing, but her fondness for wayward Rich Seaborne made it a terrific effort to sit here as if calmly sipping tea with such a surprise package of visitors was an everyday occurrence.

If Rich had cut himself off from friends and family and his privileged life for the sake of these rather delightful little demons for some reason only he knew, it stood to reason he would move heaven and earth to get them back again. Why Lady Freya Buckle and her aunt had custody of them at the moment was beyond her, as was a great deal about a haughty minx like Lady Freya turning into a perfectly bearable young lady she would like to know better.

'I wonder if you are too old to play with my little daughter and her cousin? He's only a baby, but Thomas Henry thinks he's capable of conquering the world if he chooses, so I'm quite glad he can only crawl about his nursery as yet,' Jessica mused aloud.

'How old is your little girl, your Gracefulness?' Miss Craven asked at a pause in her determined consumption of milk, now she'd been persuaded it was good to drink after all.

'Just two years old, Mistress Craven,' Jessica made herself reply solemnly, although she was longing to laugh out loud at such a novel form of address and, considering how seldom anyone called her graceful, decided to treasure it instead.

'*I'm* three and a quarter,' the little girl proclaimed importantly and looked happy to queen it over another after being born after her brother and being told about it far too often.

'Gracious, you are a big girl,' Jessica said admiringly.

'Well, I am five and three quarters,' her brother told her even more importantly, adding an intriguing fact to the buzz of them being added up and wondered over in Jessica's head while she managed to look even more impressed.

'It would probably be asking too much for you to join your sister in the day nursery, then,' she said, as if pondering the huge problem of finding him suitably mature company. 'There *is* a rather fine rocking horse in there, of course, and I believe the games and toys my husband Jack and his cousin Rich used to play with when they were boys are stored away somewhere, waiting for Thomas Henry to be big enough to play with them instead of sucking them to see if they taste nice.'

'My name is Henry as well,' the boy declared and somehow Jessica wasn't at all surprised Rich had named this bright boy after his father, even if he wasn't of his begetting.

'Should you like to visit him for a few minutes, then, to make sure you won't be too bored in such young company?' she asked as if he was really the mature gentleman he quaintly thought himself to be.

'I believe I should,' he agreed, with a look at Lady Freya, as if she was his anchor and he had no intention of letting her disappear when his back was turned.

Intrigued, Jessica rang the bell for someone to conduct her youngest guests upstairs and awaited whatever surprise came next.

'Then you must certainly do so, Hal,' Lady Freya encouraged him with a smile that understood his fears. 'I shall stay as long as you want me to.'

'Good, 'cause I don't ever want you to go,' he said with a rare demonstration of love and vulnerability that touched Jessica and no wonder she caught a glimpse of tears swimming in Lady Freya's unusual golden-brown eyes.

Well, no wonder they were there in *this* Lady Freya's eyes. Jessica would have laid odds on the one of three years ago being incapable of unselfish tears and decided she must learn to give the benefit of the doubt more often in future.

'Off you go then, my loves,' Lady Freya managed to say lightly enough, but Jessica suspected there was more sorrow behind her encouragement they should find happiness in the company of others than joy. 'Aunt Carolina and I will both be here when you get back,' she added as even impulsive little Miss Craven looked doubtful for a moment, then nodded happily and went with Hughes to be conducted to the nurseries like important visitors, rather than the mere children other noble households were inclined to dismiss their brightest hopes as, until they were old enough to make a bow or curtsy to the world.

Jessica let silence gather for a moment, offered the decimated plate of cakes to her visitors again and waited patiently for some sort of explanation. Lady Freya nibbled absently on her sponge cake and looked thoughtful now the children weren't here to shield them from each other. She also looked a lot better and, if Jessica hadn't known better, she might sympathise with the uneasy stomach and revulsion to food at certain times of the day and cravings at others that always afflicted her during pregnancy. Unthinkable that Lady Freya Buckle would let herself be taken advantage of and left with child by a rogue. Jessica told herself it must be carriage sickness and dismissed the notion from her mind.

'You must wonder why we are here,' Lady Freya finally ventured.

'You are very welcome, of course—' Jessica began, only to be interrupted.

'Please don't lie, your Grace. I don't see how I can be when I behaved so appallingly towards you last time I was here. Words cannot be enough to apologise for my ill-natured pride and arrogance towards you on that occasion and far too many others,' Lady Freya insisted and Jessica concluded the changes went far deeper than a realisation of how unpopular she had been when she visited Ashburton with her domineering mother that summer.

'So *that*'s why you didn't want to come here,' her aunt said impulsively and Jessica could see the puzzlement she was beginning to share in the lady's troubled grey gaze.

Evidently Lady Freya had no idea she was bringing at least one of Rich's children as near home as made no difference and Jessica felt her heart sink after its wild dance of joy at the thought of Rich back here and his family with him. Something deeply significant must have caused this turn about in Lady Freya's every thought and action to reveal the person under all that chilly pride. If that something was Rich, as she was beginning to suspect, how would the lady react to being deceived about Richard Seaborne as surely as the rest of the world had been these last six years?

'I behaved very ill towards her Grace when she was still Miss Pendle, Aunt Carolina,' Freya explained and caught the anxious look the other women exchanged. 'I was jealous of her and bewildered by the Duke's complete uninterest in me. Mama and I were quite sure he only invited everyone else to his house party for the sake of form, you see? To us it was unthinkable he'd choose any but the youngest and most well-bred of the young ladies gathered for his approval. That proves more about us than about the Duke of Dettingham, who had the excellent sense to choose a wife on more personal criteria.'

The Duchess blushed at the thought of how personal their reasons for marriage had become one heady June day more than three years ago now. Freya envied her only the strong love and commitment between her and her Duke now. The way she and her strong-minded mother had set out to find her a suitable husband had been wrong and sure to end in disaster and Freya was deeply grateful Jack Seaborne had been so unimpressed by her now. He had behaved as if she wasn't here when she was at her most pettish and demanding in a doomed attempt to gain his wandering attention. She wouldn't trade her week of passionate fulfilment with Orlando for a lifetime of marriage to a man who didn't even like her, let alone love her as he clearly had his chosen Duchess.

'The old Earl made your mother a very poor bargain as a husband, Freya my dear,' her aunt intervened with an excuse to soften her bad behaviour. 'You mustn't blame yourself for being too young to know Beatrice was battling to marry you off before anything happened to her and left you to your half-brother's dubious mercies. She couldn't realise or let herself see that mutual advantage was a bad basis for marriage when being a Countess meant so much to her.'

'A shame I couldn't reason all that out for myself though, don't you think? It would have saved the years it took me to realise I couldn't marry for convenience and children.'

'You only had examples of ill-advised marriages to learn from, Freya,' her aunt told her acerbically and she nodded meekly, surprising herself with the conclusion she was the luckiest Buckle of all to find love, even if she then lost it almost as soon as she had found it.

'Jack and I have been scandalously happy together, despite your behaviour so long ago, so maybe you helped drive him into my arms, Lady Freya,' Jessica Seaborne said with a wicked smile that invited her to find that a blessing as well.

'I can't imagine I did much to endear me to either of you even so.'

'Maybe not, but we're all three years older and wiser now and you have changed a great deal. Can I call you Freya? Lady Freya is such a correct aristocrat I might find it difficult to be friends with her and I'm astonished to be able to tell you I would very much like you as my friend now, Freya.'

'Thank you,' Freya said, realising how short a friendship it would be and regretting it.

'Then do call me Jessica. I can't get used to being a Duchess and my grandmama-in-law scoffs at the thought I stand in her shoes, since, as she points out whenever she thinks I'm getting too sure of myself, I can barely stand at all for the state occasions she enjoys most.'

'Standing about for hours and hours at Court and kow-towing to all those poor, dull princesses, when it would be far better if they married before they all go as mad as their poor papa from sheer frustration? I should think you are deeply relieved *not* to be asked to take on her royal duties, my dear Duchess,' Miss Bradstock said, her scorn for the sort of state the ancient Dowager Duchess revelled in designed to counter Jessica's insecurity about her damaged leg and agreeing to be Jack's lame Duchess, despite her misgivings.

'I do like you, Miss Bradstock,' she said with a delighted smile and Freya wished she had found her new friend sooner.

'There's a couple of gypsy-looking rogues coming galloping across the parkland this time, your Grace,' Hughes declared with a long-suffering sigh. 'Shall I call Hopley to open the gun cases and arm the footmen?'

'Not yet, but get the keys from the Duke's study, would you? Lest they should be needed in a hurry,' Jessica replied coolly.

Freya reminded herself this wasn't her

house, so she couldn't grab the nearest weapon and use it to protect those she loved from all comers. Nevertheless she sped to the doorway and got ready to run upstairs if there was any threat to the children and be ready to fight it with whatever came to hand.

'I will retrieve his Grace's Mantons from his study while I'm there, your Grace,' Hughes said as if it was an everyday occurrence and left the room to arm himself.

'I always expect him to get his tongue in a knot with all those your Graces, but he never does,' Jessica observed calmly.

Freya could quite see why Jack Seaborne had seized her and refused to let her out of his sight until she agreed to be his wife now. As chatelaine and protector of his realm, his lady was calmly assured and Freya only wished she felt half as serene herself.

'They could be after the children,' she cautioned and hesitated between rushing upstairs to protect them and staying here to judge how serious the threat could be.

'And that's a story I can't wait to hear,' Jessica replied a little distractedly as Hughes returned with the elegant but deadly weapons and handed one of them to the mistress of the house. 'I had four brothers,' she explained as she tested the weight of the pistol and seemed satisfied with its fine balance.

'They must be more fun than mine if they taught you to shoot,' Freya said ruefully.

'Having met Lord Bowland, I can safely promise you that they were.'

'Dull as cold porridge,' Miss Bradstock agreed and Freya fought an attack of the giggles she told herself was nine-tenths nerves.

Now they could hear two sets of hooves on the hard-packed track across the park and Freya drew in her breath and braced herself for whatever shocks were to come. Aunt Carolina had been right to insist they came here. Every last man would fight to protect four vulnerable children and their Duchess, never mind if Lady Freya Buckle had done nothing to endear herself to them last time she was at Ashburton. Her heartbeat thundered in time with the noise outside as she caught a glimpse of Reuben Summer riding a fleet-footed hunter as if the devil was on his tail.

'I must go to the children,' she gasped and ran for the stairway, seeing Reuben only as Cleo's husband for a panicked moment. She heard the patter of small feet racing downstairs as if their owners might tumble down them in haste. 'Stay where you are,' she urged desperately as the thunder of hooves stopped suddenly and she imagined Reuben jumping to the ground in a running dismount only the finest horsemen could achieve, then getting ready to storm into the house and overcome all opposition.

'Papa. It's our papa!' Hal shouted at her as if joy was about to give him wings and Sally simply concentrated on getting to the wild-looking figure who dashed past Hughes and into the hall as fast as her legs would take her.

'Papa!' she yelled as he looked frantically about for them.

'My darling girl, my Sally,' he shouted and scooped her up into his arms to hug her so tightly even Sally protested. Hal got to his father just after his sister and flung himself at his legs as they were the first part of him he could grab hold of. 'Son,' Orlando managed in a voice that broke with love and all the endless terror for them he must have lived with from the moment he found his children gone.

Hitching his daughter to one side, so he could tow his son up with his other arm and hold him close as well, Orlando seemed deaf and blind to the rest of the world while he greeted his beloved family and Freya told herself it was little and mean to feel jealous. He had never promised her more than those days and nights in the forest and she could never be the third most crucial person in his life. Feeling she was eavesdropping on a very private reunion, she turned to go back to the Duchess's sitting room and wait until she could depart with dignity, now he was here to protect his children from harm and didn't need her any more.

'You!' he barked as if her movement reminded him there was a world outside the charmed circle of him and his. 'How much did it cost my cousin to ransom them from you then, you heartless bitch? I suppose Cleo is skulking somewhere close by, so she can claim her share of the fortune Jack has just paid you to get my children back?'

Freya had imagined all sorts of reunions with her lover during the long three months spent apart, but never one like this. In a few words all the slights she'd handed out as an aristocratic lady were revenged on her a thousand times over. Every organ in her body froze with a whole winter of pain and coldness before she managed to force breath into her lungs and not faint at his feet. She wouldn't give him the satisfaction of knowing he'd made her very world a wasteland, so she swallowed the furious defence on her tongue and shot him one of Lady Freya's iciest looks of disdain instead.

'I don't know you, sir and you clearly don't know me,' she informed him coldly. 'I shall await you in the stable yard, Aunt Carolina, so we may set out on our interrupted journey all the sooner. I thank you for your hospitality and kindness, your Grace,' she said. She gave a dignified nod of the head to her hostess, which she hoped Jessica knew was all she could manage without losing her dignity in furious tears, then she swept out of the house as if she couldn't wait to shake the Seaborne dust from her serviceable skirts.

'Before God, Richard, I'm not sure if I'm delighted or dismayed to see you. It seems you have become a witless fool some time over the six years since I saw you last,' Jessica told him sharply, then hurried after her new friend to urge her to ignore her boorish cousin-in-law and stay at least for tonight and rest from her hasty journey.

'I knew it!' a stiff-backed elderly lady with the coldest dark eyes Rich Seaborne had ever met informed him with a severe nod, then followed Perdita and Jessica into Jack's stable yard, as if it was the most fashionable place for a lady to visit this autumn.

'It seems you've made an even more almighty fool of yourself than usual this time, Orlando,' Reuben informed him with a shrug that said all men were so when it came to their women, but at least Rich had now joined him as one of the biggest.

'Prudie!' keened Sally mournfully and wriggled fretfully in her father's arms.

'*We* like her, Papa,' Hal informed him with manly dignity.

'I don't think there's much chance the lady will ever like *you* again after that, my friend,' Reuben said with a cheerfulness Rich found almost unforgivable.

'How come she's here to offer you to my cousin for ransom, then?' Rich asked his son more in puzzlement than fury now the initial burn of betrayal had died down.

Was Reuben right again? Had he made the biggest mistake of his life by chasing Perdita out of his life yet again? Despair rushed in on the heels of the burning fury that shot through him at the sight of her, safe here with his children as if they'd been attending a ladies' tea drinking while he was eating his heart out for her and his children all the time they'd been gone.

'You ain't got a cousin, Papa,' Sally said distractedly and Hal managed to wriggle away and slide to the floor.

'Nor a ransom,' Hal added, looking all at sea about the whole business now his delight at seeing his father was turning to puzzlement over his tirade and Perdita's hasty departure.

'I dare say Perdita and Cleo are to share that between them,' Rich said stubbornly.

'Prudie don't like Cleo an' we don't like Cleo,' Sally insisted, hesitating between her father and her rescuer.

'Cleo's bad as bad and Perdita isn't, Papa. We hate Cleo now.'

'You're not the only one, son. So how did you come to be with Perdita if Cleo didn't get her to bring you here so the Duke could ransom you?'

'We ran away. I waited 'til we got to a big town and made Sally spit out the milk Cleo gave us whenever she went out and left us alone. We climbed down a ladder from the loft over the stables and I gave Sal a piggyback so we could get far enough away and hide.'

'Then what?' Rich asked, dread eating at him as all that could have happened to them

next flashed through his head in a kaleido-
scope of nightmares.

'We ran fast as we could, then hid in an
old tree like the one in the forest. It was ages
before Cleo came after us, but when she did
she couldn't stand up properly and looked all
wobbly. We stayed quiet as mouses until she
went right away, then we got down and ran
until Sally couldn't run no more.'

'Any more,' he correct automatically, but
Rich wondered why Hal's grammar mattered
when he was miraculously safe and well after
all that.

'That's right. Then it got light and we ran
and ran right into the city and it was a very
long way, Papa. I remembered how Kezzie
said if everything got dark and grey it helped
to speak to God about things so he could put
them right and we went inside the biggest
church you ever did see, Papa. A nasty man
tried to keep us out, but we got past him and
then Perdita came. Everything was all right
again after that.'

'How can you be sure Cleo didn't send her
after you?'

'Don't be silly, Papa; they never even liked
each other. We hid in Perdita's room all day
and didn't make so much as a squeak when

anyone else but her and Miss Car'lina could hear until the coach was on its way here and Miss Car'lina said it was safe to put the blinds down and talk. They had ham and cheese and cake at the nice inn, but we don't eat cheese now because Cleo gave us some that made my belly hurt. The milk she gave us wasn't good either, but we drank some the Duchess gave us just now and it was almost as good as the kind Kezzie's brown cow gives us.'

Hal's account of their recent adventures reminded Rich he was only a boy and had left out so much his father wanted to know. He'd still heard enough to tell he was a vile idiot and Perdita would never forgive him.

'There's room on the back of my horse for a gallant man like your son, Orlando, if you're coming back to the forest? Miss Sally can ride in front of her papa and convince him he's not the worst man in it as you go, despite what the rest of us think.'

'That's a task beyond even my Sally, but I can't leave,' Rich said gloomily.

'You're staying here then, my friend?'

'I have to. I thank you, friend, for all you've done to help find my children.'

'My woman wronged you, *veshengro*. We gypsies have enough children of our own and I couldn't have you thinking we really steal them from the *gorgios*. Blessed be, my brother,' the handsome gypsy lord said with an impudent grin, 'you're going to need all the help you can get.'

'I have my family back and that's all I deserve now, but thank you, my brother,' Rich made himself say quietly.

He would have to be content to have his little family back again and kiss the fantasy of Perdita and her slender-limbed brats added to the mix goodbye after what he'd just done.

'Then fight for what you don't deserve, *veshengro*,' Reuben urged before he leapt on the best horse's back and turned it with a wave of farewell before heading back to his tribe.

'Look after Keziah for me?' Rich called after him and Reuben waved dismissively. He'd learnt enough about the complex rogue these last few days to know he wouldn't visit the sins of her child on a woman he honoured as he did his mother-in-law.

'Aren't we going home then, Papa?' Hal asked.

'Perhaps.'

'What about Perdita?'

'I don't think she'd live with us now if I begged her to,' Rich replied wryly.

'Never mind, Papa, I still love you,' his son told him as if he was the adult and Rich the child, and after today he could be right.

Chapter Fifteen

Freya didn't need sympathy so much as something fragile and breakable to throw, so it smashed into shards on the cobbled stable yard and relieved some of her tension. Several breakable somethings would be even better. Since she was going to get it anyway, she fought back her fury and the bleakness threatening to blank out even that tearing emotion and did her best to smile.

'I am perfectly well,' she assured her aunt and the Duchess, then felt tears sting as Sally barrelled into the yard and ran up to her. 'Hello, my love, have you come out here to wave me off?' she made herself ask as cheerfully when she felt so breakable it hurt.

'No, don't go, Prudie,' the little girl ordered with a fearsome frown.

'I have to, darling. You have your papa to look after you and Hal now and will be safe with him and Kezzie back in the forest.'

'Cleo lives in the forest.'

'I doubt she lives in that particular part of it any more,' Freya said as she recalled Reuben galloping to rescue the children at Orlando's side. He clearly had all the generosity of heart Cleo looked as if she should have, with those lazy, heavy-lidded eyes of hers and the seductive laugh designed to draw men in like bees to honey.

'If you lived with us, Cleo couldn't watch Papa as if she wants to eat him any more.'

'I don't think that would stop her,' Freya said and tried not to think of returning to that apparently idyllic life and birthing her own child with Sally and Hal eagerly waiting for a new brother or sister downstairs. It was all impossible now and probably always had been.

'I love you, Prudie,' Sally said emphatically.

'I love you too, Sally,' she told her solemnly, then made herself pull a ridiculous face, 'but so do Kezzie and your papa. You must hurry back to them before they both start crying from missing you so badly and can't stop.'

'Papa doesn't cry,' Sally said doubtfully.

'He could easily sit on the yard and do just that right now,' Orlando said from behind them and Freya was shocked again at how quietly he could move.

'Prudie's leaving,' his daughter informed him with a disgruntled pout.

'You can't leave. It's not safe,' he barked as if he had the right.

'I delivered your children to the safest place I could find and owe you no duty. I sincerely thank Duchess Jessica for her kind hospitality and far more understanding than I deserve, but I have a journey to accomplish and time is a-wasting. Good day, Mr Craven, we shall never meet again.'

'But, my dear, haven't you realised yet?' her aunt asked as if there was something about Orlando that Freya should have seen for herself long ago.

'Realised what?'

'He's not Mr Craven, although after that outburst earlier he might more properly have christened himself Mr Clunch. This is Richard Seaborne, cousin to the Duke of Dettingham.'

Freya marvelled at her stout nerves for keeping her standing after this latest felling blow. Later she would be thankful she had retained what little dignity he'd left her, but right now a pleasant faint and renunciation of all this painful reality could be almost pleasant. The idea of him discovering her pregnancy when a doctor was sent for to treat the Duchess's guest made her determined not to let anyone near enough to suspect she was other than a proper maiden lady—anyone apart from her great-aunt and the wretch who already knew she was no such thing and he wouldn't be coming within a hundred yards of her ever again.

'Of course he is, how stupid of me,' she managed as if her words came from some frozen region where Lady Freya kept her wilder emotions.

'I should have told you, Perdita,' he said and she peered at the huge oak tree on the hill in the distance, because she refused to let him see how much she hurt right now.

'Who is Perdita?' Miss Bradstock asked with a shake of the head for two bumbling idiots who'd got into such wanton mischief.

'I am. Why run about the countryside advertising my true name so I could be kept against my will until Bowland turned up to ransom me? I would very likely have waited to be an old woman while he made his mind up if he wanted me back.'

'Are you Lady Bowland, then?' Mr Richard Seaborne asked her blankly.

'Of course I'm not, you idiot,' she fired back as if it was the final straw.

'She's his sister, or half-sister if we're being exact about things, as I rather think we ought to be after the knot you two seem to have got yourselves wound up in,' Miss Bradstock continued under the fascinated gaze of the Duchess of Dettingham and the stable lads.

'Lady Freya Buckle, meet Mr Richard Seaborne,' the Duchess said irrepressibly.

'Lady Freya,' he said with an elegant bow that was all Richard Seaborne arrogance and not enough Orlando Craven, so she concluded he was mocking her.

'Mr Seaborne, I cannot say it has been a pleasure meeting you and I am unable to stay here to further the acquaintance, I am very pleased to say. Good day to you.'

'Stay,' he pleaded.

'I'd rather be eaten by bears,' she said with what she felt was excusable melodrama.

'There aren't any bears left in Britain, Perdita,' Hal spoilt her grand gesture by pointing out earnestly, as if she needed to know before she made more rash statements.

'I could hire some from the circus,' she

pointed out, unable to ignore the little boy she had come to love so much it hurt to leave him and his sister behind. She wasn't even going to think about his father—that would be a thought too far just at the moment.

'If you won't stay for my sake, please stay for his?' Richard Seaborne pleaded sneakily.

Freya hesitated and both of them took ruthless advantage. Hal turned into a pathetic waif in front of her eyes and his father slanted a look that promised to tell all sorts of secrets he couldn't possibly say out loud in front of his children and the stable boys if she didn't.

'And if not for them, do it for me,' her aunt said with a weary sigh and Freya knew how hard she'd driven herself for her great-niece's sake these last few days.

'Are you very tired, then?' she asked anxiously.

'Exhausted,' Miss Bradstock managed with a long-suffering look at her new friend the Duchess that made Freya wonder how such a robust lady could go from prepared to take on the world to a fragile old lady in a matter of minutes. She sighed wearily but gave in, just in case her aunt was telling the truth, for once.

'You knew, didn't you?' she accused to let

Aunt Carolina know she wasn't a complete idiot.

'Knew what, my love?'

'Who the children's father had to be?'

'It's written all over the youngest imp's face for anyone to see, my dear,' her aunt admitted with a shrug. 'Seabornes always breed true.'

Freya hoped they wouldn't do so in her baby, or everyone would know who its father was and word might get back to him somehow. 'If your Grace will kindly have us as her guests for tonight, I suppose we could set out tomorrow morning instead,' she conceded and hoped it was clear she was only staying for her aunt's sake and would prefer to put as many miles as possible between herself and Mr Richard Seaborne before it was dusk and too dark to drive any further.

'You are very welcome to stay as long as you like, Lady Freya,' Jessica said cheerfully and Freya believed her, a revolution neither of them could have expected a few hours ago.

Orders were given with such ridiculous natural authority that Freya marvelled she'd ever been fooled this Richard Seaborne was the son of a poor gentry family and Hal dragged her back inside the great house he seemed not in the least bit awed by. Father and son had all the arrogance of their kind and Sally had always been a great lady in the making. Freya felt a fool for taking them at face value back in the Longborough Forest.

'You need a bath and the loan of some of Jack's clothes, Richard,' Jessica told him mildly and raised her eyebrows to remind him he must at least look the gentleman under her roof when he looked ready to argue. 'Then I can ask your mama and Penelope to join us for dinner without fear they'll fall into hysterics at your villainous appearance.'

'What about Marcus? If he's in town it seems a bit over-eager of him just yet.'

'How very much there is to tell you after six years of stony silence,' Jessica said and Freya enjoyed watching him squirm under the cutting irony of the lady of the house.

'Begin with telling me where my little brother is and proceed on to Jack and Alex Forthin, so we can join together to protect our families against the threat to come.'

'All in good time,' Jessica insisted and Freya almost clapped at the frustrated look in the arrogant wretch's distinctive green eyes.

Why had she never let herself see how very distinctive they were? If only she hadn't blocked her thoughts against every Seaborne who ever lived after that awful house party, she might have saved herself bitter humiliation and seen his clear green gaze for the warning it was from the first. He was so like his ducal cousin and yet so otherwise. Even Jack Seaborne was more straightforward than his wily cousin, she concluded, and shot the deceptive wretch a disgusted glare. Jack's hair was also dark as a raven's wing while Richard's had a hint of his sister Persephone's darkest of red tones in his almost-blond hair. His face was also bonier and less classically handsome. The thought of her old nurse saying 'handsome is as handsome does' popped into her head and made her pause her catalogue of ways in which Richard Seaborne lacked the grace and charm of his cousin.

Some things he did very handsomely indeed, her wicked inner self reminded her. Like raising his children with such dedicated selflessness he'd lost so many of the privileges he'd been born into to do so, Lady Freya reminded Perdita. Ha, Perdita mocked and reminded herself back why it would be folly to fall for his lying charm ever again. She would leave for her new life tomorrow, and however difficult it was to shake the Seaborne connec-

tion off her tail, she would do it, or risk them
finding her when she least wanted them to.

Reminding herself to make certain she had
a very frank conversation with her aunt before they went down to dinner, she meekly allowed herself to be conducted to an airy guest
bedroom so blissfully peaceful she eyed the
feather bed with wistful longing. No, time
enough for sleeping when a whole houseful of
Seabornes weren't about to descend on the vast
mansion and make it seem too small to Lady
Freya Buckle, faced with another lot of people who thought her the spoilt little snob she
had once been while her one-time lover looked
on. She thanked the neatly dressed maid who
came to tell her a bath was being filled in the
dressing room next door and reluctantly refused her aid, asking her to come back once
she was dressed and help to arrange her hair.

She dared not let another female see her
naked for fear she might realise Lady Freya
wasn't usually this buxom, or noticed her
once-tiny waist would soon be a distant memory. Freya sighed and wondered how many
more eggshells she must tread tonight. She
supposed it was worth it as her aunt *might* be
exhausted and the children needed time to realise they were truly safe without her.

Freya took off her plain travelling gown and decided nothing in Mrs Oaks's modest wardrobe was splendid enough for dining at Ashburton New Place, so she would have to do without the cunningly cut silk gowns she had once worn to dazzle far better men than Richard Seaborne. She reminded herself she didn't want him dazzled now and doubted she'd reduce him to manly frustration dressed so richly even if she did. Whispered discussions about Rich Seaborne's wild affairs were creeping into her mind, along with a list of all the stormy beauties he was credited with keeping in his rackety bachelor days.

Returning from her bath already halfway dressed in shift and a short corset, she sighed at the plain but beautifully pressed dark-blue gown, made high to the neck and long in the sleeves as befitted soon to be widowed Mrs Oaks, waiting for her. Sinking on to the rug by a fire lit against the mild chill of a late September evening, she waited for her weighty mass of brown hair to dry and allowed herself a harmless enough fantasy.

Tonight she was the much-loved lady of a country gentleman of modest means. He was nothing like Mr Richard Seaborne, with his large estate and even larger fortune and uncanny ability to lie that black was white. Rather than an army officer, this time her phantom husband could be a hard-working country squire, busy about his acres in order to improve his competence and provide all their children with a sound education and a start in life. They had a worthwhile life, far away from the extravagance and opulence and lies of the *ton*, and focused their energies on each other and their growing family. Recalling how delightful a simple country life could be in the right company, she set her chin on her bent knees and stared into the fire as if her fantasy might form there if she willed it strongly enough.

Fool to picture her everyday husband as splendid Richard Seaborne, she chided herself crossly and, reaching for the simple wooden comb he'd whittled for her that she kept purely because it was practical, she began the tedious business of combing out her heavy mass of hair and wondered if it might be easier to have it cut. Soon she wouldn't have the luxury of time to sit by the fire dreamily untangling her annoyingly mid-brown locks while she tried not to think of times when Orlando had done it for her, as if he loved every last

smooth and shining strand. She was relieved
when the maid returned, ready to brush, then
skilfully secure the heavy mass into a neat chignon that suited Freya better than the elaborate
nest of ringlets her mama always insisted on.
She watched in the mirror as the maid deftly
adjusted her simple gown and decided it became her better than the unsuitable splendours
of Lady Freya Buckle ever had.

By the time she discovered the little Seabornes were nearly asleep after their busy day,
it was time to go downstairs and face the ex-
tended Seaborne family. It would be so much
easier to ask for dinner to be sent to her room,
but that would be cowardly so she squared
her shoulders and descended the grand Tudor
staircase as if she owned it.

'Good evening, my dear,' her aunt greeted
when Freya swept into the family drawing
room and Miss Bradstock didn't look in the
least bit exhausted now. 'Most becoming,' she
whispered as if she thought Freya needed encouragement.

'Good evening, Lady Freya,' the Duchess
greeted her with a warm smile.

'Good evening, your Grace,' she said and
shyness threatened to undo her new ease with

her hostess and never breach her old formality with Lady Henry Seaborne.

'I have to thank you for rescuing my precious grandchildren from what they assured me, when they got over their shock at having a grandmama to tell, was a very bad woman indeed,' Lady Henry said and Freya didn't think she'd ever seen her ladyship so happy.

'Anyone would have done as much, your ladyship. My aunt deserves more thanks than I do for keeping a cool head through it all,' she said with a wry smile for her own panic every time she thought Cleo might have alerted whomever she was taking them to that the children had been counter-abducted as they flew here as fast as horses could bring them.

'I wasn't the one who rescued them when they were alone in a strange city, Niece. You must learn to take praise where it's due,' Miss Bradstock ordered, as if being too humble was as irritating as the arrogance Lady Freya Buckle had once been so famous for.

'And I can never thank you enough,' Richard Seaborne added quietly from the corner of the room he was lurking in to help his mother and sister to glasses of sherry wine.

'No, you can't,' she agreed shortly.

'That might be taking things a little too far the other way,' Aunt Carolina observed.

'He doesn't deserve anything better from me,' Freya said haughtily.

'Well, no, but it might be more comfortable for the rest of us if you pretended during dinner,' Jessica said mildly.

'Perhaps I shall, then,' Freya conceded and gave him an ungracious nod.

'I will abase myself more privately later, my lady,' he said and she glared at him, hoping he knew hell would have to freeze over before she allowed it.

'I'd buy a ticket to witness that,' his mother told her wayward son rather sternly and someone must have told her what he'd accused Lady Freya of doing. Freya's cheeks burned at the memory of standing there with her mouth open while he raved at her.

'No doubt Lady Freya will sell you one for a very small fee,' he said wryly.

'If it saves me from being alone with you, sir, the whole household is welcome to shadow my every move until I leave here as early as possible in the morning.'

Mr Richard Seaborne frowned and looked hunted when his little sister demanded why he'd grown so bear-like during his long absence as if someone had to take pity on him.

'He was always gruff and disagreeable like this when he knew he'd done something wrong as a boy, Penny,' her mother intervened, as if she understood the tension and anger snapping like summer lightning between Lady Freya Buckle and her prodigal son.

'Memory must have gilded you in my eyes, Richard,' Penelope informed her eldest brother without noticeable awe.

'Unlikely it will do so in anyone else's after today's events,' he admitted.

He was so heartbreakingly different from Orlando tonight, his borrowed evening clothes fitting a little too tightly over the shoulders to indicate he was broader there than even powerful Jack Seaborne. Their height must be comparable though, since the dark coat and knee breeches enhanced the fine masculine figure both cousins boasted. Orlando's wild and overlong locks were trimmed and tamed into something very close to the famous Brutus cut made so fashionable by Beau Brummell and the Prince of Wales. Jack must have left his valet behind to produce such a pattern card of a Corinthian out of such wild material in such a short time, Freya reflected, and wondered which was the real Rich Seaborne. This one, she supposed glumly, and longed for the dear ease of her lover over the elegance of this stranger.

They processed into dinner at last, Richard escorting his mother as the rest of them found spaces at the round table in the family dining parlour. Every course was a finely produced triumph and Freya managed to eat enough to keep her growing babe happy as the gentle hum of conversation Jessica instigated relaxed her frayed nerves. They adjourned to the family sitting room afterwards to listen to the reasons why Richard Seaborne had hidden away for so long and Freya and her aunt tried to leave the family to hear the tale, but he insisted they stay and both were curious enough to do as he asked, this time.

Rich wasn't even halfway through his tale of a wicked and murderous nobleman, a lovely damsel in distress and his very different life, designed to keep his wife and son from harm by their enemies, deep in the forest before a trio of travel-worn and weary gentlemen interrupted him and he had to begin all over again for the benefit of Jack, Duke of Dettingham, Alex Forthin, Earl of Calvercombe and mysterious Mr Frederick Peters, whom

Rich introduced as his very good friend and preserver after shaking him by the hand, as if there weren't words enough to say what service this man had done him in the past.

'Jack,' he said simply when he was done greeting his friend and Freya's eyes watered as she took in the wordless awe both cousins felt at finally being together again.

Lord Calvercombe stood by and watched proceedings with a cynical eye, as usual, but seemed genuinely glad to see Rich home when he wondered aloud why such a rogue as Alex Forthin had been invited to share in ducal hospitality for the night.

'Because I married into the family to be assured of it whenever I need to escape my tumbledown inheritance, Diccon,' Alex observed cynically, but Freya could see a new ease about him that spoke of supreme contentment with his wife and his lot in life.

'My sister would have something scathing to say about that order of priorities and so would I, if I believed a word of it,' Rich responded.

'All very well, but what have you been about and why are you here when we three have been riding the length and breadth of the country these last few days in order to save your sorry skin?'

'I was explaining all that when you so rudely interrupted me.'

'Then go back to the beginning, so we'll all know exactly what you've been up to,' Alex ordered laconically as he accepted a selection of pies and cold meats Hughes and his minions brought, then gently but implacably ordered them to be gone and not listen at doors.

'Do make yourself at home in my house, won't you?' Jack said mildly as he sat on the sofa next to his lady and stretched his booted legs out towards the fire with a satisfied sigh.

'I'd much rather be in my own with my darling wife, but since I'm here I might as well make myself useful,' Alex said with an easy grin Freya hadn't thought the austerely formidable former soldier capable of until today.

'How far have you got with your tale, then?' Mr Peters reminded Rich and the mood sobered as Richard Seaborne resumed his tale of attempted murder and an unimaginably wicked scheme to deprive his beloved stepson of life before Hal was even born.

Freya was so outraged by the tale she almost gave herself away by doing as the Duchess did instinctively and rubbing a gentle hand

over her pregnant belly to assure herself all
was well with her own baby. The fury she
felt at anyone endangering an unborn child
helped burn away her last whisper of jealousy
of Rich's wife. Imagining what the painfully
young girl had been through while she pro-
tected her child as best she could, then nursed
a gravely injured young buck back to health
made her understand why Annabelle then let
Rich sacrifice so much to keep them safe. Of
course the girl would have fallen for the real
man under all the cynical charm and restless
dash a younger and less tried Richard Seaborne must have rejoiced in—how could she
not when older and wiser Lady Freya Buckle
had done exactly the same six years on?

'You didn't dare admit your son's identity in
case the supposed Lord Lundy gained guardianship of him, I suppose?' she asked when
Richard reached the end of the tale he was prepared to tell with today's events and hers and
Aunt Carolina's rescue of his family.

'I still can't,' he said bleakly.

That wouldn't matter to a woman who loved
him, Freya concluded. She could quite happily accept Hal as Richard's heir in place of
her own child, should it be a boy. If only there
was a chance she could be Richard Seaborne's

beloved second wife she would accept his children joyfully. She recalled the dark accusations he'd made this afternoon and knew she couldn't marry a man who thought so little of her, even if he wanted her to.

Chapter Sixteen

'We three may be able to help you announce Hal's true parentage to the world and still be safe in your own home, Seaborne,' Mr Peters said in his usual quiet way.

'Listen to him, Rich,' Jack urged to silence the denial he sensed on Rich's tongue that he would ever put his son in danger. 'It's the most damnably unlikely story I ever heard, but I was there when it played out so I suppose it must be true.'

Jessica tutted at his language, but Lord Calvercombe nodded to confirm his presence as well and add his four-pennyworth to the debate and Rich stood tense as ever in front of the fire, warming his manly coat tails and looking so endearingly familiar Freya almost forgave him for not being Orlando for a moment.

'All three of us visited my chambers on our way through town to make sure no urgent messages had arrived from an agent I had trying to prove who was behind the attempts to lure you out of hiding and capture your supposed son three years ago,' Mr Peters began.

'He *is* my son in every way that matters,' Richard bit out stiffly.

'Of course he is and none of us wish him otherwise,' Lady Henry said as if it wasn't ever in question from the moment she knew about Annabelle's son.

'Unless he demonstrates the murderous tendencies of his cousin, of course,' Alex Forthin put in laconically.

'Hal doesn't have it in him to be so evil,' Freya flew to his defence and felt his lordship's thoughtful gaze on her as if she'd written a banner declaring her infatuation with that entire offshoot of the Seaborne clan and waved it under his aquiline nose.

'Francis Martagon arrived at my chambers as soon as whoever he had watching them got a message to him that I was back in London,' Mr Peters went on doggedly with his story and

Freya cast him a grateful look for distracting everyone so effectively from her blushes.

'What the devil did he want, then?' Rich growled.

'A peace treaty apparently,' Lord Calvercombe said with a frown that spoke of his mixed feelings about the bizarre idea. 'He's willing to trade information about his father-in-law's kidnap of Mr Telemachus Seaborne three years ago and his subsequent efforts to track you down and dispose of you and the true Martagon heir, in return for our promise not to prosecute him for the attempted murder of Mrs DeMorbaraye-Martagon and her unborn child and the attack on you six years ago.'

'Why the deuce should I promise any such thing?' Richard argued.

'If Francis relinquishes all claim on the Lundy title, estates and monies, then you can return to your old life and Hal will be safe,' his mother pointed out gently.

'He tried to kill Annabelle as well as Hal. He needs to die for that alone and how can I ever be sure my son will be safe while Martagon is alive and at large?'

'In a half-hearted sort of a way,' Jack surprised them by pointing out when he would usually be the first man to condemn such a heartless act. 'He's a weak fool and even I couldn't bring myself to hate him as I wanted to, Rich,' the Duke explained with a wry shrug that explained his bafflement better than words.

'He intends to sue his wife's latest lover for criminal conversation and divorce her. His only hope of doing so safely, considering who the lady's father is, has to be with our help,' Alex said impassively and, warrior that he was, he obviously found it easier to keep hating his enemies than the Duke of Dettingham did.

'Strider will fight him with every mean trick and moral blackmail he can lay his hands on and he's got enough money to buy the best,' Rich said.

'Nothing will make his daughter a Marchioness again if Martagon admits he isn't the true heir and never has been,' Lady Henry pointed out pragmatically.

'How could I be certain Hal is safe with Strider running about loose with revenge on his mind? The man doesn't have a conscience or a heart,' Rich said, the stark choices he faced over the last years clear on his face once more.

Freya felt her own heart threaten to soften,

so she reminded herself what strong and abiding love this man still felt for his late wife and how little he had for her. Nobody listening to him accuse her of that venal scheme this afternoon would suppose he'd made love to her as if his next breath depended on making it wondrous and magical for both of them. She could hardly believe it herself. Any doubt she had suffered that she was right to take herself and her unborn child out of his life and stay away had been scoured away by his mistrust.

'Mr Francis Martagon also offers you enough information to keep Strider busy fighting for his life and his fortune against a host of charges, from embezzlement of Home Office funds, blackmail, murder and treason down to swearing false oaths. If the man has any sense, he'll flee on the next ship he can find to anywhere the British law can't reach him—if you agree to Martagon's bargain, of course,' Mr Peters concluded.

'And what of the unreliability of his testimony? He was the one who arranged for my wife to be murdered and her unborn son destroyed along with her in the first place.'

'That's the beauty of his evidence,' Alex grudgingly intervened. 'None of it comes directly from him and flows from a prolonged examination of his father-in-law's shady business dealings on his part.'

'What an uncomfortable nest of vipers Lundy Court must have been these last few years,' Penelope Seaborne observed quietly.

Freya was reminded how acute all these Seabornes were when schoolgirl Penelope saw things more clearly than most seasoned adults. She must leave as rapidly as possible come morning, before one of them put two and two together about her and Richard Seaborne and reached the answer she dreaded.

'So he gets away with it, then?' Rich said with a fierce frown.

'The bargain we drove lets him take his elder daughter with him. He believes that child is actually his, and promises to live in seclusion with her on a small Irish estate I doubt Hal will ever miss. He seems to genuinely love the little girl and believes it his duty to save her from a mother who hates her as well as her latest daughter. I pity the poor mite who finally brought all this about, but the erstwhile Marchioness's lover, Menkinthwaite, is willing to take the babe into his household and bring her up as a poor relation, since she carries his stamp as strongly as I'm told your little girl carries yours, Rich,' Jack explained.

'It sounds too easy a bargain on Martagon for my taste,' Richard responded bleakly and Freya thought she wasn't the only one who set his reluctance to agree down to the attack on the wife he obviously missed so deeply he longed to be avenged on her would-be murderer.

'Then think of the alternative, Richard,' his mother urged and surely that wasn't sympathy and understanding in her eyes when they briefly lighted on Freya? 'You'll face a sensational court case where little Henry's birth and his mother's character and conduct are publically pulled to pieces, then picked over by the gossips. Then there's your hasty marriage to her before her first husband's babe was even born to explain and all the legal tangles and scandal that will provoke and your poor wife not even here to defend herself.'

'Never fear, I am here to do that,' Alex argued with a combative glint in his blue eyes that made Freya shudder for his future safety.

'I can only imagine what my sister Persephone would say about such a reckless and witless statement, Calvercombe,' Richard replied and Freya let out a sigh of relief. 'We both loved her, Alex. I'm so very sorry that we couldn't save her when my Sally decided to come into the world feet first, or get word to you of her death.'

'I knew she was dead somewhere in my heart when I came home to find her gone without a single word to me for so long, Seaborne. She would have found a way to let me know all was well with her if she was still alive. Annabelle wouldn't let anyone suffer if she could prevent it and knew I would miss her. If Annabelle loved you, I suppose you must have hidden depths the rest of us can't see.'

'High praise indeed,' Rich replied with a rueful grimace.

'More than you deserve after today,' Jessica told him severely.

Freya saw all the Seabornes who weren't here to witness Rich's homecoming wait for enlightenment and decided she couldn't endure reliving the terrible moment when he showed how little he thought of her this afternoon.

'If you will all excuse me, it has been a very long day,' she said with as much dignity as she could muster and an open yawn. 'We were up at dawn, so I suppose it's little wonder the children fell asleep as soon as they were safely tucked up in bed tonight.'

'And it's about time I was tucked up in mine

as well, my dear, so we'll go up together,' her aunt said as she stood up to support her niece. Freya knew how lucky she was to have Carolina Bradstock as her dear aunt by now and gave her a grateful smile.

They said their goodnights while Freya ignored Rich as best she could. Tomorrow she must convince her aunt nothing could change between them, but tonight she was weary beyond physical tiredness. Richard Seaborne, with his careless elegance and assurance of his own superiority, wasn't her lover. This hard-faced aristocrat was as remote from Orlando as his woodland home was from the gracious Palladian mansion she now recalled being pointed out to her as Seaborne House, the home of Lord Henry Seaborne's eldest son.

Away from him and alone at last, Freya drifted about her comfortable room carrying out the little tasks she once took for granted someone else would do for her. It was foolish to feel so weary and not go to bed, but she knew she wouldn't sleep. She ran a hand over her still-relatively-flat belly and wondered if her tiny child slept when she did and woke when she was awake. It amused her to think of a very individual being finding its mother's odd way of doing things unacceptable and going its own way even before it was born. If Aunt Carolina was right about Seabornes, it would do plenty of that once it was in the world, so she might as well get used to the idea of another arrogant and determined Seaborne doing its best to rule its mama's life and be ready to remind it she was no pushover herself.

At least sitting dreaming of her child distracted her from the aching hurt Richard Seaborne had dealt her earlier and she couldn't let herself examine that right now. She took the pins out of her neat chignon and tried to remember how it was arranged so she could copy the style herself. Once the heavy mass of it was free she combed it lock by lock, then began the hypnotic business of brushing until it was a smooth and shining mass about her shoulders. The routine soothed her into a place where she could think about the father of her baby and not hate him for refusing to love her. She could even feel sorry for him at this distance. Grief for his lost wife and natural stubbornness meant he would never meet his latest child.

She would carry his babe alone and the very idea of wedding Richard Seaborne simply to ensure this child bore his name revolted her. She would have wed Orlando Craven as equal partner in his simple existence. She could endure a life where she was his helpmeet and not his darling but, without that mutual need and shared labour to bind them together, marriage to rich and impeccably connected Mr Richard Seaborne would be nigh intolerable to her.

Lady Freya couldn't endure her old life back now Orlando's simple lifestyle had taught the wealthy daughter of an Earl to value her privacy and independence, but there was no Orlando. Rich Seaborne was about as noble as a man came without a title to label himself with and a dynastic marriage could never be enough for her now. A quiet knock came on the door and she called an absent invitation to enter, expecting the maid sent by her hostess, who was clearly unaware proud and finicky Lady Freya Buckle had learnt to dress and undress by herself since they last met.

'I can manage perfectly well, thank you,' she said without turning round to encourage idle conversation.

'Almost too well, I suspect,' a deep masculine voice said and Freya gasped and swivelled on the dressing stool to glare at him for invading her privacy.

'Leave!' she ordered furiously.

'In a minute,' Rich told her as if he had every right to stay.

'Now. The Duke and Lord Calvercombe will drag you out of here by your ears when I rouse the household with the scream I'm about to shriek if you don't go immediately.'

'I'm sure they would love to, but if you were going to scream you would have done so by now,' he said with the assurance of a rake certain charm would get him what he wanted.

'I shall leave you to a petty triumph then, Mr Seaborne. I hope it amuses you to know you harried a single lady from her bedchamber in the middle of the night,' she said as she reached the door.

'Stay,' he gasped and tugged on her hand so she swung round to meet his eyes and saw a desperate plea there. 'Only hear me out, Perdita; then I'll leave you in peace.' She stayed silent, wondering why she was tempted to let him explain the inexplicable. 'Please?' he added sneakily and won at least that by not arrogantly demanding she listen to him.

'I will stay for a while,' she conceded and let him close the door because she wanted this conversation in private, or so she assured herself as the latch clicked into its well-honed notch and they were private once more. 'I can't imagine you have anything to say that I wish to hear and my name is Lady Freya Buckle. Perdita didn't exist.'

'Then I have a fine imagination,' he said softly and she called on Lady Freya to face him with all the hauteur and scepticism at her command.

'You have, *Orlando*,' she said with as much irony as three words could bear.

'A man can't live another life for so long without becoming what he pretends when he begins it.'

'I almost understood that. Rumour was right about your glib tongue at least.'

'Apparently my fame precedes me, then.'

'You're infamous, Mr Seaborne, and now free to take up your old life.'

'Perhaps I don't care about the things Rich Seaborne found diverting now? Do you pine for your old dreams six years on, Lady Freya? I suppose you were in the schoolroom when I was out in the world earning my wild reputation.'

'I shall be two and twenty in a month, if you're trying to discover my age.'

'A mere babe, then,' he joked and Freya felt her heart ice over at the thought of him discovering her real one, rather than his unlucky figure of speech.

'And how many years do you have in your dish, Mr Seaborne? A reputation like yours cannot have been earned in a day.'

'Nine and twenty,' he said as if they were wasting time he didn't have to spare.

'You were but three and twenty when you met Miss DeMorbaraye and married her?'

'And despite my rakish reputation it took me a whole month to persuade her without her in my life I would be nothing. I wanted her to myself from the moment I set eyes on her, battling like a tigress to save herself and Hal from the devils Martagon sent to kill them. By the time I woke up from the fever she nursed me through after the wound I got helping her beat them off became infected, I was so deep in love with her I could never recover. I can't lie to you and pretend I didn't love Annabelle deeply, Lady Freya. I wouldn't have missed her for the world, cherish her memory and dote on our children.'

'I know,' she said and turned away to resume her interrupted *toilette*. She carefully combed her hair into two halves, then threes and set her fingers the task of plaiting it that was now so close to second nature she didn't need to look in the mirror, which was as well considering the sadness she would see looking back at her if she did.

'It took only moments after you'd gone to realise loving Annabelle only trained me better for loving you, Perdita. Fool that I am to let you leave in the first place,' he said softly.

She couldn't doubt his sincerity when she risked a glance at him and saw he meant it, for now. 'Perdita is dead,' she told him bleakly.

'I hope she's only asleep and dreaming of me.'

'If she was, you killed her this afternoon.'

'I don't have words to say how sorry I am for what I said then, Freya,' he said so seriously she fought the urge to childishly stick her fingers in her ears and pretend to be deaf.

'No man could love a woman and call her the names you did me,' she replied flatly.

'This one can.'

'Don't,' she demanded fiercely, 'don't dress up what you feel for me in pretty words. All you ever felt for me was lust and, strong and heady as that was at the time, that isn't love. You feel you dishonoured a single lady and I understand you must propose marriage to Lady Freya Buckle, when Perdita only warranted your purse and a ride to the nearest town. Save yourself the trouble, Mr Seaborne, because I won't have you,' she said regally, waving aside any argument about her summary of the differences between Perdita and the high-born lady she truly was. 'I wanted what happened. I enjoyed our nights and days together immoderately and cannot regret them even now. I also watched your cousin woo his bride, so I will never be unguarded with a Seaborne so set on his quarry, whatever she might say to the contrary, as the Duchess was. You had your chance to wed me three months ago and didn't take it.'

'I was waiting for Fred Peters to find a way to free me from the forest when I got the news Cleo had kidnapped Sally and Hal. I brooded endlessly on the day I could do as most men can without thinking and find the woman I loved to beg her to marry me. Ask the children if you don't believe me, because I was like a bear with a sore head after I let you leave. The reason Cleo was able to take them was because they spent so much time at Keziah's to avoid me. Cleo was long gone by the time Keziah realised what the wretched female had done and came running to find me.'

'Then why did you so instantly believe I

was in league with Cleo? How could you think such a thing of me?'

'I don't know,' he admitted and shook his head at his own stupidity.

Freya kept her face coolly blank and let silence prod him into saying more.

'I spent so many days futilely plotting and planning ways of finding you that I was half-mad even before the children were stolen away.'

'I could never profit from the misery of two children I love.'

'I know, but how can I explain what I said then when I don't understand it myself?' he asked with a defeated shrug and turned to go as he'd promised he would if he couldn't convince her. 'I'm sorry, Lady Freya.'

'So am I, Richard Seaborne,' she said sadly, desolation eating away at her certainty she must live without him, when the emptiness inside her warned that, despite their child and her aunt's wonderfully irreverent company, she would miss him the rest of her life.

'He and Orlando Craven adore every stubborn inch of you, Freya, especially the streak of wildness in you that made every day we spent together a mystery and a wondrous journey all rolled into one,' he told her as he turned back and watched her with all of it open in his deeply green eyes.

She remembered them full of shadows and mysteries as they loved—every move, every touch on sweat-slicked and fascinatingly other skin reflected in her lover's eyes.

'For three months I burned with the loss of you, tore myself to pieces for letting you go, then had to sit and wait on others until I could find you and beg you to let me love you again with everything I am and every breath I take.'

'Yet you loved your wife the instant you met, did you not?'

'All the more reason to resist loving you, Perdita. I knew the agony of loving so much, then having to exist without Anna as if I was only half-alive.'

'I can see how her loss might make you wary, but you didn't trust me, Richard. Once upon a time, I came to this house a proud and selfish lady with no thought in my head but marrying your cousin for his title. Even when I was that arrogant, vain and silly I would never have harmed a child or stolen one from a loving father.'

'I didn't know Jack had run his eyes over you while he was finding Jessica,' he said with a fiery possessiveness that almost warmed Freya's icy heart.

'I don't think he did so very seriously, but I thought a fine marriage would make me count in my father's eyes and, even when he died, I couldn't let go of the idea I must make one to matter.'

'He had a daughter any sane man would be proud of.'

'I was born a girl,' she said flatly, 'a drawback he never forgave me.'

'Can you imagine any Seaborne being considered lesser for that?'

Freya thought of Lady Henry's lovely and lively daughters and the Duke and Duchess's adored first child, Lady Nerissa Seaborne, and knew Sally would never feel a failure or a burden on her family because she was a mere female. 'No,' she agreed.

'Then risk bearing me some leggy and precious girls in your own image, Freya? Give me a chance and I swear I'll cherish our girls, along with any boys and the son and daughter we already have, for the rest of our days.'

'My aunt claims Seabornes always breed true. That's probably why she insisted we came here with the children, since she already suspected Sally was one. I can't imagine why I didn't see it as soon as I laid eyes on her myself.'

'Breed me some little Seabornes, then, and we'll find out if Buckle blood is stronger after all, although I don't think it can be, since Bowland has a Friday face and gooseberry eyes and very little resemblance to you.'

Torn between knowing she was already well embarked on that particular experiment and the temptation of succumbing to the heat and wanting in his eyes at the very idea of her carrying his child, she hesitated.

'No, I can't trust you,' she said sadly and clenched her hands into fists at her sides as she fought the memories of how wondrous it felt to love and live with him, to lie in his arms and feel the world spin away as if nothing mattered but him and her and the children safe and asleep upstairs.

Chapter Seventeen

$\sim\!\!\mathcal{C}\!\!\curvearrowright\!\!\mathcal{D}\!\!\curvearrowleft\!\!\sim$

'Or is it yourself you don't trust, my lady?' Richard said huskily, as if he sensed defeat and the very idea of it was tearing his heart out and making him fight all the harder for what he wanted. 'You think yourself unlovable and nothing could be further from the truth, Freya. You tell me you were once a selfish snob, hell-bent on making a marriage of convenience, yet I never meet a more open and democratic female in my life than the one you became in Longborough Forest before my very eyes. How could I *not* love you when every hour that passed seemed such a huge revelation to you? You paint yourself as charmless and self-absorbed, but even when you scold me it's charming. You played and cooked and

mended and strove for my children, despite
the fact another woman bore them and their
father was your lover.'

'That was then—now I know how you really
see me, Mr Seaborne. I can't live with you while
that knowledge eats away at any trust we managed to build in each other, back when I thought
you were Orlando and you thought me Perdita.'

'Then come back there with me, if that's the
only way to get you to love me again. We'll
live that way and Hal and Sally will just have
to learn to be lady and gentleman from observation and theory. Now and again we'll have to
come here and be Mr Seaborne and my lady,
but I'd live for ever a woodsman and a car-
penter if it would persuade you to marry me,
Lady Freya.'

'You would do that, for me?' She tried to resist the picture of this man humbling himself
to life such a life again, not because Hal would
be in acute danger if he didn't hide away in the
forest now, but because it was the only way to
win back her trust. Probably just as well if he
didn't know he already had her love and had
almost from the beginning.

'Anything rather than lose you,' he promised so simply and fervently she felt a flutter
of hope leap in her heart after all.

'Such a little life for a great gentleman and landowner to live for the sake of my Lady Freya,' she said, her voice a little wobbly at the thought of any man making such a huge sacrifice to prove how much he loved her, let alone this one.

'For her every bit as much as for Perdita,' he promised huskily. 'Marry me,' he begged her. 'I'm proud and stubborn and wrong-headed as a mule when I'm in a temper. I say hasty things to those I love the most when life catches me on the raw and this won't be the last time you have to forgive me for it, but I will always love you, even when I don't tell you about it or rage at you as if I've a right to be right so you have to be wrong. I could promise to guard my wretched tongue and tame my temper for you, but I'd only make myself a liar next time you decide your way is better than mine and stick that proud chin in the air and defy me with every bone in your body. I can only say I'm sorry, Freya. I can't unsay those terrible words I said in pique and temper and exhaustion when I saw you calmly standing there as if I'd been dashing about the country day and night for days for no reason at all. I can't tell you how much I wish I could snap my fingers and make it not so, but not even a Seaborne can do that.'

The realness of what he said and offered broke through her hurt as charm and magic and moonlight might not have done and made her hesitate. She had convinced herself she had to live without this man long before he said what he had today, but what if she'd been wrong?

Her hesitation went on long enough for him to sense she was weakening. Wolf as he was by nature and breeding, that was enough for him to seize the advantage and kiss her. At first his mouth moved on hers in a plea, then with increasing firmness and confidence as she held still and then responded. She couldn't bring herself to flinch away and manufacture a 'no', when she had yearned for his kisses since the day they parted and now they were warm and real on her lips.

'Neither of us can resist the other and I really do love you, Freya,' he assured her very seriously indeed, once he'd managed to raise his mouth from hers long enough to say anything that made sense. 'I never felt such pain in my life as I did while I railed and raged at you like the madman I felt when I saw you this afternoon.'

'Really?' she asked, the terrible loss of his

first wife in her mind even as she ordered herself not to make the comparison.

'I raged at the devil the day Annabelle died, of course, but misjudging you made me totter on the edge of lunacy, love. I wanted to tear at myself and smash down the walls, then sit in the rubble and weep because I'd lost you through my own efforts. I'd held the hope of you in my heart all these weeks and months and as soon as I saw you again all I could do was shout at you for rescuing my children for me and being you.'

'Hmm, it does sound as if you've suffered a little, Mr Seaborne,' she mused, as if she could be cool and detached about him when she was warm in his arms as she hadn't truly felt since the day she left him, feeling as if every step dragged with leaden reluctance.

'A little? Can you really love me if you believe it was only a little when I thought I'd truly lost you this time, Perdita?'

'I can, but will you love me once I tell you all my secrets, Orlando?'

'Aye,' he promised as if he'd opened himself to the essential rightness of them now, so all he could do was love her. She hoped he was right and made herself tell the biggest one of all before he got any further with seducing her again and found out for himself.

'I'm carrying your child, Richard Seaborne,' she made herself say as she met his gaze while holding her breath against the anticipated storm.

'Good God, are you?' he asked and confounded her by chuckling, then grinning at her as if he was a tom cat with an awful lot of cream on his whiskers.

'Stop pretending you're solely responsible for my shameful state. It was very much a joint effort.'

'I remember every single shot we made at the project in vivid detail,' he said and leered another stray-cat grin. 'Would you like a demonstration to remind you?'

'I'm not sure—how much will it cost me?'

'A wedding ring, lover,' he said, the grin and rakish poise quite gone as his green eyes were suddenly completely sincere and very serious indeed.

'And what will the children say?' she asked the question she had dreaded facing if her wildest dreams ever came true, for it was one thing to be their friend, quite another to become their stepmama.

'It's about time, I should think, if they were

old enough to have a firm opinion on the subject when at the moment they only love you. So what's your answer, Freya-Perdita?'

'Yes, all right then,' she breathed on a long and contented sigh.

'Your aunt assures me a special licence could settle the whole business inside a week, if only I find a bishop ready to grant me a second chance at loving you abidingly, Lady Freya,' he said, his eyes brilliant with triumph and joy, as if he was only holding in a wild whoop of joy because it was now very close to midnight.

'Does she now? She is a very devious old lady and I shall tell her so in the morning.'

'Since Bowland doesn't deserve the honour of being asked for your hand in marriage, I thought I might as well request it from the only other member of your family who matters to either of us,' he told her with a sly Seaborne smile she didn't trust an inch.

'Considering I came to bed convinced I would never marry anyone and least of all you, she's obviously a very crafty aunt indeed, then.'

'Don't expect me to argue. I had to swear I loved you as passionately as Romeo ever loved his Juliet, or any of my assorted sisters, brother or cousins love their chosen mates, before she agreed I might make you a tolerable husband, in spite of everything I'd done today and in the past to make myself the last man on earth you would ever agree to wed.'

'And do you?' she asked dreamily.

'Do I what?'

'Love me that much?'

'If you doubt it, why not let me show you?' he whispered and kissed her so deeply and passionately she forgot what the question was and launched herself into this familiar, but, oh, so deeply missed and mourned, loving without any edges to it.

So this was real love, she decided hazily as she felt his questing mouth and wicked fingers undoing her in so many more ways than one. Until now, she hadn't let herself dream it would ever come back at her even more generously than she gave it out. He found the new fullness of her breasts and she felt his breath stutter with all sorts of complex emotions as he reined himself in like a trembling thoroughbred and just let the tip of his tongue delicately whisper over her sometimes too-sensitive nipples. Burning with need, tender with loving and revelling in his heady exploration of her changing body, she was on fire and more desperate than she had ever been to take him into her and love in every sense of the word.

He shucked her gown off her shoulders and unlaced her not very tightly laced corset, even as her busy hands dealt disrespectfully with the ducal finery he'd borrowed and couldn't return now they'd done their worst with it. At last they were both in the same state of nature and he could explore her changing body with tender reverence. She splayed her hand over his as he tested the slight changes in her waistline where their child was growing and realised how special the bond between a man and woman could be. He would never be revolted or less than fascinated by her changing body and his child and she felt all the dreams she'd never let herself dream in her cold days as Lady Freya come true anyway.

'When do babies quicken, Orlando?' she murmured as she felt him try to hold himself a little away, so she wouldn't feel intimidated by the hugeness of his need of her, and frustrated such ridiculous ideas by pushing her neat *derrière* back into his braced body.

'Another few weeks yet,' he said distractedly and she luxuriated in the shaken restraint he had managed to clamp on his eager sex for her sake.

'Can we love without harming our babe in the meantime?' She asked the question she needed answered right now.

'With me like this and you more or less as you are we can,' he said thickly, as if words were becoming too demanding to say easily, 'or the way we did that last night when I was ungallant enough to gag you lest you woke the children,' he managed in a rush of interesting information that undid his most gallant desires to protect her from his rampant needs, so he demonstrated in as wild a race as he dared gallop with her already three months along with his child and she enjoyed every wanton inch of the race and the joyously hasty rush to completion as they shot to ecstasy their painful wait for each other had only made more inevitable and boundlessly wonderful.

'Well, that all seemed to work very well, don't you think?' she asked when he had pandered to his gentlemanly instincts and carried her almost-boneless body to the spacious and comfortable bed the Duchess had allotted her so considerately.

'My practical Perdita,' he muttered on an unsteady laugh she shushed, as if their gasps in the extremity of their satisfaction wouldn't already have alerted anyone close enough to hear that Lady Freya was behaving in a most unmaidenly fashion with prodigal Richard Seaborne once again, and enjoying it mightily.

Luckily Miss Bradstock and the other guests were a wing and a floor away and the Duke and Duchess occupied the ground floor room in the most splendid part of the original Tudor mansion and the only ones disturbed by their lovemaking were any ghosts haunting Ashburton and the last traces of Lady Freya's chilly dignity.

'Who are we to be from now on then, my love?' she murmured as she snuggled into her lover's shoulder and sighed like a contented cat as he played with her hair.

'Husband and wife,' he informed her lazily.

'Not that, idiot. What shall we call each other, as we have two names to choose from?'

'Well, I intend to be Rich Seaborne most of the time we live at Seaborne House and I farm my acres and you ever so gently bully my staff and discuss our children, our estates and our hopes and dreams with me. When we're in Longborough Forest, I shall abandon him and be Orlando again. I'll have to build another wing on the cottage to accommodate our growing family and give Hal a room of his own now he's a young gentleman.'

'We shall have to spend time at Martagon Court as well,' she reminded him with a grimace, finding the rest of his programme very much to her taste and wishing they didn't.

'Of course, we owe Hal and his parents that much at least. Chance is a very odd beast, don't you think?' he asked as he stroked her long silky hair down over her slender back, then even lower and made her think she might not have it cut after all.

'In what way?' she managed despite the long shiver of awareness prickling delightfully down the length of her spine.

'If Colton Martagon hadn't been killed in a reckless ride to try to win enough money to set his wife and child up in comfort without his guardian knowing he had either, I would never have met Annabelle and Hal and loved them so deeply I was still hiding in Longborough Forest the night you needed me to find you there.'

'So all my terror and confusion was worthwhile after all?' she mused.

'Never, I wouldn't have you run a step in such fear if only I'd been able to prevent it, but I wonder if Lady Freya would ever have fallen for Rich Seaborne half as freely and honestly as Perdita did for Orlando.'

'Probably not. Is Lady Freya going to get in the way of you loving the rest of me?'

'No, how can I *not* love all of you, Freya Buckle? You're my lover and you'll soon be my wife and the mother of my child. Anyone who cares to argue with the woman at the very heart of my life will have to fight me first.'

'I can win my own battles,' she reminded him.

'I know, but why do so alone when we can fend off our enemies together, my love?'

'Why indeed?' she said with a luxurious shiver and lost interest in battle altogether.

Now her fifth and sixth grandchildren had been safely baptised in Ashburton Church, Lady Henry Seaborne gave a contented sigh and watched Rich proudly show off his very different twins to the assembled guests. Meanwhile Freya was doing her best to distract Sally from loving her little brother and sister so heartily they would begin to scream again. At three months Miss Miranda Carolina Seaborne's eyes were already lioness amber and Master Matthew Frederick Seaborne watched the company with fascinated green eyes the exact shade of his father and big sister's.

Her son exchanged a quick joke with the darkly handsome young devil someone whispered was a gypsy king among his own people and the little tanned woman Freya had insisted must be one of her daughter's godmothers, who nodded knowingly at whatever her son-in-law had said and added some pithy observation that made Rich roar with laughter. Melissa felt intensely blessed to be able to stand among her family and watch her beloved elder son live and love and laugh again at last.

Her darling Telemachus meant so much to her and she loved her daughters dearly, admired their husbands and thought all her grandchildren quite ridiculously wonderful and talented, but with Rich back home it felt as if something had clicked back to rightness about the Seaborne clan as it hadn't been since the day her own beloved Henry had died. She watched Richard's own young Henry, Marquis of Lundy, and his son in every way that counted, lean against his side and whisper something significant to the monstrous great dog Rich insisted had the right to follow his family everywhere they went nowadays and was glad nothing about Rich and his Lady Freya's life was conventional or predictable.

He was never one for rules and schedules and neither was his lady, now she dared be her true self, and Melissa knew her daughter-in-law enjoyed their different ways of life as much as he did.

'You'll have to revise your opinion of how clearly the Seabornes stamp their mark on their progeny now,' she informed Miss Bradstock with a very happy smile as that lady emerged from the crowd of very mixed guests.

'Aye, our latest young miss has her own views on the subject,' the little girl's great-great-aunt agreed, clearly very happy Miss Miranda looked so much like her mother.

'The younger generation should always defy the expectations of their elders,' Lady Henry said with an affectionate glance at her daughter-in-law, who had certainly confounded anyone who remembered Lady Freya Buckle, husband hunter, by wedding a commoner, even if he was Rich Seaborne and very uncommon indeed. 'Only think what a poor marriage she and Jack would have made if he had proposed to Lady Freya four years ago instead of Jessica.'

'They were wrong for each other in almost every way,' Freya's great-aunt scoffed as she watched Lord and Lady Bowland sceptically as they made a few weak attempts to join with the radically mixed throng of guests at a Seaborne christening with a difference.

'Rich loves it when Freya puts on her queen-of-all-she-surveys look and does her best to put him in his place. She and Jack would have brought out the worst in one another.'

'So now we're surrounded by a pack of disrespectful whelps and their ridiculously besotted wives and must endure a constant stream of impudent Seaborne and Forthin brats disrupting our peace and quiet morning noon and night.'

'I know—isn't it wonderful?' Lady Henry said with a blissful sigh.

'Aye,' the vital lady Lady Henry would never regret inviting to share her home admitted. 'My Freya is as happy as a pig in muck and I've seldom felt less bored in my life.'

'And my errant son has become the man I always prayed he might be. There seems little left for a mother to wish for.'

'Then you're not planning the most sensational come out a girl ever experienced for that flighty young miss of yours in a few years' time, I suppose?'

'Maybe, but Penny will follow her own path

to happiness, whatever plans her proud mama makes for her. The Seabornes always did insist on going their own way, whatever I had to say about the matter.'

'And they travel with such style while they're doing it,' Miss Bradstock admitted as she eyed the assembled pack of partially tamed wolves with their extraordinary wives and the promising families they all doted on.

'True,' said Lady Henry, a Seaborne wife with remembered stars still in her eyes, 'but it's a journey whomever they startle, charm and seduce into sharing it with them will never forget,' she confirmed.

'I can't argue with that, considering Alex Forthin, Antigone Seaborne and my lovely Freya look as if they don't know how they managed to be so happy.'

'Aye, and my Helen is growing up with her fine young lord and Jack's more in love with his Duchess than he ever dreamt he could be in his worst nightmares.'

'Five down, one to go,' Miss Bradstock said with a wickedly conspiratorial smile.

'What mischief are you two hatching?' Jack asked as he subjected his own far-too-innocent-looking aunt and Lady Freya's frankly devious one to the acute green gaze they'd been talking about just now.

'The best sort, my love,' Lady Henry said sweetly.

'What a terrifying prospect,' he said with the relaxed resignation of a man who had already experienced the best and worst a matchmaking conspiracy could drag him into for his own good.

'Rich and his Freya don't look as if they've suffered unduly from our interference,' Rich's proud mama said as her gaze once more rested on her eldest son, as if she would never tire of looking at him after six years of being deprived of the sight.

'Since they found each other without any help from either of you, I can't see how you can claim the credit for that match.'

'A good enough *grande dame* will always claim the credit for any good thing that happens within a hundred miles of her, my boy,' Miss Bradstock informed him sagely, 'and it took a great deal of guile to push the two of them back into each other's arms where they belong, once your totty-headed cousin was fool enough to let my niece get away from him.'

'At least I had the sense to know my fate

when I met her,' he said as if meeting and marrying the love of his life had been his idea all along and two great ladies exchanged knowing glances.

'Of course you did, my love,' his aunt told him soothingly and smiled delightedly when Freya came to join them with Sally trotting determinedly along behind her so she didn't lose her beloved Prudie in the crush.

'Happy now?' Miss Bradstock said and Freya smiled a blissful assent.

'More than I ever dreamed I could be the day I got lost, then found Orlando Craven in the wild wood.'

'Papa,' Miss Sally Seaborne said wisely.

'My Sally,' Rich agreed as he followed with Hal proudly holding his littlest sister and Master Matthew Frederick making it very plain he wasn't intending to relinquish their father's attention before he finally had to give in and sleep. 'Was ever a man so undeservedly blessed?' he asked nobody in particular.

'Never,' his wife informed him with a sharp nod to remind him how undeserving he'd been on more than one occasion before he realised it.

'Or so recklessly brave in taking on a proud and arrogant female like you as his lady,' he taunted her with a conflagration of desire and love for Lady Freya and her eager alias in his hot green gaze.

'That wasn't bravery—it was the coming of wisdom,' she informed him and met his challenge with one of her own.

'You will excuse us, won't you?' Rich asked as he somehow signalled to his family's eager helpers that his youngest children were both as near asleep as made no difference at long last and young Lord Lundy and his enterprising little sister not much better after so much excitement.

'Why should we? It's your house and your party,' Jack argued with a disgruntled stare at his own love and his six-month-old heir, surrounded as they were by admirers.

'Because I'm a Seaborne and she was a Buckle and we arrogant aristocrats deserve each other,' Rich said with an unrepentant grin that admitted he was indeed intending a detour to their aristocratic bedchamber as soon as the children were safely asleep and Jack would just have to envy them until he came up with an excuse to get his Duchess alone.

'True,' said the Duke of Dettingham with well-contained ferocity and stalked off to contrive one at the double.

* * * * *

A sneaky peek at next month...

HISTORICAL

IGNITE YOUR IMAGINATION, STEP INTO THE PAST...

My wish list for next month's titles...

In stores from 6th September 2013:

- ☐ Mistress at Midnight — Sophia James
- ☐ The Runaway Countess — Amanda McCabe
- ☐ In the Commodore's Hands — Mary Nichols
- ☐ Promised to the Crusader — Anne Herries
- ☐ Beauty and the Baron — Deborah Hale
- ☐ The Ballad of Emma O' Toole — Elizabeth Lane

Available at WHSmith, Tesco, Asda, Eason, Amazon and Apple

Just can't wait?

Visit us Online

You can buy our books online a month before they hit the shops! **www.millsandboon.co.uk**

0813/04

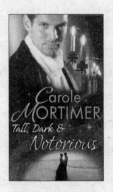

Join the Mills & Boon Book Club

Want to read more **Historical** books?
We're offering you **2 more** absolutely **FREE!**

We'll also treat you to these fabulous extras:

- 🌹 Exclusive offers and much more!

- 🌹 FREE home delivery

- 🌹 FREE books and gifts with our special rewards scheme

Get your free books now!

visit www.millsandboon.co.uk/bookclub
or call Customer Relations on 020 8288 2888

The World of Mills & Boon®

There's a Mills & Boon® series that's perfect for you. We publish ten series and, with new titles every month, you never have to wait long for your favourite to come along.

Blaze.
Scorching hot, sexy reads
4 new stories every month

By Request
Relive the romance with the best of the best
9 new stories every month

Cherish™
Romance to melt the heart every time
12 new stories every month

Desire™
Passionate and dramatic love stories
8 new stories every month

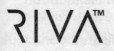